William Shaw was born in Newton Abbot, Devon, grew up in Nigeria and lived for sixteen years in Hackney. For more than twenty years he has written on popular culture and sub-culture for various publications including the *Observer* and the *New York Times*. He lives in Brighton.

He has won wide acclaim for his Breen & Tozer crime series set in sixties' London: *A Song from Dead Lips*, *A House of Knives* and *A Book of Scars*; the fourth novel, *Sympathy for the Devil*, is published in 2017. *The Birdwatcher* is a standalone novel that introduces the character of Alexandra Cupidi, who will feature as the star detective in Shaw's next new crime series.

THE BIRDWATCHER

WILLIAM SHAW

riverrun

First published in Great Britain in 2016 by riverrun
This paperback edition published in 2017 by

riverrun

an imprint of
Quercus Editions Ltd
Carmelite House
50 Victoria Embankment
London EC4Y 0DZ
An Hachette UK company

A CIP catalogue record for this book is available from the British Library

Paperback ISBN 978 1 78429 724 4
Ebook ISBN 978 1 78429 721 3

10 9 8 7 6 5 4 3 2 1

Printed and bound in Great Britain by Clays Ltd, St Ives plc

For my brother Christopher
and all the other boys who climbed trees

ONE

There were two reasons why William South did not want to be on the murder team.

The first was that it was October. The migrating birds had begun arriving on the coast.

The second was that, though nobody knew, he was a murderer himself.

These were not the reasons he gave to the shift sergeant. Instead, standing in front of his desk, he said, 'God's sake. I've got a pile of witness statements this deep to get through before Thursday, not to mention the Neighbourhood Panel meeting coming up. I haven't the time.'

'Tell me about it,' said the shift sergeant quietly.

'I don't understand why it has to be me anyway. The constable can do it.'

The shift sergeant was a soft-faced man who blinked as he spoke. He said, 'Ask DI McAdam on the Serious Crime Directorate. He's the one who said it should be you. Sorry, mate.'

When South didn't move, he looked to the left and

right, to see if anyone was listening, and lowered his voice. 'Look, mate. The new DS is not from round here. She needs her hand holding. You're the Local District lead, ergo, McAdam says you're on the team to support her and manage local impact. Not my fault.'

It was still early morning. It took South a second. 'Local impact? It's in my area?'

'Why else would you be on the team? She's outside now in the CID car, waiting.'

'I don't understand. What's the incident?'

'They didn't say, yet. It's just come in. Fuck off now, Bill. Be a pal and get on with your job and let me get on with mine.'

It was an ordinary office in an ordinary provincial police station; white paint a little scuffed on the walls, grey carpet worn in front of the sergeant's tidy desk from where others had come to haggle about the duties they'd been allocated. The poster behind his desk: *Listen. Learn. Improve. Kent Police.*

'Could you delegate it to someone else?'

'It was you he asked for.'

'So if I show her round today, will you get someone else on it for the rest of the week?'

'Give me a break, Bill,' said the shift sergeant, blinking again between words as he turned to his computer screen.

Over twenty years a policeman; a reputation as a diligent copper: but South had always avoided murder.

Maybe it would only be for a day or two. Once the new

DS had found her feet, he'd go back to normal duties, back to the reassuring bureaucracy of modern police work, and back to getting things done in his patch. He was a good copper. What could go wrong?

William South paused before walking through the glass door at the front of the station. Outside, the blue Ford Focus was parked in the street, engine running. Behind the wheel sat the new woman, and right away the sight of her made him nervous.

Late thirties, he guessed, straight brownish hair, recently cut; a woman starting a new job. Her fingers tapped on the steering wheel impatiently. She would be running outside inquiries for the murder investigation; a new arrival, first case on a new force, keen to get on, to make a go of it. Lots to prove.

A good copper? There was a part of him already hoping she wouldn't be.

He sighed, pushed open the door. 'Alexandra Cupidi?' he called.

'And what should I call you? Bill? Will?' she answered.

'William,' he said.

'William?' Was she smirking at him? 'Well, then, William . . .' She stretched his name to three syllables and nodded to the empty seat beside her. 'I'm Alexandra, then.'

He opened the passenger door and looked in. She wore a beige linen suit that was probably new too, like her haircut, but it was already crumpled and shapeless. And the car? It was only Tuesday, so she could barely have had it for a day so far, and already it was a tip. There were empty crisp and cigarette packets in the footwell and wrappers and crumbs all over the passenger seat.

'Sorry,' she said. 'Bit of a late one last night.'

He sat down in the mess, buckling the seat belt around his stab vest. She'd been with the Met, he'd heard, which was enough to put anyone on their guard.

DS Cupidi reached out, took a gulp from the coffee cup in the cup holder, then said, 'So. You're Neighbourhood Officer for Kilo 3, yes?'

South nodded warily. 'That's right.'

'Good.' She switched on the engine.

'And there's been a murder there? Shouldn't I have been informed?'

'You're being informed now. What's the quickest way?'

'To where exactly? It's a large area.'

'Sorry.' She dug into the pocket of her linen jacket for a notebook, opened the clip and flicked through until she had found the most recently scribbled page. 'Lighthouse Road, Dungeness,' she said.

He turned to her; examined her face. 'You sure?'

She repeated it.

Right now, he thought, he should just get out of the car and walk back inside the police station. Say he wasn't feeling well. 'This is the address of where it's supposed to have happened?'

'What's wrong?' she asked.

'They're not pulling your leg or anything? First week on the job?'

'What are you on about?'

'That's my road. That's where I live.'

She shrugged. 'I suppose that's why the DI said it was so important you should be on my team.'

South thought for a second. 'Who is it?'

She indicated and pulled out into the traffic, glancing quickly down at the open notebook and trying to read her own notes. 'No name. Address is . . . I can't make it out. Arm Cottage?'

'Arum Cottage.'

'That's it.'

'Robert Rayner,' said South.

She raised her eyebrows. 'That must be it. The woman who reported the crime is a Gill Rayner.'

'Bob Rayner is dead?' William blinked. They pulled up at a zebra crossing where a woman in a burqa pushed an old-fashioned black pram very slowly across the road.

She turned and looked. 'I'm sorry. You knew him?'

'A neighbour. A friend.' South looked out of the side window. 'Arum Cottage is about a hundred yards away from where I live.'

'Good,' she said. 'I mean. Not good, obviously, sorry.'

South said, 'So I shouldn't be part of the investigation. Because I know the deceased.'

Cupidi pursed her lips. 'Shit,' she said. The woman with the pram finally made it across to the other side of the road.

DS Cupidi drove over the crossing, then pulled the car up on the zigzag lines on the other side, hazards flashing.

'Give me a minute,' she said, pulling out her mobile phone. She dialled and then held the device to her ear. 'DI McAdam? Something's come up.' He heard the DI's voice.

Amongst the noise of the traffic, he couldn't make out what the DI was saying. Cupidi paused, turned to South. 'He wants to know, were you a close friend?' she said.

'Close? I suppose,' said South. 'I saw quite a lot of him.'

'Hear that, sir? . . .' She looked at her watch. 'Do I have to go and drop him back at the station?' She listened some more, said, 'I understand,' a couple of times, then hung up.

When she'd replaced the phone, she reached out, put the blue light on and swung back into the traffic, cars ahead scattering in panic, mounting pavements and braking, not knowing which way to move.

'Well?' said South.

'He said you can stick with me, strictly on an advice basis. For today at least, while we find our bearings. Just don't do anything unless I say, OK?'

Unfamiliar with the local roads, she was cautious at junctions and the town's many roundabouts. Only on the outskirts was she able to build speed, heading out towards the coast.

'What happened?' he asked when the road opened out in front of them.

'I don't know, yet. Call came in from a distressed woman

about an hour ago. Scene of Crime are there doing their thing.'

He remembered. Bob had said his sister was coming to visit. She arrived there once a fortnight; it was an arrangement the two of them had.

'God. I'm sorry. Are you going to be OK to do this? I mean, if he was a friend . . .?'

'I shouldn't be involved,' he said.

'But you are, though, aren't you?'

The flats on their right-hand side gave way to council houses, then to semis and bungalows and caravan parks, the flashing blue light reflecting off their windows. The further they travelled, the more open the land became.

On the left, occasional gaps in the breakwater gave glimpses of shingle running down to the sea. The traffic thinned and Cupidi gunned the engine. Overtaking, she flashed her lights at an oncoming car.

'You actually like it here?' she asked.

'I've lived here almost all my life,' he said.

'Not that there's anything wrong with that.'

'But what?'

She was concentrating on the road ahead. 'But nothing. I just can't imagine it, really. It's very . . . flat, isn't it?'

They were passing through the marshland, its grass burnt brown by the wind. 'So why did you move here?'

'Oh, you know. Just fancied a change,' she said, but a little too lightly, he thought.

'Slow down,' he said. 'The turning's any minute.' He

shifted in the seat. Something was poking into his behind. 'Left,' he said.

The thinner road was pitted. At the shoreline, loose stones crackled under the tyres. Flat land to the north; flat sea to the south. Weather-beaten houses with rotting windows and satellite dishes dribbling rust-marks down the paintwork. An oversize purple-and-yellow UKIP flag flapping in the wind.

'Must be bitter in winter,' she said.

'Bitter all year round.' It was a wide low headland extending south from the marshes, exposed to winds from every quarter.

As they drove towards the point, South noticed some people sitting round a fire on the shingle.

'Go slowly,' he said to DS Cupidi.

'Why?'

South looked out of the passenger window. The low light was behind them and they were too far away to see their faces clearly; he didn't think he recognised any of them, anyway. Fires on the shingle were always a risk. The flints exploded sometimes in the heat, shooting hot stone splinters out at the drunks.

'Rough sleepers?' she said.

'They come down here, break into the old fishing huts and burn the wood. They haven't been around for a while though,' he said. The vagrants were huddled close to the fire, trying to warm themselves in its dying heat.

'Can't stop now,' said Cupidi. South pulled his notebook

from his vest and wrote '*3 men, 2 women?*', then replaced the elastic band around it and put it back in his pocket.

They were nearing the end of the promontory. The road veered suddenly to the right, away from the sea.

'Now left,' he said, and she turned again.

'God, it's bleak.'

'It's how we like it.'

A track led away from the main road. DS Cupidi looked ahead, at the massive buildings in front of her. 'Jesus. What the hell is that?'

'Nuclear power station,' said South.

'Wow. I mean . . . I didn't realise it was here.'

Behind the black tower of the old lighthouse, the metal and concrete blocks that surrounded the two reactors rose, unnaturally massive in the flat land. These colossal shapes were surrounded by rows of tall razor-wire fences. As Cupidi and South approached, the buildings seemed to grow still larger. Their presence made this landscape even more Martian. To their north, lines of pylons marched inland across the wide shingle beds.

'Aren't you worried it'll blow up?'

This was where he had lived since he was fourteen. A freakish, three-mile promontory of loose stones built by the English Channel's counter-currents.

The single track road led to Bob Rayner's house and, beyond, to the Coastguard Cottages. Under the looming geometry of the power station, small shacks were dotted around untidily, as if they'd dropped accidentally from the back of a lorry. In recent years, the millionaires had arrived. Some huts had been rebuilt as luxury houses, with big glass doors and shiny flues. Others still looked like they were made from scraps pilfered from a tip.

'People live in those?' said DS Cupidi.

'Why not?'

South pointed to the row of houses, an oddly conventional-looking terrace a little further away from the reactors. 'My house is over there,' he said.

The car slowed. A dog was lying in the road. Alex Cupidi honked the horn at it. The dog got up slowly and sauntered off into the clumps of mint-green vegetation.

William South felt something vibrate as they bumped over the potholed road. His phone? But when he pulled it out of his pocket, the screen was blank; no one had called or texted. He was just putting it back when DS Cupidi said, 'That must be the place, then.'

He looked and saw Bob Rayner's bungalow. A small wooden construction, with two small gables, like a letter M, facing the track. A couple of chimneys stuck out of a tiled roof. The wood had been painted recently in red preservative, but it was already starting to flake. It sat on its own on the shingle, sea-kale and thin grass struggling to take hold around it. Like most of the shacks here, it would have been built originally almost a century ago as a poor man's getaway, long before the nuclear power station had arrived.

Today, there were police cars and vans parked outside the

small building. Half a dozen, crammed on every available piece of the narrow track.

'Shit,' he said, quietly.

Bob; his friend.

'Are you going to be all right?' said Cupidi, peering at him as she pulled up the handbrake. Not sure if he was, he looked away towards the sea, avoiding her gaze.

A memory. Police cars outside the house . . .

He was thirteen years old, late for his tea and running hard up the hill. He should have been home half an hour ago. Usually his mum wouldn't have been bothered, but after everything that had happened, she'd have been going mental.

It was all Miss McCrocodile's fault. She had spotted him lurking in the Spar and been all over him. 'Ye poor wee snipe, Billy McGowan. The people who did this terrible thing will not escape the wrath of the Lord. For God shall bring every secret thing into judgement, whether it be good, or whether it be evil.'

She bought him a packet of Smith's Crisps, at least.

Now he ran, past the hum of the electricity substation, past the playground where the climbing frame there had been recently painted in red, white and blue (and not by the council either), past the bored squaddies on the check-point, rifles pointed towards the tarmac, and finally on to the estate: NO POPE HERE, touched up only a few days earlier. The black ring on the grass of the field where the bonfire had been.

The McGowans' house was at the top, where the town ended and the fields began.

When he reached the start of the cul-de-sac, he stopped dead, panting.

There were two police cars outside his house. One of those big new Ford Granada Mk IIs with the orange stripe down the side, and an old Cortina that had seen better days. They were back again. He ducked behind the Creedys' chip van.

He was getting his breath back now. But he stayed there, peeking out from behind the chipper, waiting for the police cars to drive off.

He started shivering, even though it was summer. He closed his eyes tightly, wishing he had never even existed.

He should just kill himself now. They must have known. He was in such trouble.

TWO

The boxes of blue paper overshoes and latex gloves sat by Bob's shiny white fibreglass fishing dinghy. It was a good boat, a 16-foot Orkney, light enough to launch off the beach; South had helped him buy it and showed him how to use it. South dug his nails into the palm of his hand.

Cupidi didn't look any keener about getting out of the car. She chewed the inside of her cheek. 'Right then,' she said eventually. 'Here we go.' But instead of reaching for a handle, she stretched across him for a packet of cigarettes.

'You done a lot of this?' asked South.

'Quite a bit,' said Cupidi. 'It's what I did in London. You?'

'Not really. Never, in fact. Not like this, anyway.'

'Really?'

South opened his door first, and as he did so, something fell onto the tarmac. All through the car journey he had been sitting on a mobile phone, he realised. He mustn't have seen it when he got in. It was pink and decorated in nail-varnish hearts and diamanté stickers. That's what must have vibrated. He reached down, picked it up and held it out to DS Cupidi who was standing by the car, trying to light her cigarette.

'Christ,' she said.

'Is this yours?' he asked.

'My daughter's. She must have bloody left it behind.' Cupidi's eyes flickered.

'In the car?'

The detective sergeant looked away. Was she blushing? 'I know what you're thinking,' she was saying. 'Personal use of a police car. It was an emergency. I worked late last night so took the car home. Then we were late this morning and I didn't have time to go and swap the car for mine. She was going to be late for school. It's her first week. In a new town. New school. I've only ever done it once. Cross my heart.'

'I didn't say anything,' said South, holding his palms up.

'I think she leaves it behind on purpose.'

'Why would she do that?' asked South.

'You not got kids, William?'

'No.' He shook his head and handed the mobile to her. She put it in her handbag. 'Right,' she said. 'Let's get started.'

A constable South knew was keeping the site secure, standing just outside the cordon of blue tape, rubbing his gloves together to keep himself warm. Standing next to him, a couple of beach fishermen were chatting with him, rods in hand. One had a damp terrier circling around his feet. People always wanted to find out what had happened. It was understandable. The men tutted, looked concerned, tried to peer into the open front door of the house.

'Shall I wait out here?' South asked.

'Have you ever been inside Mr Rayner's house? Do you know your way around it?' Cupidi said.

South nodded. He'd been here many times.

'Would you come in with me, then?' She stubbed out her half-smoked cigarette by the car. 'I want your eyes.'

Through the windows, South could see silhouetted men at work inside the dead man's house.

'Hi, Bill,' called the copper at the perimeter.

'Hi, Jigger. You been in?' asked South. The constable's first name was James, but no one called him that.

The copper nodded. 'I was the first responder. Been here all morning, waiting for you lot.'

'What's it like?'

The constable shook his head. 'Fuckin' horrendous. Go see for yourself.'

'Is it Bob Rayner? Definitely?'

'Yep. That's what she said, the woman who called us.'

'Was she still here when you arrived?' asked Cupidi.

'Yes. She's at Ashford now. For the DNA and stuff.'

They would need to compare her traces to any others they found in the house, thought South. 'Was she OK?' South asked.

Jigger exhaled loudly. 'Not exactly. Stands to reason. When we found him in the box, she just ran out the house screaming.'

'The box?'

'Where they'd hidden his body. She was halfway to the beach, wailing like a wounded animal before I caught up with her, poor cow.'

Cupidi chewed her lip. 'What did they use?'

'Blunt instrument, they're saying.'

'Any idea why?' she said.

'Don't ask me.'

'I am asking you,' said Cupidi. 'You were first on the scene.'

The copper looked stung. 'B and E, isn't it, I reckon.'

Breaking and entering. Cupidi nodded. She was zipping up a white coverall. 'It's what we're all wearing this year,' she said. 'Get yours on, William.'

'He had told me his sister was coming to visit.'

'You knew the poor cunt?' said the constable. 'Christ. Sorry, mate.'

South nodded. When he had his suit, gloves and shoes on, he followed Cupidi to the door. 'How come he gets to call you Bill?' she asked.

'He never asked me which I preferred.'

Black-headed gulls dove and wheeled. Shrubs shivered in the wind. Police radios chattered to themselves.

'Are you going to be OK, William?' This time she spoke quietly, out of earshot of the other man.

This was his last chance to duck out of it. He could plead mitigating circumstances and go and sit in the car and have nothing further to do with the investigation.

But the front door was wide open. Cupidi went through it. South took a breath and followed her inside.

The interior of the little house was unrecognisable. Books had been yanked from the shelves, drawers spilled onto the floor, cupboards emptied.

Like most of the buildings here, it was not much more than a chalet that sat on the shingle; a living room and kitchen, a bathroom and two small bedrooms. The forensics team were busy in each of the rooms, but South's eyes were drawn to the photographer who was leaning over a blanket box under the living-room window. A flash lit up the room. Others were kneeling examining the walls. For spatters, he guessed. Another man was methodically spraying the floor with some chemical that would reveal where blood had been. Oh Christ.

South stepped forward. Something cracked under his feet; startled, he looked down. Just dried pasta; jars from the kitchen had been spilled.

Cupidi was introducing herself to the Scene of Crime Officer standing next to the open box. 'You're new round here, aren't you?' the man said.

'First week. I moved down on Saturday,' said Cupidi.

'Welcome to the job, then.' He waved his arms around the room.

'Thanks a billion.'

South watched her as she approached the open box; he noticed the small jerk of her head as she saw what was inside. The Crime Scene Officer had paused in his work too and was scrutinising her, as if checking she was up to the job. She looked at the dead man for a while, then beckoned. 'William. Do you recognise him?'

South hung back.

'It's OK. His sister already identified him,' said the forensics man. 'His name is Robert Rayner.'

'All the same, can you come and take a look?' said Cupidi quietly, looking up. South had been in this room many times and thought of himself as an observant man, but he had never really noticed the blanket box before. From where it was positioned, in the small window bay, the pine chest must have been used as a seat. There would have been a cushion on top of it, he supposed, or a rug. He tried to remember.

Bob Rayner had been a nice man, a good man who cooked badly but dressed well. He did sponsored bike rides for cancer and had volunteered at the local lifeboat station. Last summer he saved a tourist girl from drowning on the beach, though he hated anyone talking about it and refused to allow the papers to take photographs of him afterwards. He wasn't one of the rich ones who were moving in around the headland, who employed fashionable architects to remodel their fishing huts, but who only used them a few weeks a year, blocking the narrow roads with their wide cars. He was one who had come to stay here all year round. It took a sort of person. Apart from a few weekends, this was a quiet place. Most who lived permanently on the headland were private people like South who relished the isolation.

South approached the open box slowly.

'You've seen dead people before?' said Cupidi.

The first thing he saw was Bob's head. At first it puzzled him. He thought there must have been a mistake. It didn't look like Bob at all. It was the wrong shape. Too big, for a start.

It took him a second to realise that the head was swollen to almost half its size again, and dark with crusted blood that had filled the eye sockets, covering them. Every inch of skin was discoloured. An ear seemed to be missing; in its place just scab, gristle and clot.

South walked closer. The naked body was every colour imaginable. The whole of Bob's skin above the waist seemed to be bruised. It was like he was wearing a suit of orange, red, purple, black, brown and yellow. His groin was dark from bruising.

Whoever had killed him had beaten him repeatedly, brutally. He had become meat. The violence was written all over his body.

It seemed absurd. Such a peaceable, gentle, quiet-spoken man. Now this thing – it wasn't even Bob – was being measured and photographed, picked over with tweezers and evidence bags.

'What kind of weapon?' Cupidi asked.

'Too early to say. Something heavy though.'

'Nothing found at the scene?'

'No.'

There was no blood on the wood of the box. He had

been dumped inside after he was dead, South thought, looking in horror at his friend. Poor Bob. Poor, poor Bob.

'I'm sorry,' said Cupidi.

'What?'

Even if he was still looking at the dead man, he could feel Cupidi's eyes on him, scrutinising him. 'It's a shock to you, isn't it? You're upset. Do you need a minute to yourself?'

Why did he resent that consideration, right now? Probably because it wasn't really kindness at all. She would be thinking how she had lucked out; if he knew the dead man that well, he'd be even more useful. She couldn't help it, though. It was the job. She was protecting an asset. He shook his head. 'No. I'm OK.'

He backed away, but even from where he was standing, he could see one hand. The other was somewhere underneath the rest of the body. The fingers on the hand he could see were broken, lying at unlikely angles, as if he had been trying to protect himself with it at some point during the beating.

'Repeated blows,' said the forensics man, as if he could hear what South was thinking.

'How many would you say?' asked South.

'Not my department, really. Hundreds, easy.'

Cupidi said, 'Either somebody really had it in for him, or we're looking for someone mental. Or both.'

'That's the kind of brilliant insight they teach you at the Met, is it?' said the forensics man.

'William? What do you say? Had he pissed anyone off?'

'That's the point. He wasn't the sort to annoy anyone. He was the sweetest man you could meet. You barely noticed him, most of the time,' South said. 'He was just . . . just a lovely man. That's all.'

Cupidi turned to South and asked, 'What did he do for a living?'

South felt suddenly exhausted. He wanted to sit down, but you couldn't do that at a crime scene. He tried to think about what he knew. 'He was retired. Used to be a school teacher,' he said.

'Subject?'

'Um. English, I think. I'm sorry. I can't remember exactly.'

'Wife?'

South shook his head. 'Single,' he said, and realised he could not remember asking Bob about that. But he must have, surely? Was he divorced? Separated? He didn't know.

'What about a lover?'

'Look around,' he said. 'No photographs. There was no one in his life apart from his sister. No kids, either.'

He watched Cupidi do a complete methodical turn, looking around the room and the debris on the floor. Most people had family photos somewhere; a small gold-framed picture on the mantelpiece or sideboard. Rayner had nothing.

'I suppose I must have always assumed he was gay,' said South. 'You know, from that generation that didn't talk about it? Or just not interested. I thought it was a generational thing, you know? Not talking about your personal life. He was a few years older than me. I never saw anyone. He never talked about anyone either.'

'Was that odd?'

South shook his head.

'I mean, I'd find it strange, if it was me,' Cupidi said. 'You never asked?'

'No.'

'Men are a mystery to me,' she said.

'I suppose that's what I liked about him.'

It wasn't that they hadn't talked a lot over the couple of years South had known him, but Rayner never invited any questions about his personal life. And in return, Bob Rayner never asked South about his life either. As far as South went, this had been a perfect arrangement. They had talked about what was in front of their eyes; the weather, the state of the shacks and houses, the height of the shingle on the beck, how to clean fuel filters on a diesel engine and, of course, the birds. Bob Rayner had been eager to learn.

'Sign of forced entry?' Cupidi was asking the Crime Scene man.

'We haven't found any. The door was open when the woman arrived, far as I know.'

Someone Bob Rayner knew? Someone they both knew, maybe? 'Take a good look around, William,' said Cupidi. 'You notice anything different about the room? Anything missing?'

He'd never really paid a lot of attention to what was in Bob Rayner's house. It was easy not to because though it was unusual outside, the inside was perfectly normal. There were hundreds of books. Novels mostly. Dickens, Austen, a couple of Booker winners. Some nature books. A few books of prints by painters like Picasso and Chagal, the sort you'd find in any middle-class English house. On the walls, an oil painting of some ducks, a framed nineteenth-century map of South Kent.

The drinks cabinet door was open, he noticed. 'He always had a single malt. There's nothing there.'

'Good,' she said, making a note. 'Take your time. What about valuables? Do you know where he kept them?'

He looked at the floor. Many of Bob's books were ruined, face down on the floor, pages crumpled. Bob would have hated it; he was always such a neat man.

He needed to concentrate, but it was not easy. It took him a second or two, looking towards the hallway, to realise that the hook by the front door was empty. He scanned the floor around it. 'His binoculars are missing, I think.'

'His binoculars?' She nodded, made another note. 'Anything else?'

South shook his head. 'What about the bedroom?'

The bungalow had been built long before the two vast nuclear reactors had obscured the view to the west, the first in the sixties, the second twenty years later. The master bedroom would have had a great view once, looking out at the huge expanse of shingle. Bob had always slept in the smaller of the two bedrooms, the one with the window looking away from the power station. The other, facing the reactors, had been his spare bedroom and office.

The wardrobe doors were open, drawers half pulled out. Papers were scattered by the bed. There were pairs of socks, too, all over the floor.

'Maybe he came back and disturbed a burglar,' said South.

They looked into the second bedroom. Again, the drawers of a filing cabinet had been left open. A technician was fingerprinting the drawer handles.

'Or someone who wanted to look like a burglar,' she said. 'We'll come back when Scene of Crime are done, and go through all this.'

'We?'

'Don't worry. I'll arrange cover.'

'You can try,' he said. 'There won't be any cover, though. Don't know what it was like in the Met, but there's barely enough of us left down here to cover a weekday, let alone a weekend.'

'The timing of this isn't exactly brilliant for me, either. I was hoping to find my feet a little before something like this turned up.' She sighed. 'You never know. We may be able to get the worst of it wrapped up in a couple of days, if we're lucky. I'm going outside for a cigarette,' she said. 'When you're done in here, come outside and tell me if you found anything else missing.'

For a while he watched the forensics man. It was careful work, trying to tease the slightest smudge into a clue. They

24

would have to progress methodically through the whole house like this. It would be a while before DI McAdam and his team would be able to go through Bob's belongings to try and figure out what had been taken.

Outside, a man in a white coverall and facemask was going through the green bin, carefully taking out its contents and placing them in clear plastic bags. Cupidi was leaning her elbows against the bonnet of the CID car, talking on her phone. 'Half an hour,' she was saying. 'Can the DI make that?'

As South approached, she finished the call, pulled out a packet of cigarettes from her shoulder bag and offered one to him. He shook his head and looked at something behind her head. Pulling out his police notebook, he wrote down '*Juv Arctic Pom/Skua?*' and the time.

She said, 'Anything?'

'Just making a couple of observations,' he said. It was swooping at a herring gull, just at the shoreline, trying to steal its catch. As usual, he thought about telling Bob about it, then he remembered with the kind of stupid shock that happens at times like this, that Bob was dead. Bob would have liked seeing the bird.

'I've noticed. You're someone who takes notes. That's good.' She nodded. 'So? What else can you tell me about Mr Rayner?'

South tucked the book back inside his vest. 'He arrived about four years ago. He bought the cottage outright.

I didn't have much to do with him at first. A lot of the people round here keep themselves to themselves. Only he was into birds, or was learning to be, so I used to see him out on the reserve. Old gravel pits. He was there every day. He wasn't experienced, not at the start anyway, but he had all this gear. Eighteen-hundred-pound binoculars. We started talking.'

'You're a bird spotter?'

'Birder, really. Not a bird spotter.'

Cupidi made a face. 'There's a difference?'

South shook his head. 'It's not important.'

'Is that rare? Eighteen hundred quid for binoculars?'

'Not so much these days, I suppose. But it was obvious that before he came here he hadn't done much birding. Some people come here like that. You spend your working life dreaming of it but you've never actually had any time to do it.'

The police tape slapped in a gust of wind. 'Did he mention anything that was worrying him at all?'

South shook his head. 'More I think of it,' he said, 'more I realise I didn't know much about him. I mean practically nothing, really. He had been a teacher. He had a sister. That's it. I mean, we saw each other pretty much every day. I like to go out before dusk. It's a good time. This time of year it's right after my shift. I'd taken to calling on him maybe three or four days a week and we'd head out together. But we never talked much, unless it was about birds.'

'Birds?'

'Strange as it may seem.'

'Sarge,' called the Scene of Crime man standing at the bin. 'Take a look.' Cupidi walked towards him, South following. The man in the white protective suit held open a blue-and-white shopping bag for Cupidi to peer inside. 'Bandages?' she said.

''Bout twenty packets, I reckon. All unopened.' The man delved inside the bag and pulled out one of the small boxes: '*Absorbent for lightly weeping or bleeding wounds*,' he read.

'Did your friend have any condition that required him to have dressings?' asked Cupidi.

'No. Not that I know of,' said South.

'Poor bugger inside could have used a few of them, I reckon.' The man held one of the boxes between blue-gloved finger and thumb. 'Think the killer brought them with him?'

South peered into the bag. 'Is there a receipt?'

'That would be kind of weird, wouldn't it?' said the forensics man, rummaging inside the bag. 'Bringing your own bandages to a murder? No. No receipt.'

DS Cupidi's phone started ringing. 'Just a minute,' she said, and swung the handbag round to start digging in it. She found it before it rang off. 'I can't talk now. I'm on duty,' she said. Then, 'Oh.'

South saw her eyes widen.

'What did she do? . . . Are you sure? . . . I see. Only, it's not exactly very convenient right now.'

27

She walked away, lowering her voice, so as not to be heard.

South closed his eyes and tried to remember the last time he had seen his friend. He had been running after a shift; he liked to do at least a couple of miles most evenings. The light had already been going. He tried to picture Bob waving at him, to remember exactly what he had looked like that last time.

'What on earth are you doing, Billy?'

When he opened his eyes, Sergeant Ferguson was standing there by the chip van, in his big peaky hat and uniform.

'I was just on my way home.'

'Were y'now?' Ferguson smiled. 'Come on then, lad. I been out all over looking for you.'

Ferguson laid his hand on Billy's shoulder to steer him towards their house up at the top of the cul-de-sac. The sergeant was a thin man whose uniform always looked too big, but he wasn't the worst of them.

Why did his mum always dress like a teenager? It was embarrassing. She was in the hallway on the phone. 'Thank God. He's here now.' She put down the handset. 'Billy, where the hell you been? I was sick with worry. Tea was ages ago.'

'Miss McCorquadale wanted to talk to me,' he said.

His mother scowled. 'Oh yes. And what did she want?'

'She said she was praying for me. She told me I could talk to her any time.'

'Sanctimonious busybody,' said Billy's mother. 'Tell her to mind her own beeswax.' Behind her, peering from the living-room door, stood the RUC inspector who had called on them twice before: a big, veiny-faced man who smelt of beer.

Billy's mum enfolded her son in a hug, even though the coppers were there to see it. He felt the push of her breasts against his face. 'Get off,' said Billy, wriggling.

'Hello, Billy,' said the Inspector, attempting a crook-tooth smile as Billy struggled free, pushing past him into the living room. His mother followed them. The small room looked especially bare since they had taken up the carpet.

They had had to, on account of the blood. Dad's favourite chair was gone too.

The Inspector was holding a pencil in one hand and a blue notebook in the other. 'As you were saying, Mrs Mac,' he said, all familiar and friendly.

'I wasn't aware I was saying anything at all,' she said.

'I was asking for a list of your husband's associates.'

'Write down what you like,' Billy's mother said. 'But you know I am not saying anything.'

'No,' he said sadly. 'You're not. But you have to understand, after an incident, all sorts of rumours go flying around. And at times like these, rumours have deadly consequences. The sooner we find out who did this . . .'

'I have a child,' she said. 'It's just me and him now. You know I can't say a single word.'

'No,' said the Inspector mournfully.

'My husband was always a stupid idiot,' said Billy's mother. 'Getting involved in all that. And now look what's happened.'

The Inspector looked shocked. Sergeant Ferguson was more used to it.

She was not even dressed in black, like you're supposed to. They had some of the other mums round here the other day, whispering and tutting, though they do that anyway. She still dressed in skirts and platform boots, which Billy thought was embarrassing enough at the best of times. Today she was wearing that yellow sweater that showed her bra straps, God's sake.

Ferguson put his hat down on a chair and said, 'While you're talking to the Inspector, why don't I have a wee chat with Billy upstairs?'

'I don't know about that,' said his mother.

'You know me, Mary. We're good pals. Trust me,' said Ferguson.

'I don't mind,' said Billy, glad to be away from his mother and the Inspector. Fergie was OK.

'Lead the way, Billy,' said Ferguson.

'Don't say nothing, you hear? Nothing.'

'Do you have any more tea?' said the Inspector hurriedly. 'It's a great cup you make.'

THREE

'What's wrong?' said Cupidi, marching towards him on the shingle.

The world was suddenly bright as he opened his eyes again. A low sun had broken through the grey. 'I'm fine.'

'You look crap. Was it dizziness?'

'No. I'll be fine. I was just thinking. It's just been a shock.'

'Sure? We'd better make a move on then. Get in,' said Cupidi.

From where he was standing he couldn't see the sea over the bank of shingle, but the sunlight bouncing off the water seemed to light everything around him. His familiar world looked strange, almost unnatural.

'Where are we going?' said South, opening the door and sitting back down on the pile of biscuit wrappers and empty cigarette packets.

She started the engine and set off back down the track, away from Bob Rayner's house. 'Team briefing back at the station. Eleven o'clock.'

South checked his watch. It was still only a quarter past ten in the morning. 'It won't take us that long.'

'Yes. Well. First we have to drop by my daughter's school. Just five minutes. I can't bloody believe it. On her second day.'

'You have to pick her up?'

A police car was coming the other way on the single track road, lights flashing. 'Shit,' said Cupidi, pulling over and winding down the window.

DI McAdam was driving; the Chief Inspector was with him. McAdam smiled. 'Everything under control on site, Alexandra?'

'Yes, sir,' she said. 'Just heading back to print out a few things for the meeting.'

'Very good,' he said. He looked past Cupidi. 'Sorry to hear about your friend, Bill. Terrible shock.'

'Yes, sir.'

'Well. See you two back at the station, then,' the inspector said.

The roads were less crowded now. Cupidi drove fast. 'That was the school office on the phone. She's being sent home,' she said. After a mile she added, 'Keep this to yourself, will you?'

First day of a major case as well, thought South. Taking time off for family business.

'Oh come on,' she said. 'Give me a bit of slack. Single mother. New job.'

'I didn't say anything.'

'What's the harm? I'll be five minutes, absolute max.'

Without asking him, she was involving him in

misconduct. A few years ago nobody would have thought anything of it. These days, though, it didn't take anything to get yourself pulled up by Professional Standards, and before you knew it, no final salary pension and a future working in private security if you were lucky. 'Isn't there anyone else who can look after her?'

She took her eyes off the road for a brief second and looked at him, then back to the road. 'No. There isn't, actually,' she said.

They were flying along the A259 now, a long, straight causeway built through the marshland. After a couple of minutes she said, 'I requested the transfer from London because she's fifteen and I'm not sure South London was exactly the best place for her, know what I mean? This job came up, but she doesn't know anyone round here and right now she hates me for taking her away from her pals. So maybe I feel guilty.'

South should have been angry with her. 'You shouldn't. My mother did the same for me. Took me away from trouble.'

'Did she? And did you forgive her?'

South didn't answer. They drove in silence through the flat land, until the houses of the town started to appear around them again.

Cupidi returned from the school office with a girl walking behind her, backpack over one shoulder. The teenager was thin and dressed in a stiff new red school jumper, uniform skirt rolled up at the waist to shorten it, and her bleached hair showed a dark centre parting.

He could hear them talking through the open car window. 'And?' Cupidi was saying.

'It actually wasn't my fault, as a matter of fact.'

Alex Cupidi said, 'On your second day.'

'They're evil. They were having a go at me 'cause of the way I look and the way I talk.'

'Oh, Zoë.'

'They are a bunch of inbreds.'

'And you told them that?'

South pretended not to be listening; he picked at a fingernail.

'It was them that hit me and I was only joking. I wasn't being serious. I was just trying to have a laugh.'

'Oh for God's sake,' said her mother. 'You've got to try, Zoë. You've got to make an effort.'

'I was making an effort, actually. The whole cacking thing is an effort.'

'Please, Zoë.' At the crime scene she had seemed effi-cient, in charge, asking questions in a voice that demanded answers. Here with her daughter she seemed less in control. Her daughter's pale-skinned youth made her look older, somehow.

'Why have I got to make an effort?' the girl was saying. 'I didn't want to come to this dump in the first place. It's not my fault we're here.'

Cupidi's hair blew into her eyes. She brushed it out and

asked, 'What happened to the other girls who were fight-ing with you?'

'I hate them. I hate all of them. I'm never going back.'

'Did you hit them?'

'Not really. I defended myself a bit, that's all. Same as anyone'd have done.'

'Why didn't you just walk away?'

The girl said quietly, 'You don't understand anything at all, Mum.'

Outside a gust of wind buffeted the car. Winter would be here soon.

DS Cupidi was digging in her huge shoulder bag to pull out a door key. 'You'll have to spend the afternoon at home then. Make yourself some lunch.'

'Aren't you going to give me a lift?'

'I can't. Not now. This is a police car. I'm not allowed. And I'm working.'

'You gave me a lift this morning.'

'I wasn't supposed to.' Cupidi glanced at South.

'It's miles.'

'You'll have to catch the bus.'

Her daughter threw out her arms wide in protest, as if she were being crucified. 'I don't even know which bus to get. I'm not sure they even have proper buses around here.'

DS Cupidi rubbed her forehead. Sitting in the front of the car, South said quietly, 'Where do you live?'

'Kingsnorth,' said Cupidi.

'You'd have to walk up Hythe Road to the Tesco.' He told her the number of the bus.

'Thanks, William,' said Cupidi.

'Who's he, anyway?' said the daughter, as her mother handed over change for the fare and the mobile phone she'd forgotten that morning. The teenager walked away from them, backpack sagging on her shoulder, not looking back.

Ashford Police Station was a municipal brick-clad concrete building; dull and functional. A ramp led down to the underground police car park. Cupidi drove the car down, switched off the engine and picked up a folder from the back seat, heading towards the lift door without saying a word. South followed behind. She was preoccupied, he guessed, running through what she would have to say in the morning meeting.

'You OK?' he asked, in the lift.

'Why wouldn't I be?'

'Just asking.'

South went to wait in the conference room on the first floor. Bright lights. Plastic chairs. Vertical blinds on the windows. The smell of cleaning fluid, cheap carpet and body odour.

Other coppers wandered in, holding mugs and folders. He recognised most of the faces. 'Didn't know you'd joined Serious Crime, Billy?'

'They wouldn't take me even if I asked.'

'Oi, oi. Look sharp. Cupid's coming.'

'I thought Cupid was supposed to be naked with a bow and arrow.'

'Thank Christ she's not.'

A laugh.

Cupidi was just outside the doors, talking to the DI. 'She's trouble,' said one of the detectives.

'What?' said South.

The man lowered his voice. 'My brother-in-law is Scotland Yard. Apparently Cupid there had the Practice Support Team all over her arse.'

'What for?'

But Cupidi was entering the room now, pushing the door open with her backside, a mug of coffee in one hand, a bundle of papers in the other. Ignoring the other men she went straight over to South and said quietly, 'Question. You live alone?'

'Yes. Why?'

Before she could answer, the Chief Inspector was in the room, clapping his hands. 'Come on, boys and girls. Let's get going. Lots to do.'

Cupidi moved to her place at the side of the room, in front of a whiteboard, while DI McAdam outlined what they knew so far. When the body was discovered. Presumed cause of death: trauma with blunt instrument to the head. Presumed time of death: 24 to 36 hours ago. 'It was an extremely violent murder,' said the DI. 'Mr Rayner was bludgeoned to death over a prolonged period.'

Cupidi took two digital prints and put them onto the whiteboard.

South looked away. He could hear the intakes of breath around him.

'Multiple beatings over several hours.'

'Jesus,' somebody said, finally.

'This is rage,' said Cupidi.

'Precisely,' said McAdam. 'It takes a lot of work to do this kind of damage. This kind of attack gives us a profile. Anyone?'

'Someone who literally cannot control themselves, or doesn't want to,' suggested Cupidi. 'Someone who is so consumed by anger they cannot stop. Unfashionable though it may be to say so, the culprit is almost certainly male, given the force and nature of the attack.'

Even in this weather, the Chief Inspector looked sweaty in his grey suit. 'Whoever did this is a very dangerous person,' he said. 'Almost certainly someone who's committed violent acts before. We don't know what made him angry, or much else at this stage. Was he angry at Mr Rayner? Or something else entirely?'

The Chief Inspector had given up smoking last year, but looked no better for it. In contrast, the DI was one of the new generation, younger than Cupidi, a man who cycled to work and changed out of his Lycra in the men's room into pristine plain suits. When his hair had started thinning, he simply shaved it all off. McAdam said, 'Sergeant William South here was a friend of the victim's. We've asked him to join the murder squad for the initial phase of the investigation. Give us an idea who the victim was, Sergeant.'

Everybody in the CID room was looking at South now. He could see the raised eyebrows and the looks of concern. The Chief Inspector sat at a desk at the side of the room, chewing on the inside of his cheek, watching South; he cocked his head expectantly. South tried to think straight. How much did he know about Bob Rayner? Little, considering the hours they'd spent in the hides up by the reserve.

'Bachelor,' South began. 'Late fifties. Retired. Former public school teacher. Taught English, I think. Must have had a few bob because those properties go for a fortune, now. Did fundraising for the RNLI. Interested in nature conservation . . . He had a sister who came to see him once a fortnight—'

'The sister that discovered the body?' said someone.

South nodded. 'And apart from that, I didn't see a lot of visitors. Any, in fact. He was a loner. We spent some time together looking at birds, but he wasn't that much of a talker. He was . . . a quiet man.' He looked around the room. Everyone was looking at him. He felt he should be saying more, but realised there was not much more to say.

Cupidi interrupted, rescuing him. 'A pair of expensive binoculars have gone missing, plus a bottle of spirits—'

'Whisky,' said DI McAdam.

'And a lot of the drawers were open, which suggests a burglary of some kind. Rayner may have disturbed the intruder.' Cupidi added a DVLA picture of Rayner to the board.

'Anything else from the house search?'

'Bit strange but Rayner's bin is full of bandages. About twenty packs of them. All unused. Like he was expecting a beating or something.'

'Unless the killer brought them.'

'Why would he have done that?' asked Cupidi.

'I don't know. A threat maybe?'

'Right. Let's get down to actions,' said McAdam. 'Alexandra?'

Cupidi pointed at a young woman in a smart business suit. 'Sorry, Constable. I forgot your name. Laura? Right. You find out everything you can about Rayner. We'll need to question his sister as soon as we can. We've got her details, have we? Don't let her go home. I'll need to speak to her too before she goes anywhere. Find out anyone else we should be contacting. Liaise with William South here.' She turned and wrote on the board: 'ONE. Friends and family.'

Inspector McAdam was standing just behind Cupidi, watching her, sizing up this new woman from the Met. 'OK. Task number two. You –' Cupidi was pointing to another constable – 'the moment Scene of Crime are out of the house, you're in charge of going through everything. Look for anything obvious that might have gone miss-ing: jewellery, watches, cameras, stereo. Make a note of everything you see, room by room. List what's there, and what you think might have been there but isn't. Dig out any personal items, letters, bills, receipts, bank statements. Find his mobile phone. I presume he had a computer?'

'Yes,' said South.

'Bring that in. Can we get a computer specialist? Do we have one locally?'

'This isn't the Outer Hebrides, Sergeant.' The inspector smiled.

Cupidi wrote on the board: '*TWO. House.*' She continued: 'Three. We think the pair of binoculars have gone missing. You —' pointing again — 'we need to find anyone who might have been offered them for sale. Anybody who handles stolen goods. All the pawnbrokers and Cash Converters. What make were they?'

'Swarovski. 8.5 by 42s,' said South.

'Worth?'

'A little under two grand, new,' he said.

'Bloody hell,' said one of the constables.

'There you go,' said Cupidi. 'That's a possible motive already. Four. Contact all branches of Boots. See if any branch remembers selling twenty packets of bandages to a man recently. Get a description.' She looked at her notebook. 'Savlon Alginate Dressings. Pack of five. Got that? Fifth on this list: records. Go through the basics, NI, banks, then use what we find in the house. Any other bank accounts, pensions, will, dependants, all of that. Anything that might suggest a financial motive for this.'

If she was putting on a show to try and impress DI on her first case, it was a good one. 'Six, local search. We need feet out there. Two teams. Team one goes door to door to ask if they saw anyone around Rayner's property in the days leading up to the killing, if they saw anyone suspicious, if they've had anyone trying to break into their own properties. And finally, we need a search of the area. So far Scene of Crime say the weapon was not present in the house. We're looking for something like a baseball bat. A blunt instrument but something with a bit of weight. We're going to need as many officers as we can get. How many can we have down there?' She turned to the DCI.

'We'll give you everything we can,' he told her.

Cupidi stood there, whiteboard marker in her hand. 'And what does that actually mean in terms of numbers?'

There was a pause. Everybody looked at the Chief Inspector. The smile thinned. 'It means we'll give you everything we can.'

'How many people, exactly?'

'Count them,' he said, waving his hand across the room.

South counted. There were eight people in the room, not including the inspector, the DCI and him. Cupidi's mouth opened as if she were about to say something. Before she had a chance McAdam said, 'And I'm sure the duty sergeant can rustle up three or four more special constables for the next shift. What we have to remember is, it's not about numbers. It's about efficacy.'

'Right. Well let's be as . . . efficient as we can then.' And she did her very best, South noted, to smile back at the DI. Then she looked right at South. 'You live close by, don't you, William? Can we use your place as a base tonight while we're there? Can you spare a room for us? It makes a lot more sense to have somewhere local. Otherwise we're driving back here all the time.'

South blinked. 'Well,' he said.

'You know the area. It would be useful. If there's a problem . . .?'

He felt the gaze of every person in the room on him; the inspector too. Cupidi seemed to think it a reasonable demand. Like Bob, he was a private man. He wasn't in the habit of inviting people back to his house, but Bob had been his friend. 'That'll be fine,' he said.

The DCI turned to the room. 'OK? Any questions? If not let's meet at Sergeant South's place at five and see what we've got.'

Cupidi held out the marker to him. 'Write your address down on the board,' she said. 'Then head back there. We need to go back to the scene, quick as we can.'

Above the noise, McAdam called out, 'Before any of you people go anywhere, Alexandra here is going to get these all issued as HOLMES actions, OK? Don't forget to stop by the incident room and pick yours up before you leave.'

Coffee still in hand, Cupidi grimaced, then pushed her way back out of the door again, followed by the inspector.

South went to the whiteboard to write down his address. 'Sorry about your mate,' one officer said, putting his hand on South's shoulder.

Another said, 'We'll get the cunt, don't you worry. Promise you that.'

South nodded. Coppers were a sentimental bunch; it was them against the world, and now this wasn't just any murder, it was one connected to one of their own. South felt the weight of the CID man's hand.

The CID officers remained in the room with South, staring at the list of tasks on the whiteboard.

'That new one. She's very . . .' one of them said.

'Assertive,' another completed.

'Dominant.'

'You like that, don't you? A bit of domination,' said one of the women.

South watched Cupidi through the glass. She dressed like someone who was no longer trying to impress. The crumpled linen suit she wore was practical rather than feminine. She was on the phone, talking angrily to someone, rubbing her forehead with her free hand.

Presumably the other men just saw their new DS being assertive and dominant. South reckoned she was probably just arguing with her daughter again.

Coastguard Cottages was a white terrace that would have once faced out to sea. South's house was in the middle. He moved books off the dining-room table. 'Will this room do?'

'You sure it's OK, us taking over your house like this?' said Cupidi.

'You said you just wanted a room.'

'Just this room,' she said. 'And maybe the kitchen for tea and stuff. I don't think we'll actually need the bedrooms.' She started to help him clear the table, picking up another pile of books. 'I was joking about the bedrooms,' she said.

'Leave it.' He nudged her out of the way of the table. 'I know where they go.'

She stood back, arms raised, leaving the books where they were. 'Divorced?'

'No.'

'Gay?'

'No,' he said, a little more abruptly this time.

'Sorry. Just curious. I am, as you probably guessed. Divorced I mean, not gay. God I envy you, living alone,' she said. 'So uncomplicated. You keep it very nice. Do you have coffee?'

Did he have coffee? He remembered a jar at the back of a shelf. 'Instant.'

Cupidi made a face. 'I'll send out.' She opened her laptop and placed it on South's table, searched around for a socket, hitching up her skirt and then crawling beneath the table to plug it in. South took a little too long to look away.

As her laptop booted, she called the CID office, giving out South's landline number. 'Reception here is horrible,' she told whoever she was speaking to. 'Pass that number round, will you?'

When she put down the phone, she pointed out of the window and said, 'Doesn't it scare you, them being there?'

45

'The reactors? Nope,' said South.

She sat down at the table, glancing at her laptop. There was a splash of nail varnish on the keyboard. 'Right. Let's go.' Looked at her watch. Opened up a document. 'What are the chances of other people round here having seen him?' she asked.

'Him?' said South.

'I mean the killer.'

'I know you said that at the briefing,' said South. 'But isn't it a bit early to decide that it's a man?'

'Don't look at me like that. I've been in the business long enough. It would have taken a lot of work to kill your friend. That kind of pattern of rage is a man. Completely sure of it. I'm not being feminist saying that, although I am one, if you want to know. It's just that sometimes, some men do that. Not all men. Some men. But women? Women kill, for sure, but have you ever heard of a woman behaving like that? No. So, what are the chances that some-one will have seen him?'

'This time of year? Not great. Most of these are just summer houses. People come down for the weekends. In the week it's pretty quiet.'

'What about the people who work in there?' She nodded her head towards the huge power station beyond the glass.

'We can ask, but they don't come this way. They get to work down Access Road which is separate from the rest of Dungeness, so unless they're going for a walk after a shift or something, they wouldn't go past Bob's house.'

'But we should ask, right?'

'It's a nuclear facility, so there's a Met Police unit stationed there round the clock.' The Met had been stationed there in case of a terrorist attack that had never come. 'And they've nothing else to do. Get them to do it.'

'Good.' Her mobile phone rang. She picked it up and started talking. 'When will she be here? Don't let her go without me speaking to her.' Then, after ending the call, she said to South, 'OK if we bring his sister here to interview her?'

They had removed the body and Gill Rayner was on her way back to her brother's house to pick up her car. Before he could answer, she said, 'You have a lot of books.'

He smiled. 'Too many.'

South followed her eyes. *Bird Populations. Essential Ornithology. Ten Thousand Birds.*

'You used to go birdwatching with Mr Rayner a lot?'

'I go whenever I can. He was the same. You get pretty hooked. There's a lot to see around here.'

'And what? You count them, or something?'

The reason he liked the company of other birders was that you never had to explain to them. 'This place, it's all about this time of year,' said South. 'And the spring too. You get to see all sorts coming through. Millions of birds come through here. Every year it's different depending on which weather systems blow them across. And then there are the winter visitors.'

'Clapham Junction for birds,' said Cupidi.

'Kind of.'

'When did you last go out with him?'

'Sunday, I suppose it must have been. The day before yesterday.'

'And . . .?'

'We saw some redstarts. I remember because we'd never seen them this late in the year. A huge flock of goldfinches. Saw my first goldeneye of the season. Don't laugh.'

'I'm not. Honest. What I meant was, did he talk about anything? Was he worried?'

South tried to think back. 'Thing is, we only ever really talked about birds.'

'Men are so bloody weird,' she said.

South said, 'You're talking from personal experience, then?'

'Oh yes. Plenty of that. Think back. Anything at all that may have been different about how he behaved? Anything at all?'

South tried to remember. On the day before they had gone over Springfield Bridge to Christmas Dell hide.

'Some people had left litter on the path there; empty vodka bottles and cigarette packets. Bob had been angry about it, I remember. It was unusual. He said something about how some people wreck the world for everyone else. But mostly he was pretty up. He was probably look-ing forward to seeing his sister. You could tell they were close. He was always happy when she was coming.'

'Nothing else?'

'He said that he wouldn't be around for a couple of days. She wasn't that keen on birds. To be honest, now I think about it, he never talked that much about anything else.'

She stood, looked at her watch. 'Because he didn't have anything to say? Or because he had something to hide?'

He would have to watch her, he thought. 'The second, I think, maybe.'

'Why?'

He thought for a minute. 'There was so much he didn't talk about, in retrospect.'

She returned his look with a curious smile on her face; he turned away to avoid her gaze.

Billy's house was a two-up two-down on the edge of the estate. He had the back bedroom next to the bathroom, looking up towards the mountains.

'Careful,' Billy said to Sergeant Ferguson. 'The carpet's loose.' Mum had kept badgering Dad to nail it back down but he never had.

Billy pushed the door to his bedroom open; the copper stepped inside. 'So, I guess that you like birds?'

'Yep,' answered Billy.

'I never knew that.'

Almost every spare inch of the walls was covered in pictures of birds, some from magazines, most drawn himself with coloured pencils. He preferred the photos. The ones he had drawn himself were a bit rubbish. And his hand-writing underneath, naming each bird, was crap.

A sudden panic as he realises the can of Flamenco Red spray-paint is lying there, in full bloody view, right on his floor. Everything started with that can of red paint. He wishes he had never nicked it. Billy looks up anxiously, but Ferguson hasn't spotted it. He is peering at a drawing of a pied wagtail. With a gentle kick, Billy nudges it under the bed, and hears the tiny ball bearing rocking back and forward in the can as it settles.

'Nice,' Ferguson said, pointing at the drawing.

How can Ferguson not have heard that?

'What do you do when you run out of wall? Start on the ceiling?' He grinned at the boy.

'They don't stick to the ceiling. They fall down,' said Billy.

'Course they do. Stupid idea. You know all the names and everything?'

It was just conversation, Billy thought, to make him feel better. 'Yep,' he said.

'I never knew. And your mates at school? Are they into this?'

'Not much. They don't get it, really.'

'Know what I heard? There's a snowy owl been spotted up on the mountains there.' He nodded towards Billy's window.

'I heard that too. I been going up there to look for it at weekends. Got soaked last Saturday. Mum says I'm mad.' He grinned.

'That would be something, wouldn't it, seeing that?'

Billy nodded.

'Did your father like birds too?'

Billy said, 'Not much.'

'No. I suppose not. Not that kind of fellow.'

Hated them, in fact; had thought his son was a fucken sissy for liking them, but Billy didn't say anything. Dad had wanted him to like cars, like he had. Sergeant Ferguson shook his head and looked at him in a way that Billy thought meant he must be feeling sorry for him. That made Billy feel angry, embarrassed. No one should be feeling sorry for him.

He went over to his chest of drawers and fiddled with a Corgi car that sat on top of it and then turned. He could still just see the lid of the can of paint in the gloom under his bed.

If this was *Starsky and Hutch* the policeman would have spotted it now, thought Billy.

FOUR

'What's the matter? Why won't they let me in?' Gill Rayner asked. 'It's my brother's house.'

They had walked down the short lane to Bob's house to meet her there. 'The Crime Scene team say they're going to need a little longer, I'm afraid,' said Cupidi.

Gill Rayner was what South's mother would have described as a no-nonsense woman. Short, manageable hair, little or no make-up, a clear complexion and dark brown eyes. They were bloodshot, presumably from crying.

'It's frustrating for us, as well,' said Cupidi. 'We need to get in there too.'

Poor woman. South wanted to reach out and take her trembling hand and hold it. 'Have they found something?' she asked.

'Too early to say,' Cupidi said.

'Oh.' Gill seemed to be considering this.

South stepped forward. 'My name is William South. I knew your brother. I liked him.'

She examined him. 'He talked about you a lot,' she said.

'Did he?' said South.

'He always said he found you a very interesting man.'

Cupidi stepped in before South had a chance to say anything else. 'William has a house up the road. Perhaps we can go there and have a cup of tea?'

'Why?'

'I would like to interview you about your brother.'

'But I already spoke to a woman at the station. I need to go home. I'm very tired.'

'I'm part of the investigation, Miss Rayner. I realise it's difficult . . .'

'Do what you have to, I suppose.'

South noticed that her accent was very different from her brother's. His had been BBC English, the kind you'd expect from a public school teacher; hers was more estuary: Kent, or maybe Essex. Bob would have grown up speaking like her, he assumed, but disguised his roots as he grew older. Maybe that was another reason they had hit it off so well. Birders were practised at concealing themselves.

The three of them walked up the road. The grey clouds forming out at sea had a diagonal haze beneath them. Rain was coming.

'I'm very sorry about your brother,' said South. 'He was a very good man.'

The woman gulped air, but didn't speak. She looked fragile, as if she would fall to the ground at any moment, or the wind could blow her down. He reached over and took her arm and guided her towards the house, feeling her weight leaning into him for support. Beneath the wool of her jacket, he could feel her shaking, and he felt her immense sadness passing into him and, like her, just wanted to be alone with it. But he was a policeman; he was working.

Back at South's house, the ground coffee had arrived. Cupidi returned with two cups. 'It may have a few bits in it,' she said. She had improvised with a pan and a tea strainer.

'I don't suppose I'll sleep anyway,' said Gill Rayner, taking one.

Out of her shapeless woollen coat, she was surprisingly slim. She was one of those women who dressed to hide their looks, rather than accentuate them. They sat on dining chairs in his bare front room, Gill Rayner staring up at the cramped bookshelves. 'I see why Bob and you got on,' Gill Rayner said, looking at his books.

DS Cupidi said, 'What else did he like?'

'DS Cupidi is not a bird lover,' said South.

'I need to know what kind of person Mr Rayner was.'

Gill Rayner was sitting very straight in her chair. She said, 'I don't know what to say.'

'He was a teacher, apparently,' said Cupidi. 'What did he teach?'

'English literature. The classics. Some maths too. And he is a science teacher too. Was.'

'Good. Where?'

'At a preparatory school in Eastbourne. I told this to the

other policewoman already. I'm very, very confused and tired. I just want to go home now.'

Cupidi reached out and took her hand. 'I'm sorry. I'll let you go in just a minute. You visited him here regularly?'

'I visit him every fortnight.'

'Had you spoken to him over the last few days, to make arrangements about your visit? Had he mentioned anything out of the ordinary?'

'We didn't speak. We didn't need to. It was an arrangement.'

'I know that this is hard for you, but can you think of anyone who would have any reason to use violence against your brother?'

She shook her head hard, then wiped her eyes with the back of her hand.

'Think about it in your own time. Anyone with a short fuse?'

South watched Gill's hands shaking gently. She looked destroyed.

'Had he expressed any concern about anything? Any money troubles?'

'He was OK for money. He never borrowed.'

'Do you have any tissues, William?' Cupidi asked.

When he returned with some toilet paper from the downstairs bathroom, Cupidi had moved her chair next to Gill's and was hugging her, enfolding her completely in her arms. Gill's shoulders were shuddering as she cried. When he handed DS Cupidi the wad of tissue he'd torn from the roll she rolled her eyes, as if to say, *Is that all you've got?*

'Any friends. Old teaching colleagues?'

She shook her head.

Cupidi frowned. 'No one?' Cupidi made a note on her pad, then said, 'A girlfriend or lover? Divorced? Some big ex?'

She shook her head, pulled her chin in a little. 'No. Why would you think he would?'

'It's just a standard question, Gill. I mean, it's not always usual for a man to live on his own, unless there's some reason for it.' Cupidi paused, looked at South. 'Present company excepted.'

'He was just a very private man.'

Cupidi leaned forward. 'What about anyone else? When you arrived there this morning, did you see anyone else around?'

The woman frowned. 'I don't think so.'

'Try. Please.'

Gill Rayner snapped. 'Look, I wasn't expecting to find Bob dead. So, I'm sorry, but I really wasn't paying any attention.'

Cupidi recoiled, startled by sudden loudness of the other woman's voice. 'You live in London?' Cupidi asked. 'We have your address and contact details?'

'I left all my details at the station.'

Cupidi said, 'We can drive you home if you like. You can pick up your car another time.'

'No. I'll be all right.' She opened her handbag and stuffed the wet tissues into it.

South said, 'It's not always a good idea to drive after you've had such a shock. I can drive you to a station.'

She looked up, eyes pink. 'I just want to go home now. I just want to be on my own.'

South stood. 'I'll walk you to the car, then,' he said.

'Right,' said Cupidi. 'Good.'

Gill Rayner's car was parked just inside the police tape; the constable had to untie it to let her out.

As she opened her handbag to look for the keys, he said, 'I was wondering. What did you think they had stolen? If you looked in the box, you must have been looking everywhere.'

Gill Rayner frowned, as if surprised by the question. 'To be honest, I can't even remember why I looked in it. It seems odd now, doesn't it? I suppose something must have been wrong with it,' she said. 'Maybe the lid wasn't down properly. I really can't remember.'

He nodded. 'If you ever want to talk . . . not just as a policeman.'

She looked down at her plain brown shoes.

'I'm sorry. It's probably not appropriate,' he said. 'But he was my friend. I'm going to miss him a lot.'

Turning away, she said, 'Maybe,' but the word was mangled, as if she was trying not to cry again.

He stood in the lane as she drove away in an old green Polo. A thin drizzle was starting, though this would just be the beginning. It would rain hard this evening.

As she drove past him standing by Bob's gate, she turned her head and gazed at him. He gave her a little wave, but she looked away.

She knew more than she was saying, he thought to himself. Had Cupidi noticed it too? Was she the kind of woman who spotted things like that?

He could see Gill Rayner looking in the rear-view mirror now, back at her brother's house as she drove down the rutted road.

When he got to the house Cupidi was pinning an Ordnance Survey map to his wall. She looked at him, guiltily. 'I'll fix it up later, don't worry.'

'You should have used tape,' he said.

'Sorry. I couldn't find any. We're going to have to do a fingertip search for the murder weapon.' She stood back and looked at the map. 'Christ. It's huge, isn't it?'

Twelve square miles of shingle and scrub stretched to the north and west of them. It was called Denge Beach, though little of it was anywhere near the sea. 'We'll need someone to help the Police Search Adviser. Can you do that?'

'Whoever did it could have just chucked it in the sea. Or in one of the pits.' The shingle was dotted with old gravel pits that had filled with water.

'We've still got to try, haven't we? They'll be back from the door-to-doors any time now. Start the search as soon as there are enough of them.' Tongue between her teeth, she pressed a red pin in, marking the location of Bob

Rayner's bungalow. South heard the plaster crack beneath the paper.

'I was thinking. What if I get one of the specials to nip to the shop and get a couple of loaves of bread and some ham and put together some sarnies in your kitchen?' She paused, looking at him. 'I mean, I could just make them work through if you're not happy about that.'

In situations like this, coppers would miss their breaks. Making a copper skip lunch never made the senior officer popular. Being new, an outsider, Cupidi wouldn't want to be the one to tell them to work on.

'OK,' he said.

'We could have the afternoon meeting here too. Save going back and forwards to Ashford.'

'Here?'

'We've got so few coppers on the ground, I don't want them going back and forwards to the nick. We have to make the most of all their time.'

South looked around his room. It suddenly felt very small.

He noticed someone standing outside the window. Eddie, dressed in the same wax fishing hat he wore, inside and out, was peering at them both. He rapped on the glass. 'Is everything all right, Bill?' he called. 'What's going on down at Bob's house?'

'Who's he?'

'A local.'

Eddie was a young birder, eager to prove himself. He

was writing a PhD on changing migration patterns and global warming and was going out with a dippy girl who made dreamcatchers and tried to sell them from the caravan he lived in, parked behind one of the old shacks. South stepped outside the front door. It was starting to rain. He told Eddie what happened, watching his face as he did so.

It was no good telling himself that a man like Eddie could never have done this. Eddie, an eager young biologist in his twenties, girlfriend in Dover. At times like this you had to suspect everyone.

'Who? Why?' The blood had left Eddie's face.

'Did you see anyone unusual around? A man? Any cars you didn't recognise?'

Eddie was crying as he shook his head to each question, tears dribbling down his face into his scanty, dark, young man's beard. Things like this didn't happen here.

The coppers were ambling back from the door-to-doors now, miserable with cold, dripping wet footprints down the hallway, piling waterproof jackets onto the banister as they came in to report to Cupidi.

'Wipe your bloody shoes,' he complained.

'Sorry, skip.'

But the next one came in and did exactly the same. South found a copy of the *Kent Messenger* and spread its pages out on the floor.

The coppers approached Cupidi one by one, notebooks open, turning over damp pages as they reported back.

Cupidi listened, making notes herself. As South had said, only a handful of the houses were occupied at this time of year. None of the occupants had noticed anyone at Rayner's cottage. Apart from the rough sleepers, nobody had noticed anything unusual. Most of the people they'd spoken to didn't even know who Bob Rayner was.

Cupidi chewed on her lip thoughtfully as the coppers perched on any free chairs in the kitchen. They had taken over the living room too, gnawing on the sand-wiches and chocolate bars, dropping crisps on the carpet. There weren't enough cups for everyone so there was a rota for tea.

Outside, the rain was beginning to come down hard. The sooner they got going the better. Time means everything in an investigation. The rain would be washing evidence away. Facts slipping away between stones.

Sergeant Ferguson sat down on Billy's bed. 'I want to ask again about your daddy. Is that OK? You found him, didn't you?'

'I told the other policemen about it loads.'

'I know. But I just have to ask. I just want to try and work out what time it was.'

'I don't know.'

'It must have been a shock.'

His daddy, strong as a JCB, sprawled out in the chair

61

under the portrait of Her Majesty that hung above the fire-place, a half-finished bottle of Mackeson's on the table next to him. He had been drinking all afternoon, stacking tyres onto the bonfire in the field.

'Had your father been working in the garage?'

'I suppose.' Dad had been a mechanic. He was always in the garage. Loved the big American cars with all those Indian names, like Pontiacs and Cadillacs.

'But he was home when you got back?'

'Mm.'

'I was wondering, was the telly on?'

Billy nodded.

'Do you remember what the programme was?'

'I don't know, maybe the news?'

'You sure about that, Billy?'

'Don't know.'

'Your dad had enemies, didn't he?'

Mum had told him to say nothing. Billy concentrated on the toy car he was holding, a Buick Regal, like the one Kojak had. 'Wouldn't know.'

'Anyone unusual who came to the house in the few days before he was killed?'

Billy shrugged.

'Did you hear him, maybe, speaking to someone on the phone? Was he up to anything, you know?'

Billy shook his head.

Ferguson sighed. 'So. What had you been doing at your friend's house?'

'It was the bonfire. Eleventh Night. Only, Mum wouldn't let me go because she said there was going to be aggro.'

Those days there was always aggro on Eleventh Night. Every July the older lads would burn Irish tricolours and look for Catholics to fight. 'Mum was at the bingo, so she said I could go round to Rusty's. So we was just watching the fireworks, you know? From my friend's window. You can see them from his mum and dad's bedroom.'

'That's just a couple of doors away, isn't it?'

Billy's bedroom faced towards the back of the house, so you couldn't see Rusty's house from there. 'Over the road,' he said.

'And you didn't hear the shot there?'

Billy shrugged again. Nobody heard the shot. There were fireworks.

'Who was you there with?'

'Just Rusty and Stampy. You know. His older brother.'

'The one with the gammy leg?' said Ferguson. 'He doesn't go out on Eleventh Night either?'

Billy shook his head. 'Stampy says he hates all that. Besides, he can't run so fast now.'

'Fair play.'

Stampy Chandler liked to tell the younger children he walked with a limp because he had been kneecapped by the IRA for dealing weed, but really it was because he'd been hit by a car last year, crossing the road outside school.

'And tell me, Billy, when you came back from your

friend, Mr Chandler's house, did you see anything strange? Before you let yourself in the door, that is.'

Billy shook his head, curling his lower lip down.

'Nobody hanging around in the street outside?'

'No.'

'No unusual cars.'

'Nope.'

'Think, Billy. Think really hard. Because we've asked everyone and no one else in the street was out and about that night. You were the only person out there at that time. You're the only person who can help me.'

Billy squinted at the car, the way you did when you were trying to pretend that it was real. From his trouser pocket, Ferguson pulled out a packet of Spangles and offered one to Billy. It was a new tube. Billy took one between finger and thumb.

'No. I didn't see no one.'

For a while Fergie said nothing, then, weirdly, he reached out his arm towards Billy; Billy flinched back, but Ferguson's hand kept coming towards his face and just when Billy thought he was going to try and touch him or something weird, he just lifted the fringe away from Billy's forehead and said, 'That's a nasty cut you got there.'

Before he could stop himself, Billy lifted his fingers to the scab that hid at his hairline. 'Nothing much,' he said.

'Who did that to you?'

'I fell,' said Billy. 'On the stairs.'

'Yeah?'

'The other day,' said Billy.

'Sure about that?'

Billy carefully unwrapped the sweet, put it in his mouth and nodded, conscious that the copper was staring at him.

'One more thing. You told the Inspector you got home at nine fifteen? That would make sense if it was the news, and all.'

Cautiously, Billy nodded.

'Yet nobody called the police until . . .' Sergeant Ferguson took out a notebook and flicked through it. 'Gone ten, when your mammy got home. That's a long time to be on your own with your dad . . . you know. Like that.'

Billy spun the wheels of the car.

'Are you sure?'

Billy sucked on the sweet.

'Sit down here, Billy.' Ferguson patted the bed next to where he was sitting. 'I got a feeling about you, Billy McGowan. You're a good lad. I've got a feeling you're not saying everything. You have your reasons, most like, but I promise you this. Anything you tell me is between the two of us. Cross my heart and swear to die. This isn't me as a copper. This is me as a friend of your mammy's. A special friend I hope. I got a lot of time for your mother. Her and me go way back. She was always the best-looking girl round here. Still is. Did you know me and her used to walk out, when we were at school?'

'You never?'

Ferguson grinned. 'True. Before she met your dad. She and me were close, back then. Real close.'

Billy considered for a little while.

'Your mum. She's special, Billy. I think a lot of her. I promise I'll never do anything to hurt her. Or you. I just want to find out who did this to your father. That way I can keep you both safe.'

Billy concentrated even harder on the car. All this talk about his mother was embarrassing.

Ferguson said, 'See, I don't believe a boy like you would have just stayed in the room with his dad, like that. Not all that time. Not for almost an hour.'

Billy didn't answer. He just spun the wheels of the car round and round for a while as Fergie sat there next to him, watching, like he knew something.

FIVE

The Search Adviser turned out to be a tall woman in her thirties who wore her glasses on a string around her neck.

'All this area is just scrubland?' the woman said, peering at Cupidi's map.

'Twelve square miles of it,' said South.

'Christ on a bike,' she said.

'Precisely.'

She handed out gloves and explained that, because of the openness of the land, they were going to circle anti-clockwise around the house, walking in a line. 'Me too?' said South.

'I want you there, just in case,' said the woman. 'I don't know this area.'

'He was already at the crime scene,' said Cupidi. 'He could contaminate it.'

'Right,' the woman said. She dug around in a carrier bag and brought out another coverall, overshoes and mask. 'You'll have to put them on then. Just in case. And keep your distance, OK?'

She explained they should make a note of what they

found – anything from clothes or gloves to any litter that the killer might have discarded, as well as anything that might have been used as the weapon. Once the pathology report came back they'd have a better idea of exactly what they were looking for, but that could take days.

Wind hummed in the telephone wires as it drove the rain in from the east. Standing in the rain, South watched as they walked around Bob's house. The rain was sometimes at their backs, other times straight in their faces. The advantage of the landscape was that little was hidden. In long grass or wasteland you could only afford to be a couple of yards apart at most. Here the line spread out thinly, pausing only for officers to poke sticks at clumps of gorse that grew where it could. The ground around here was pitted with rabbit scrapes.

'Here!' A woman constable shouted, raising her arm.

An old fence post, lying on its side. It looked too large and unwieldy to kill a man with. A SOCO, clad from head to toe in white like South, ran over and started photographing the object, flash-lighting up the stones around.

'OK,' said the search leader, shouting above the wind. 'Keep going.'

They closed up the gap in the line and moved on. Once they had trudged around Bob's house twice they came to the power station's perimeter fence. There were notices fixed regularly along the length of it: *Nuclear Installations Act 1965. Licensed Site Boundary.*

From behind the fence came a constant, deep noise, a bit

like a kettle starting to boil. You didn't even notice it if you lived here. At the wire, they turned around. Now, instead of doing circles, they began doing C-shapes, first one way, stopping when they reached the perimeter, then the other way, each arc wider than the last.

Now the circle was large. Each arc was taking thirty or forty minutes. A few more sticks and a short, rusty metal bar had been found, tagged and photographed, but none of them showed any signs of being used to kill anyone, or having been put there recently. South was used to being out here when it was like this – he liked to be out in any weather – but the other policemen looked tired already, blinking in the rain and hunching into the weather. The uninterrupted wind slowed them, making their muscles stiffer.

'What do you reckon about the new girl, Sarge?' a constable to his right called, from a clump of broom he was prodding with a stick.

'Sergeant Cupidi?' South shouted back over the noise of rain on his waterproofs.

'Bit pushy, in't she?'

'Kind of.'

They had reached the houses and huts on the far side of the road now.

'Do we need to do the bins?' the coppers complained.

It was already getting dark by the time they reached The Pilot. Inside the lights were on. Afternoon drinkers were standing at the bar.

'You know the publican?' the Search Adviser asked.

'Of course.' It was the pub where visiting birders gathered to discuss what they'd seen.

'Tell him he can't chuck anything more in those bins,' she said. 'I'll get them sealed and SOCO can do them later.'

A drinker noticed the policemen fanning out in the car park, came to the window, pint in hand, and watched them as they methodically worked the ground around the pub.

'Bastard,' said one copper. 'Just doing it to taunt us.'

'Fuckin' soaked, I am. Supposed to be waterproof, this coat. My arse.'

The light was going. There wouldn't be much point continuing for much longer.

'Look busy. Here comes Jesus.'

South looked up. A police BMW was driving towards them, lights on full beam. It would be the Chief Inspector coming back to join them for the afternoon meeting. The car paused by the pub car park and lowered an electric window.

Inspector McAdam was sitting next to the Chief Inspector in the back seat. He leaned across the larger man and asked, 'Have they found anything, Bill?'

'Don't think so, sir.'

'This meeting is in your house, I gather, Bill.'

'Yes, sir.'

The window wound back up and the car moved on. The search leader blinked in the rain, checking her watch, and shouted, 'Ten more minutes, then all back inside.'

From the pub, the line of police officers was moving southwards, across the road. The beach was wide here. There was so much debris at this time of year it was hard to know what to pick up. A few locals had tried to preserve the old sheds that housed the fishing boats' winding gear, nailing fresh wood on to stop them from falling apart, but mostly the weather was taking them now.

South wandered away from them towards the beach. In the lee of one of the sheds South saw the blackened stones from where a fire had been. He remembered the rough sleepers he had seen that morning.

They had left the place in a mess. The shingle was littered with blue Tennent's Super cans, torn cardboard strips and a broken bottle.

The drinkers had long gone. They would be sleeping it off somewhere. South squatted down. The fire had burned out, turning the shingle a grey-ish pink. The ash had washed away into the stones. In a circle around the coloured shingle, the half-burnt sticks and planks.

Leaning over to shelter himself from rain he pulled out his notebook. '*3 men, 2 women?*' he'd written. '*10.10 a.m. No rain.*'

It was all to do with the birding. Writing everything down: the time, the place, the weather conditions, the look of things; it was a discipline all birders worked to acquire. When he'd started he'd used Alwych All Weather notebooks, like all the birders did. Over a year or so, he would slowly fill a book with the record of everything he saw and where he'd seen it. It was as much about birds as a record of a life. But somehow, as a copper, he began to find it more natural to use the smaller police books instead of the Alwyches. It wasn't just that they fitted more easily into a pocket; but somehow it was the deliberate blurring of a practice.

He leaned down, took his eyes off the book and peered instead at the pieces of unburnt wood, circled like a child's drawing of sunrays around the ash. Most were old weathered pieces of flotsam they'd picked up. One half-burnt stump looked newer. A paler, heavily varnished new wood. A gust of wind hit him just as he realised, with shock, that he was looking at an axe handle, the sort you'd buy in any tool shop.

'Here,' he said.

A gust of rain carried his voice away.

He remembered the tremble of Gill Rayner's arm by his side. Now he looked closer at the axe handle: was there something dark smudged on it?

It could just have been soot. But there was also something caught in a crack at the unburnt end; he knelt, leaning as close as he could. It looked like a single, human hair.

Quickly he took off his cap and held it over the stump of wood, to protect it from the steady downpour.

For the first time he noticed the label on the broken bottle. It was Balvenie. A single malt. He shouted again, 'Here.'

The other coppers were already too far away.

'Here,' he screamed, waving his free arm. Rain was in his hair, already trickling down his neck and into his shirt. His whole body was shivering.

'Quick.'

From between the sheds and shacks, the sound of boots on stones. From all around, coppers were running towards him now, wind and wet in their faces.

On the doorstep, the Inspector said, 'I know what things are like, Mary. The way things are round here.'

'Ye don't,' his ma said, staring past him.

Billy waited in the kitchen. Sergeant Ferguson hung back, too, until the Inspector was gone.

'He means well, I suppose,' said Ferguson.

Across the road, Mrs Chandler peeked out from behind her nets at them.

'He's scared there's going to be more of this. What's happened to this place, Mary? When we were kids it was never as bad as this.'

A mile or so to the south lay the bad lands. Theirs was a Protestant estate, but the countryside around them was Catholic and thick with paramilitaries. The Irish border was only five miles beyond.

One summer night when he had been about six or seven, at the start of the Troubles, his dad had woken him from his bed and said, 'Come on, we've got work to do.'

73

Dad had been drunk. Together they had walked down to the little lane at the bottom of the estate. There his dad had handed him the torch and said, 'Shine it on the tarmac.'

Dad had pulled out a paintbrush. There had been something clumsy about the way the big man had worked, tongue protruding through his teeth as he concentrated. Occasionally he had muttered, 'Fuck,' as he dripped paint on his ancient brogues.

When he'd finished he'd stepped back to review his handiwork. NO POPE HERE. The letters had been uneven, diminishing in size as they went.

Billy remembered how his father had frowned at his rotten handwriting, disappointed that it hadn't turned out better. 'As long as the Taigs can fucken read it, I suppose.'

'One thing,' Sergeant Ferguson said to Billy's mother, picking up his cap from the chair. 'You said, "They killed him." Tell me honest, Mary, who do you think "they" is?'

His mother pushed the sergeant towards the door. 'Goodbye, Inspector Van der bloody Valk.'

'Listen, I should tell you this, only I'd appreciate you keeping it to yourselves, but I think it's important. It's about the gun they shot him with,' he said.

'What?' said Mary.

Ferguson lowered his voice. 'It had been used before.'

'So?'

Billy's eyes widened. 'How do you know that?' he asked.

Ferguson looked at the boy.

'Billy. Go upstairs,' said his mother.

'Why should I?'

'No lip. Go up and wash your hands. They're filthy.'

Billy left the room and thumped his way up the stairs, so she would think he'd gone up, then tiptoed straight back down again. His mother was saying, 'I know you're trying to help, Fergie, but I don't want to hear any of this. The less I know the better.'

'You should. For your own safety.'

'For my own safety? What do you mean by that, Fergie? I was never anything to do with what my husband got up to. I always said he was stupid for getting caught up.'

'Let me tell you this, Mary. The bullet they found in him? Well, they matched it up with others they found from other killings. They can do that, you know? Wee scratches on the bullet. They're just as good as fingerprints.'

'Leave me now, John Ferguson.'

'This is important, Mary. The gun had already been used in two murders. One in '76, and another a few weeks back. A Catholic taxi driver and a young lad picked off in the street. The UVF claimed responsibility for both. Hear that? The UVF. So we know it was the Volunteer Force, most likely.'

'One of our own? You're kidding me?' she said. Billy could hear the tremble in her voice now.

'No, I'm not. See now? That's why the Inspector's so bloody anxious. This isn't IRA, like everybody is saying. It's UVF killed him. And if that's the case, this is like a civil war in a civil war, Protestant killing Protestant. And I don't want you caught up in any of this. Was there a falling out between him and the Volunteers over anything?'

'You'd know better than I would. Half the Constabulary are in the UVF, aren't they?'

'That's why the Inspector is so shite-scared. Think about it. This could be real bad if it's a copper.'

Billy's stomach rumbled so loudly he was sure they would hear it, but they kept on talking. So the gun that killed his father had already killed at least twice before? He longed to tell someone why that piece of information was so amazing to him. Why it turned his world upside down. But he couldn't. To say anything at all would be to give his own secret away.

'Everybody knows your man was UVF, Mary. One of Joe McGrachy's bully boys.'

'I don't know anything about that.'

'Course you don't, Mary. Most of my mates in the RUC say exactly the same. Fuck sake. Three wise monkeys. But how long can everyone go round pretending, Mary?'

'Oh, Fergie, leave us alone for a bit, will ye?' Mary McGowan sighed. 'I know you want to help. But what good's it going to do anyway?'

'I know, I know.' There was a pause. Then: 'Are you managing OK, Mary? It must be hard.'

His mother said something, but quietly, and Billy couldn't hear it.

'I could come round some evenings if you like? Keep

you company. Help out with the lad. Remember how we used to sneak off to the Frontier cinema together, when we were sweethearts?'

'We were never sweethearts really, Johnny Ferguson.'

'Whatever you say, Mary. But I mean it.'

Billy crept back upstairs. From the window at the top he watched Ferguson's car drive away, down into the grey town, passing over the words his dad had written: NO POPE HERE.

SIX

DI McAdam was all smiles. 'Good job, Bill,' he said. 'You know Sergeant South, don't you, Chief Inspector?'

The front room was crowded with coppers, steaming in the warmth. One of the younger policemen was coughing every few seconds without bothering to cover his mouth.

'Excellent idea, using your house as a base,' said the Chief Inspector, looking around.

'It was Sergeant Cupidi's idea, sir,' said South.

Across the room, Cupidi winked back at him. The Chief Inspector was peering around in the crowded room for somewhere to sit. Seeing one of his neighbourhood PCSOs perching on one of his dining-room chairs gazing at her mobile screen, South nudged her, motioning her to stand. Blushing, she jumped up to make way for the Senior Inspecting Officer.

The air was pungent with the reek of damp socks. South had asked the policemen to leave their boots in the hallway. Only the SIO and the inspector had left their shoes on. 'OK, girls and boys,' the inspector said, loudly enough to get everyone's attention. 'Good work, everybody. Fantastic results for a first day. From what we've learned, this looks more and more like an opportunist. Especially if that bottle Bill found turns out to be the one missing from the cabinet.' He'd taken his jacket off and was rolling up his sleeves as he talked. 'We can concentrate our resources looking for substance users, homeless people, alcoholics. Bill says he saw three men and two women, but didn't get much of a chance to see their faces.'

Looking east towards the morning sun was like trying to identify a bird when the light was behind it.

'Maybe they'll have sobered up and figured out what they've done. Or maybe they're on another bender already. We're looking for homeless people who were in this area over the last forty-eight hours,' he was saying. 'Any CCTV around here?'

Cupidi said, 'Some on the pub. I've already asked for it. A couple of homeowners, only the houses are empty so it'll take a while to contact them.'

'We'll need a multi-agency approach. Coordinate that. Contact the council's housing and homeless department.'

'Done that already, sir,' said Cupidi.

'And the local homeless charities and Social Services. Someone will have a list. We need to find everyone who's been sleeping out around here.'

'Yes, sir,' said Cupidi, tight-lipped. The more the inspector talked, the less she was smiling. 'I was thinking maybe tonight, sir. The hostels will have duty officers on. Maybe

I can take an officer around with me. Find out what they know? For all we know he's in one of them now.'

McAdam smiled. 'No need for overtime yet, Sergeant. I'll suggest the duty sergeant puts a couple of the night shift on calling round the hostels.'

'Yes, sir,' she said quietly.

'Good. So, when did forensics say they were going to get back to you about the weapon?'

'They're calling up first thing tomorrow to say whether it's human hair or not and whether there are decent prints on the broken bottle. Take a few more days to confirm whether they're Rayner's or not.'

McAdam nodded. 'But they will be, won't they?'

'Hard to say with all the rain,' said Cupidi.

'I can't see that as too much of a problem,' said McAdam. 'I'm convinced that whoever did this is behaving chaotically. They won't have thought to cover their traces properly. Check all the DIY stores. Get their CCTV. Look for anyone buying an axe handle.' He looked at his watch. 'OK?' he said. 'Meet back here 8.20 a.m. tomorrow?'

'What about searching the rest of the area?' said Cupidi.

'We'll see what manpower we have available tomorrow.'

'Only, we don't know for certain that what we've found is the murder weapon, sir.'

'I'll bet you a tenner it is.'

'All the same. We need to properly examine the area around the discovery site.'

'Naturally. I'm sure Sergeant South can help you liaise

with the Police Search Adviser on that. Anything else?' Another big smile. 'Good work, boys and girls. Good work. Anything you want to add, Chief Inspector?'

The SIO said, 'Everyone knows, last few years, there's been a significant rise in homelessness round here and all the associated problems. Ruins our patch's reputation. We need to stamp on this. Speed. Faster we act, the better our chances. And the quicker you all get home.'

South walked McAdam to the front door of the house; the Chief Inspector was out there already, waiting in his car.

At night, the nuclear plant was illuminated. Against the blackness of the Channel behind it, its orange lights were dazzling. 'Extraordinary place,' McAdam said. He paused at the door and turned to Cupidi.

'Are you OK?' he asked her.

'Me, sir? Fine.'

'Look Alexandra. I know you're keen to make a good impression. Your first case here. Keen to get everything sorted in a few hours. One thing I've learned. Work with what you have. Don't you worry. We'll have it wrapped up in a couple of days.'

'Very reassuring, sir.'

'Certain of it.' When he smiled back at her, South wasn't sure if he was just ignoring the irony in her voice, or had missed it altogether.

On the road, a few hundred yards away, a lone copper sat in his car, running the engine, interior lights on.

To prevent anyone disturbing the scene, they had put up

a tent over the spot where the fire had been. In the morning the Scene of Crime Officers would be back. For now, the one policeman would have to spend his shift sitting alone in his car, guarding the site.

The Chief Inspector's car sped past it, away home.

'Say it,' said South.

'What?' She looked up at him. The other police had gone now; their shift was over. Cupidi was sitting on his front step smoking a cigarette.

'Say what you really think of DI McAdam.'

'Did it show?'

'Just a bit.'

'Is he always so obsessed with his budget?'

'I suppose he has to be. Besides. You should probably go home. Your daughter will be on her own.'

The rain had passed over now. She stubbed out her cigarette on his stone step. 'Don't tell me how to be a parent, William, OK?'

'I apologise.'

She sighed. 'Speed is everything. The more resources you throw at something like this in the first hours, the better the result. It's always the same. The longer it takes, the harder it gets.'

She moved over and he sat on the step next to her.

'Are you OK?' she asked. 'Staying here? Your friend was killed just a hundred yards away.'

South said, 'I'll be fine.'

'Really?'

'I don't know.'

'Tell you what. I haven't had time to buy any supper. I was going to take Zoë out to a Nando's. Would you like to come?'

South blinked. 'Well, that's very nice of you. But . . .'

For the first time that day, she laughed out loud. 'I'm not trying to proposition you, William. I want to talk about the case, that's all. I'm not used to just going home after a day like this. It feels ridiculous. And I don't think you should be alone. You've had a rough day. Your friend was killed.'

'What about your daughter? Don't you need to talk to her in private?'

'To be honest, she'd probably be grateful there's someone there as well as me. It doesn't have to be Nando's. There's a Pizza Hut there too. It's very cosmopolitan.'

Cupidi unplugged her laptop and got in her car to drive ahead to collect her daughter. South stayed behind, putting the mugs in the dishwasher and mopping the mud off the kitchen floor.

The shopping complex sat beside the M20, north of the town. The Nando's was one of half a dozen chain restaurants positioned around the car park of the huge multiplex.

South got out of his elderly Micra and stood outside the restaurant. The air was heavy. Gusts blew at the puddles. It would rain again soon. Ducks from the Baltic would be taking advantage of the easterly.

He thought about Bob Rayner: he would be lying in a cold storage unit somewhere. They should have been together watching the birds arrive. Instead, they would be cutting him open soon to examine his organs and measure his wounds and contusions. A little way off, the motorway roared; its lights shone on the low cloud above him. He considered just calling Cupidi's mobile and saying he would prefer to be alone this evening.

The restaurant was almost empty. Cupidi and her daughter sat at a table at the back with a bowl of nuts in front of them. Cupidi had a lager and the girl had a Coke.

'Sorry I'm late. I had to clean up the house.'

Zoë, Cupidi's daughter, leaned her head on one side slightly and said, 'I don't know. He's not that good-looking.'

'What?'

'Oh God. Shut up,' said Cupidi. She hadn't changed out of the linen suit, or put on fresh make-up, but she looked more relaxed here, at least.

The fifteen-year-old leaned forward, across the table. 'She was saying, before you came, she thought you were really fit.'

'Zoë!' hissed Cupidi. 'Behave. William's had an awful day.'

'Single mother. Divorced. I suppose she's had to lower her standards a bit,' said South.

Zoë clapped her hand over her mouth and laughed: a surprisingly low, loud laugh, given her slight frame.

'It's a complete lie,' said Cupidi. 'She's just making it all up to embarrass me. I didn't say anything about you. Stop it, now, Zoë.'

'She's the liar. Not me,' said the teenager.

'See why she's always getting into trouble? She's such a shit-stirrer.'

'I'm not the only one who gets into trouble. Tell me, William, which one of us do you believe?' said the teenager.

'I know you think it's funny. But it's rude. Would you like a beer, William?' said Cupidi, waving at the waitress. 'She's just in a sarky mood because I was telling her off.'

'Who's her?' said the girl.

'Because I was telling you off.'

A waitress appeared. 'I'll have a Coke,' said South, and ordered chicken wings.

'Don't you think this is the weirdest place on the planet?' asked the teenager.

South looked around at the restaurant.

'No,' she said. 'This whole place. All of it.'

'William grew up here,' said Cupidi.

'You'll get used to it,' said South.

'Hope not,' she said.

'You're being rude,' said Cupidi.

'She's fine, honestly,' said South. 'It must be strange, after London.'

'Thank you,' the girl said, dipping her hand into the bowl of nuts.

'Zoë is in a bad mood because I have been asking her

about a fight at school and what caused it and she won't tell me.'

'Zoë is right here,' said the teenager. 'It was just a stupid fight. Don't want to talk about it.'

Cupidi put down her knife and fork. 'Tell me about the inspector,' she said.

'McAdam? He's a career boy,' said South. 'Oxbridge. Loves targets. But he's OK.'

'Key performance indicators. Equality impact assessments. Development reviews.'

'Mum doesn't always hate inspectors,' said Zoë. 'Sometimes she thinks they're lovely.'

'What's wrong with you, Zoë?'

'Can I have some wine?'

'No you can't,' said her mother.

'Why did you move here?' Zoë asked South.

William paused. He looked at his Coke. 'My dad died. My mother wanted a change.'

'Yeah, but why here?' said Zoë.

'She wanted to go to France, I think, but we never made it across the Channel. This is as far as we managed. It was a long way away from where I grew up, I suppose,' he said.

'Where was that?'

South pretended he hadn't heard, and said, 'Are you annoyed at the inspector for getting stuck in this afternoon?'

Cupidi smiled. 'It's his prerogative. I'm just a lowly sergeant. It's what he's supposed to do.'

'But you didn't like it, did you?'

'I'm new. I'm just learning to keep my head down. Stay out of trouble. But I'm good. I know I am. I want him to know that.'

'You did well. He knows that. If you hadn't insisted we carry on despite the weather, we'd never have found the murder weapon.'

'If it is the murder weapon.'

'Don't you think it is?'

'Almost certainly, actually. It fits with the profile of an opportunist. We will get him. I promise,' she said, and she put her hand on his.

Zoë noticed. She looked down at the hands, then up at her mother. 'What murder weapon?' said Zoë. 'What are you talking about?'

'Sorry, love,' Cupidi said, pulling her arm back. 'William's friend was killed. He only found out today.'

'Oh.' She looked at him, then said, 'Sorry.'

South nodded.

'That's why Mum says you're having an awful day? I thought it was just . . . you know, work. How was he killed?'

'Zoë. Leave him alone.'

'We think he was bludgeoned with a stick by an intruder.'

'How gruesome.'

Cupidi said, 'You mustn't go talking about this at school. This isn't London. In a place like this everyone probably knows everyone.'

'God, Mum. What do you think I am?'

'I think you're a fifteen-year-old girl who gets into fights at school because she can't keep her mouth shut, that's what I think you are.'

'You don't know anything about it. Sometimes I hate you.'

'Ditto.'

'She doesn't mean it,' Zoë said to South. 'She loves me really. Was he a good friend?'

'I suppose he was,' said South. 'I'm only beginning to realise it.'

Zoë picked up her drink and sucked on her straw thoughtfully. Cupidi stood and said, 'Excuse me. I need the toilet. Be nice.'

When she was gone, Zoë said, 'I'm really sorry I was being a brat. I didn't realise. Banter, you know?'

South said, 'So, why were you fighting? At school.'

Bored staff chattered next to the till. There was pop music playing in the background.

'It was nothing.'

South said, 'I bet it wasn't.'

'You'll tell Mum,' said Zoë.

'Can't promise I won't,' he said. 'But I know what it's like, moving to a place like this.'

'Just don't, OK?' She leaned forward, talking more quietly. 'You know my mum dropped me off at school this morning in the car? Just as she was dropping me off she put the blue lights on and the siren in front of everybody and just literally shoved me out. All the other girls were saying

88

goodbye to their mums, and mine was driving off going *nee-naw nee-naw*.'

'She would have just heard about my friend Bob,' said South. 'That's when they discovered his body.'

'Oh God. I'm sorry. What happened to me is nothing. I'm being such a selfish idiot.'

'No. You're fine. I asked.'

'It was my second day, today. New school. Can you imagine what that's like? These . . . cows started taking the piss: "Your mum was so keen to get away from you she had to put the siren on."'

He nodded. 'They can be cruel.'

'They don't like coppers. They don't like coppers' kids. That's what it was about. There are some psychos there. The girl who attacked me in the toilets says they're going to get me. Please don't tell Mum. She'll only go in to the Head and complain or something stupid and make things a trillion times worse.'

'I won't,' he said.

'Promise?'

Cupidi was coming back from the toilet already. She said, 'What are you two talking about?'

'William was telling me about what it was like when he first came here,' said Zoë.

'I was going to ask,' South said. 'Why did you decide to move here?'

Cupidi said, 'I wanted to move Zoë out of London for her GCSEs. This job came up.'

'It was because of your stupid job,' Zoë said. 'I was fine in London.'

'No you weren't.'

'Are you two always like this?'

'Just don't go pretending it was because you wanted me to move out of London when it was nothing to do with that.'

'Keep your voice down, love.'

'I'm the one who's lost all my friends and have to start again.'

'They weren't very good friends.'

The girl said, 'How can you say that they weren't very good friends? At least they wouldn't have dragged me to this hole because you'd—'

'Enough.' Cupidi's voice was suddenly loud.

The other diners stopped talking and stared. Apart from the Take That song playing in the background, there was silence.

'Sorry, Mum,' said Zoë. 'I didn't mean it.'

'I think we should call a taxi,' said Cupidi.

'I'll drop you,' said South.

'No. It's fine.'

'I don't mind. Honestly.'

'What about pudding?' said Zoë.

Out in the car park Cupidi waited as her daughter ambled towards them across the wide tarmac. 'I'm sorry. I thought we could have a relaxing evening to get your mind off things. She's taking a little time to adjust, that's all.'

South just wanted to get home now.

'What she said about why we left . . .'

South shook his head. 'You don't have to explain.'

'Thanks,' she said, looking at the tarmac.

South's Micra was a two-door car. He looked away as the teenage girl squeezed herself into the back seat.

'What's this?'

'It's a tripod.'

'You take photographs?'

'It's for a telescope.'

'William is a bird spotter,' said Cupidi.

'Really?' said Zoë.

'Don't start,' said Cupidi.

'Cool. How many different birds have you spotted?'

'Around three hundred and fifty.'

'That doesn't sound that many.'

'Three hundred and fifty-six, in fact.'

'How do you tell the difference?'

He turned towards the back seat. 'The trick is to know what you're seeing. You can take people who've never been before and they can't even see what you're pointing at, sometimes.'

'A bit like being a copper, then,' said Cupidi. 'Noticing the stuff no one else does.'

DS Cupidi's house was three miles out of town. The night was black and thick. Cars came towards them, lights on full beam.

The housing estate was on a right-hand turn. South had

to wait a long time at the junction, cars careering towards them at crazy speeds, before there was a long enough gap in the traffic.

Cupidi directed them to a cul-de-sac. 'Here,' she said.

It was a new house, recently completed on a new estate; pale brick and white wood windows. The new grass outside it had turned to mud in the heavy rain. It would have to be re-turfed.

'Thanks. See you tomorrow,' said Cupidi. She ran to the tiny porch with the front door keys. As Zoë pushed her seat forward she said, 'Will you take me bird spotting one day?'

'You?'

'Why not?'

'I suppose,' he said, unsure of himself. She was the teenage daughter of a colleague. 'If it's OK with your mother.'

Zoë snorted loudly and stepped out of the car.

The constable was still enduring his miserable shift alone in the car. South offered to fetch him a cup of tea but he said he was OK.

South's car crawled past Rayner's house, all dark now, a *Strictly No Entry* notice on the door. He tried not to think of Bob being battered slowly to death while South had almost certainly been in his house, close by. He had been beaten 'over a prolonged period', the report had said. Had he cried out to South for help? He must have done. But South hadn't heard; no one had come.

The terrace was dark now, lit by a single street light.

Letting himself into his own house, he paused for a second and listened. He felt for the handle of the baseball bat he kept by the front door and stood there for a second in the darkness, listening, a weapon in his hand.

Just in case.

At night, he lay in bed, blankets up around his chin. His mother was downstairs, fussing. A full moon was inching slowly across the sky outside the window. To stay awake, Billy pressed his fingernails into the palm of his hand. Tonight, when he needed her to sleep, Mum was busybodying around the house. She was starting to throw stuff out.

Finally, he heard the clinking of empty milk bottles on the front step outside; then the creaking stairs, taps turned on in the bathroom, teeth brushed. A toilet flush.

He waited until her light was off, then tried to count to a thousand, but he lost his way in the two-hundreds. He recited the Lord's Prayer. He counted his teeth with his tongue.

In the end he decided his mother must have fallen asleep, so he put on his slippers and his parka, opened the door to his bedroom and crept downstairs.

For a while he stood in the hallway. Something about the house was different, he realised, now it was just the two of them. It wasn't just that they ate meals in front of the TV now Dad wasn't around, either. Some invisible quality was different. Even the air was lighter, easier to breathe.

The crowbar was under the stairs where his dad had always left it. Billy took it, went to the kitchen, turned the key in the back door and yanked at the bolts. Unable to shift the top one, he carefully lifted a stool, placed it by the door and stood on it.

The bolt was stuck. He tugged. Then shifted his weight so he could push. This time it shot across, loudly. Billy tottered on the stool, but didn't fall. Heart jittering, he stood, listening for footsteps from upstairs. Silence. His mother had not woken.

The back garden was oddly warm tonight. In the moonlight, he tucked the tip of the bar under the edge of the manhole cover, just as he had spied his father doing from his bedroom window.

It was a hell of a weight to shift. His father had made it look so easy.

The first time, the jemmy slipped and the manhole cover thumped back down again. 'Oh crap,' he whispered to himself. He looked up, waited a few seconds to see if a light came on, but none did.

He forced the steel rod back under and lifted. When it was high enough, he peered down into the blackness.

It was too dark to see anything down there.

Fergie had said the gun had killed two men before his father. Maybe they were not so different, his dad and him, after all. The idea made him feel nauseous.

He was reaching down inside the manhole when a light came on in the kitchen.

94

Oh shit. Billy dropped the jemmy down into the manhole and let the cover drop back down. The kitchen door swung back.

'Billy McGowan. What in hell's name are ye doin' out here in the cold at one in the morning?'

SEVEN

The next morning the weather broke. The rain stopped and a cool low sun turned the sea slate blue. South spent the morning with three other coppers combing as wide an area as he could but they found nothing more. He noted two firecrests and he was sure he'd heard the thin call of a redwing, but hadn't been able to see it.

No rough sleepers, though. The sight of police everywhere would have been enough to put them off. The inquiries at the night shelters in the region hadn't turned up anything so far.

He headed back in just before midday, legs stiffening from the cold, and was boiling a kettle when DS Cupidi arrived, talking on her mobile phone. She reached past him and took her pack of ground coffee from the shelf.

When she ended the call she said, 'They've got fingerprints on the bottle fragments. And possibly on the axe handle. Almost certainly DNA too.'

He understood the appeal of a murder investigation. Unlike most policing, the sort he was used to, the objective was a clear and simple one. With luck there would be a match. Old-fashioned fingerprints were often quicker to match than DNA results, which could take several days, and these days pretty much any rough sleeper's records would be somewhere on the PNC database.

'Any luck with the shelters?'

'Nothing yet. I've got a list of soup kitchens and food banks from Social Services,' said Cupidi. She held out a bit of paper. 'Would any of your lot go to those?'

'My lot?'

'The rough sleepers we saw yesterday.'

South scanned the list. 'Maybe. Mostly not. There's a food bank in Lydd too,' he said. 'It's not on the list. That's the nearest one. But the type of users you see here don't use food banks. They're too far outside of the system for that.'

She took the paper back from him and frowned at it. 'What about users?' she asked. 'Pound to a penny the killer was on drugs. Any dealers round here?'

He put down a half-drunk cup of tea and reached for his coat.

They started at Wiccomb caravan site. 'Careful how you go here,' said South. 'She doesn't like police much.'

'Her and me both. You think she'll know anything?'

'She'll know something. It's whether she'll tell us . . .'

The caravan was in the middle of the static site. It was a luxury model with a brand-new Audi A3 parked outside. 'How much do you reckon that car's worth?' said Cupidi.

'I don't know.'

'Around seventy grand,' said Cupidi. 'I don't suppose whoever owns that sleeps out much.'

Chained to a propane canister, a Dobermann and a Staffordshire had worn the grass bare in an arc in front of the caravan. The dogs started barking the moment South stepped out of the car.

The chains tensed and clanked. Behind the main window, the nets twitched. She was in.

'Judy. It's Sergeant South. I need to speak to you.'

The door stayed closed.

'Judy. I just want a word.'

South had the sense they were being watched, not only by whoever was in Judy Farouk's caravan, but by most of the other residents too. No one showed their face though. They were used to Judy here. They had learned not to interfere.

The caravan park was looking scrappy. Foxes had torn open bags of rubbish, scattering the debris over the grass. One mildewed caravan close to Judy's had been unoccupied for years, its door wide open. A wheelless car sat up on bricks.

Six years ago, this had been a nice place. Elderly people who wanted to live by the sea had retired here. Then Judy's family moved in. In the first few years there had been a serious assault and a couple of arsons, one resulting in a death. An elderly man who'd kept budgerigars had been burned alive in his static home. A few days before his death, he had complained to the police about drug dealing on the site.

South had interviewed him. They had raided Judy's caravan. Nothing was ever found. And then came the fire. Again, nothing had ever been proved. Nobody could ever explain why the victim would have been keeping petrol inside his static home.

In the next few months, those who could afford to moved off the site. The others, who had put all their retirement money into buying a plot here, kept quiet.

'I'm not going away, Judy. We've got all day.'

Still nothing.

'We'll be inside the car whenever you're ready to switch off Jeremy Kyle and talk to us.' He returned to the passenger seat.

'How long is this going to take?' asked Cupidi.

'Ten minutes. Maybe twenty. She always comes out in the end. She likes to piss us off a bit, but she knows that as long as we're out here, she's not doing any business. None of her customers are going to come anywhere near with a cop car outside.'

They waited, engine running.

'Your daughter said she wanted me to take her birding.'

Cupidi looked at him and frowned. 'Birdwatching?'

'When she was getting out of the car last night. She asked me if she could go out with me one day.'

'Are you serious?' said Cupidi. She dug in her handbag for a cigarette. 'You think she's trying something on?'

'Maybe she just likes birds. People do. Why would she ask that?'

In the rear-view mirror, South noticed a white SUV drive onto the site, then brake a little way off just by the site office, with its sign: *PROPANE refills £35 with cylinder ONLY no exceptions*. Then it slowly reversed, turned and left the caravan site. South smiled. Judy would have seen it too. A lost customer, he guessed.

He opened his notebook and wrote down the registration number.

'You have good eyes,' Cupidi said, looking in the rear-view mirror on the passenger side. 'I couldn't make that out from here. Maybe I need to get tested.'

'Birdwatching,' he said. 'See what make it was?'

'No.'

Cupidi got out, walked to the car bonnet and sat on it, smoking a cigarette while the dogs went crazy, barking at her. All the time, she just stared back at them, occasionally flicking ash.

Judy never kept drugs in the caravan. She did her dealing here on the site, but to collect, the buyer would have to drive to meet some spotty teenager in a flat somewhere a couple of miles away. She changed the teenagers regularly. They were never around long enough to get caught, and if they were they never admitted any connection to her.

Cupidi walked towards the caravan, cigarette in hand and squatted down right in front of the dogs, just beyond the stretch of their chains. The dogs tugged and pulled and growled and snarled, pawing at the earth, but the gas cylinder they were tethered to wasn't shifting.

'Careful,' said South, from the safety of the car.

The fact that her face was inches from them infuriated the dogs. After a minute staring at them, she took a pull on her cigarette, then blew smoke right into their faces.

A second later the caravan door tugged open. 'Don't you dare treat my dogs like that.'

Cupidi stood and looked at the woman standing in the doorway of the caravan. She was in her forties, dressed in sweats, a towel around her neck, though the weight she carried made South suspect she hadn't taken any exercise in a long time. 'You must be Judy,' Cupidi said.

'And who the frig are you?' Judy's eyes flicked over towards the campsite entrance, as if to see who else was around.

'Get your dogs under control and I'll tell you,' said Cupidi, calmly.

South sat in the front of the car; Cupidi was in the back with Judy.

'I don't know why you think I would know anything about it,' she said.

'We're just making inquiries. There were three men and two women. We believe that at least one of them may have witnessed something important.'

Judy's thickly floral perfume filled the car. 'Don't know any of them.'

'We think the person who killed him was drug- or alcohol-dependent.'

Judy made a face. 'I'd help you,' she said. 'Only, I honestly don't know what you're talking about.'

'Any new people around?'

Judy did a deliberately poor impression of someone trying to rack their brains. 'No. Can't think of anyone. Finished now? Only I've got some daytime TV to watch.'

Cupidi took out a card. 'You know the score. If you hear anything, please get in touch. We'd appreciate the help.'

'Cupidi. Funny name. You an immigrant?'

'No. Are you?'

'My dad was. Hard workers, immigrants. Not like most of the people round here. I'm thinking of moving, being frank. Can't stick it here.'

'Alleluia,' said South.

'Maybe move down the road. I like the look of Dungeness. You live there, don't you, copper?'

South blinked. How did she know that? He reached up and adjusted the rear-view mirror; in it, she was smiling back at him.

'It's no secret, is it? I keep my eyes open, that's all.' She looked away. 'Case you wondered, I walk the dogs there every morning. It's nice. I wouldn't mind one of those places, actually. I could see myself retiring there. Bunch of weirdos and misfits. I'm sure I'd like it there, don't you think?'

'I'd make bloody sure you didn't,' said South quietly.

'And one of them's just come empty, then, you say?'

'Fuck off, Judy.'

'That's not nice,' she said. 'I'll remember that.' From the back of the car, she glanced around the caravans. 'We done?' People ducked away behind their nets.

South said, 'If this man is one of your customers, you'd be better off without him, that's all.'

Farouk shrugged. 'And I haven't got any idea what you're talking about.'

Waiting for a gap in the traffic at the gates, Cupidi said, 'Well, she's a charmer, isn't she? Do you think she did know something?'

'I know her,' said South. 'She'll never say anything to your face. But she's in business. She doesn't want some psycho junkie messing things up for her. It's always worth poking the stick in the hornet's nest.'

They drove away down the rutted track. 'I've been thinking. What if Zoë is actually interested in birds?' said Cupidi. 'I sometimes don't know her at all.'

'It's not that outlandish,' said South. He rubbed his eyes.

'Did you manage any sleep last night?'

'Not much, to be honest.' He couldn't stop thinking about what Cupidi had said yesterday about rage; the kind of anger that made you unable to stop what you were doing.

'It shakes you up,' she said. 'A thing like that. Maybe you should take some time off.'

'You weren't saying that to me yesterday,' he said.

'Yesterday I needed you,' she said. 'And you did well.'

He looked at his watch. He was due at the Neighbourhood Panel meeting in fifteen minutes. He would be late; he should call ahead to let them know. It was always so hard to find a date everyone could make. They met quarterly. It was the kind of ordinary inconsequential policing he was used to. There would be tea and digestives. Sometimes one of the women brought cake. It was provincial and utterly normal. It wasn't like Serious Crimes. The things it achieved were simple and undramatic, but they made a difference.

Today, especially, he found himself looking forward to it.

Councillor Sleight was late too. 'Family stuff,' he said. 'My son's just back from university. Cambridge,' he said, as if he'd forgotten to mention it before, but South had always liked this vanity; a father who was proud of his son.

Before the meeting began, Ella Mears was complaining about a man she was convinced was a sex offender. 'You have to tell us if he is a paedo,' she said. A squat woman with a heavy smoker's voice, she represented one of the housing associations. South knew the man she was talking about. He had moved onto the estate a couple of months ago. 'It's the law,' she said.

'Not exactly,' said South. 'You can only request disclosure if he's working with young people, or associating with children. And he's not.'

She was right though; he was on the registered sex offenders list. He wondered how she had found out. Someone had disclosed confidential information and he would have to keep an eye on the situation.

'Well the law's wrong then,' said the woman. 'What if he turns out to be a murderer or something . . .?'

'Move on, Ella,' said Sleight. 'Everybody got the minutes?'

Sleight was a good man to have on the panel; he had been in the building trade, then become a property developer before he turned councillor. He had the softened face of someone who had enjoyed his share of good food and fine wine, but he was business-like, a civic-minded man who chaired a committee with simple grace and efficiency.

The first item was traffic control at local schools, but they veered away within minutes.

'Did you see that on last night's news, Vinnie?' Ella Mears asked.

'Near you, wasn't it, Sergeant?'

'Getting so bad round here.'

'Beaten to death, they said on the telly.'

'It was a druggie, wasn't it, I heard, Sergeant?' said Councillor Sleight, then held his hands up and grinned. 'Sorry. Off topic.'

'Round our place is swarming with bloody Romanies or whatever you're supposed to call them,' said a man from the Chamber of Commerce.

'Roma,' said Julie, the exhausted-looking social worker.

'Call them what you like,' said Ella Mears. 'They're bloody taking over. And like the councillor says, they're all on drugs.'

'Levels of drug abuse among the Roma are on a par with other disadvantaged local communities,' said Julie.

'Don't know why we waste our time at these meetings,' said Ella Mears. 'If we hadn't let them in in the first place we wouldn't have half the problems. Round my way the kids are up to all sorts.'

'Order, order,' said Councillor Sleight, who was supposed to be chairing. 'We're discussing obstructive parking outside schools. I'm not sure you can blame the gippos for that.'

'Roma,' said Julie, the social worker, again.

'Just for the record,' said South, 'there is no evidence to suggest that the killer of Mr Rayner is from any of the immigrant communities.'

'Well said,' said Sleight. 'Right. Can we continue? We have less than thirty minutes.'

Julie the social worker said, 'There are issues with asylum–seeker children with poor language skills being placed in unsuitable schools, if you want to discuss that, Mrs Mears.'

'Shouldn't be here in the first place. Can't get our own kids into decent schools.'

Sleight slammed his palm down so hard on the table that the water in their glasses trembled. 'Enough!' There was a shocked silence. 'I will not stand for this. I'm a busy man. I've better things to do than listen to this kind of nonsense.'

Ella Mears looked like she'd swallowed a wasp. Sleight glared at her for a few seconds more, then his stern face melted into a smile. 'I circulated an agenda before the meeting,' he said, his voice calm again. 'Can we save any further discussion for Other Business?'

At the end of the meeting, South was still writing up the

actions he had agreed to in his notebook when Vincent Sleight said, 'In a way, Ella's right. I don't know why we bother. None of this stuff about parking and litter is solving anything. And like it or not, a lot of it is immigrants. That's the real pressure round here. Ask an eighteen-year-old lad who can only afford to take a job that pays enough to pay the kind of exorbitant rent people charge these days. Ask him what he thinks of all the Poles and Lithuanians who can afford to work for half the money.'

'Even in your neighbourhood, Vincent?' said South.

Sleight laughed. 'Fair play, but I come from one of those places like Ella's. Worse than that too.' Sleight lived in one of the big white houses in the middle of the golf course behind Sandgate. A swimming pool, a guest house and a view south, over the Channel. South had been there only once, three or four years ago, to inspect Sleight's gun safe after he'd applied for a shotgun licence.

Sleight laughed. 'Come round for dinner, Bill, sometime,' he said, as he stood, picking up his briefcase. 'The wife does a smashing roast. You ever met her?'

'I don't think so.'

'Come and meet my lad. Back at home now.'

'Thank you.'

'Good luck with the murder case, by the way. Are you going to make an arrest?'

'I think we're close.'

'Good man.' Sleight always invited him to dinner without naming a date; South recognised it as a form of politeness.

South was just a low-ranking copper. And Sleight probably knew he wouldn't have wanted to come, anyway.

Every neighbourhood had them; the big men. Sleight was by no means the worst of them, thought South.

The days after his dad died, it was like something was buzzing away inside his head, making it impossible to think straight.

'What, Mum? Sorry. Didn't hear you.'

'Poor lad. What are we goin' to do with you?'

He hadn't dare go back to lift the manhole cover. The nights kept him awake, tying the sheets around his legs as he turned and turned.

'He's sleepwalking now,' she announced to the girl on the till at the Spar. 'I caught him the other night, out in the garden. I'd take him to our doctor, only the man's practically senile.'

Mrs Creedy was standing behind them, clutching a bottle of bleach. She said, 'Poor little soldier. He's got to be brave, like his daddy was.'

Billy tugged at his mother's coat, but she was still waiting for her change.

'Our community has lost a great man,' continued Mrs Creedy. She was dressed in the housecoat she wore in the chip shop, reeking of fat, with her black hair all blow-dried upwards. Please shut up, thought Billy, but there was no stopping her. Lowering her voice, she said, 'A great defender of the Union.'

'Which union is that, exactly?' said his mother loudly, staring her in the eye. 'I know all about my husband and his unions.'

Mrs Creedy reddened. 'I was only trying to show respect,' said Mrs Creedy.

The women in the queue behind were all pretending to look away. Billy pulled harder. But his mother said, 'Respect, is it? I'm surprised you have any of that left at all. You and half the women in this town.'

Nobody said a word; the girl behind the till stared at her feet as she held out the 80p change.

'The big men,' she said as they walked away as fast as they could, pushing past the prams and shopping trollies. 'They all love the big bloody men.'

And Billy thought about the other two men the gun had killed. He imagined them kneeling at the country roadside awaiting the bullet, or chased down dark alleys.

If it had happened to him, he would have run. He was pretty fast. He had heard if you zigzag there was less chance of the bullet actually hitting you. They'd all practised running like that in the playground, him and all his mates at the school.

It was now two weeks after the funeral and he was back at school. People stared and pointed. Most attention anyone had ever paid him. At break, Patrick Hamilton caught him by the outside toilets. 'What was it like, Billy? Did ye see them shoot your da? Rusty says they shot at you too. Did they?'

After school, he and Rusty ran up past the checkpoint.

'Can I come an' play at your house?' asked Rusty, panting for breath.

All his schoolmates were making excuses to call round. They wanted to see where his dad had been killed.

'Me mam's in Armagh buying a wedding dress for my sister. I forgot me key an' I'm locked out till five. Oh g'an,' pleaded Rusty.

'Can't Stampy let you in?'

'Nah. He's off at the hospital doing fizzy therapy.'

'OK,' said Billy, Rusty tailing after. Billy was just about to turn in to walk onto the estate when he heard the car coming up behind them.

He expected it to pass them on the road but it didn't. Instead he heard it slow right down and begin to crawl along behind them. Guessing it was the police, Billy paused to pretend to do up his shoelaces to give him a chance to glance backwards. The car had stopped too. It was an old grey Morris Oxford being driven by a fat-faced man with a quiff, with a young man in dark glasses sitting next to him. Definitely not the police; worse.

He stood and started walking. The car began moving too. Oh crap.

Rusty hadn't even noticed it. He was going on about *Star Wars*. 'When the big spaceship whizzed over at the beginning . . . it was amazing.'

'Come on, Rusty. Pick it up.'

'My sister Bridget ducked. It was that realistic. She's a ninny. She cried all the way through.'

'Run, Rusty.'

'Why?'

Billy took Rusty's arm and started yanking him forwards. 'What's the rush?'

Billy broke into a sprint.

The grey Morris Oxford revved up behind them. They were almost at the estate now, where the kerbstones ahead turned red, white and blue.

'Wait for me, Billy,' called Rusty.

But Billy was far ahead of him now, at the playground, when the car passed them and stopped, just ahead.

The guy with dark glasses stepped out of the car, grinning. 'So. You'd be Billy, then?'

'Who's asking?' he said.

'Don't be clever. It don't suit ye. Your ma said to give ye a lift home,' said the driver; you could tell he was an Elvis fan from the hair. The younger man opened the back door. 'Get in.'

'I can walk,' said Billy. 'Don't need a lift. It's only over there. I'll be there in a minute.' He pointed up the hill.

'Your mammy told us to pick ye up,' repeated the man in the dark glasses calmly. Fat Elvis had got out of the car now and was walking slowly around to Billy's side. 'She said it's real important,' the driver said.

And then Billy saw a figure in dark tweed pushing her

bicycle up the hill towards them and he had never been as pleased to see Miss McCrocodile as he was then.

'Afternoon, Miss McCorquadale,' he called.

'Afternoon, Billy.' She looked at the two men. 'And who would these gentlemen be?'

Elvis said, 'We're friends of the family, aren't we, Billy?'

Billy was about to say that he'd never seen these men in his life, when the man in sunglasses took them off and said, 'Remember me, Miss McCorquadale? You taught me at Sunday school. I'm Donny. Donny Fraser.'

'Donald Fraser? My. You've grown. How's your father?'

'He's great, thank you Miss M.'

Rusty stayed a few yards off, not wanting to come too close.

'I was a friend of Billy's daddy. I promised I would help the family out now his daddy's passed away.'

McCorquadale relaxed a little. 'A terrible thing,' she said.

'Appalling.' The man who had called himself Donny Fraser shook his head. 'We were all shocked rigid, Miss McCorquadale.'

'These are shocking times, Mr Fraser.'

'Indeed they are. We better be going, though, Miss M. Come on, young Billy. In ye jump.'

The door was wide open. Billy hesitated. He looked at Miss McCorquadale, who was frowning, as if she wasn't sure things were quite right.

'We promised his mammy we'd give him a ride,' said Donny Fraser.

'Come and see me any time, young Billy. You're in my prayers.'

'Come on then, Billy. Your mammy will be waiting.'

And as he pulled away up the hill, he saw Rusty waving at him, smiling, like he was off on a jaunt or something.

EIGHT

The site investigation was done. His house was his own again.

Because he worked Saturdays, Thursday was a day off. He spent it sea watching in the beach hide with Eddie and two other birders. Over six hours they counted around fifty sooty shearwaters, almost nine hundred gannets and a single Balearic shearwater; but his heart was not in it. Today, they were just birds. For the first time, it seemed like a pointless activity; a habit he had acquired but couldn't lose. He decided to end the watch early as the wind came up. A couple of times he called the police station on his mobile to see if they'd made the arrest yet, but there was no news.

He lay awake in his bed that night, still tasting salt from the wind on his face, still hearing the thump of the waves on the beach.

Since arriving here as a child he had loved this place, but now, the killing made him wonder if it was time for him to move elsewhere. It was as if whoever had killed Bob had taken something important from him too. It wasn't just the threat of violence, the idea that the killer was out there still; something dark had been stirred up.

His duvet was knotted around him by the time he finally fell asleep and was woken, it seemed like only seconds later, by someone knocking at his door.

'Bill!' Someone was calling through his letter box.

Thick-headed, he stumbled downstairs. It was light already. Through the glass he could see a haze of yellow; one of the fishermen, he guessed.

'What's wrong, Curly?' he asked when he opened the door.

'Some cunt's nicked my fuckin' boat.' Curly had a full set of oilskins on; even the sou'wester, all shiny with rain.

There were only a handful of men left who fished off Dungeness now. Though there was still good cod offshore, the effort of towing boats onto the shingle was too much; the boats that you could launch here were too small to be profitable any longer.

'Give me a minute.'

South dressed, put on a waterproof and followed Curly down to the edge of the beach.

'Came down this morning to catch the tide and the boat was bloody gone.'

'Blue Plymouth Pilot?'

'That's the one. Eighteen-footer.'

One of the smaller boats. Fishing was as much of a hobby to Curly as anything. His father had been a fisherman here, and if you asked him he'd say that's what he was too, but the truth was he earned his money working as a builder and decorator. The rain was thick, trickling into South's eyes as they walked towards where Curly had kept the vessel.

He stopped. 'Fucking cocks,' Curly said.

South looked down at his feet. The galvanised chain lying there had been cut clean through. South knelt and examined the end of the chain. It looked like someone had used wire cutters.

'Insured?' said South.

'Not enough,' said Curly.

'Got a tracker fitted?'

Curly shook his head.

South looked up the road. 'Well, they'll have passed CCTV cameras,' he said. 'We should get a pretty clear view of the vehicle that towed it.'

'Don't think so,' said Curly. 'They took it out to sea.'

'You're joking?'

'Fuckin' not,' he said. 'Look.'

Sure enough, behind where the boat should have been there were still deep tracks in the pebbles leading down to the high-tide mark. Someone had used a vehicle of some sort to drag the boat and its trailer down to the water.

'They took it out to sea?'

'I know.'

South looked out at the water. It was one of those early mornings when the sea still seemed to be sucking all the light from the sky. 'You called the coastguard yet?'

'No. I just came straight to you.'

'When did you last use it?'

'Three days ago.'

Tuesday. The day they had discovered Bob's body. South tried to remember if he'd seen the boat since then. The theft could have taken place any time between then and now; last night, probably, as no one had noticed it missing until now and the ruts were still clear in the shingle.

'You were here on Monday, then?'

'Maybe. Don't know.'

'Either you were or you weren't.'

Curly scratched his chin. 'Yes. Think so.'

'Did you take the boat out?'

'Actually, yes. May have.'

South said, 'May have? Don't you remember?'

'What's all this shit about Monday? I definitely saw it Tuesday. Isn't that good enough?'

'Think about Monday, Curly. Did you see anyone else around here?'

Curly crossed his arms. 'Nope. Don't think so. What about my boat?'

South looked at his watch. The tide was halfway out. High tide would have been around three in the morning. If they'd stolen it last night, they wouldn't have had far to tow it to get it into the sea.

'Where's the trailer?'

'No sign. My guess is that they left it in the water. The tyres were inflated so it would have floated. Probably half-way to Folkestone by now, reckon. Fuckers.'

They stood there looking at the open sea, as if expecting the boat would suddenly appear on the water before them.

South was in the car when the officer at the station called him up on his mobile to update him with what had happened on South's day off.

He pulled over in the lay-by and opened his notebook. 'Minor burglary at Littlestone. Hit and run RTC on the 259 involving two vehicles. Minor injuries. Sending you the description of a red Honda. A resident on the Wiccomb caravan park has been complaining about the dogs barking. Usual old bollocks.'

'I got a fishing boat nicked here. I'll come in with the details this afternoon. About twenty grand's worth. Wiccomb you said?'

'Yes.'

South considered that, then said, 'Any news on the Rayner murder?'

'Nothing I heard.'

Cupidi would be frustrated, he thought. She'd wanted to wrap it up fast but it was now the third day after the body had been found. How hard should it be to track down some homeless man? But this was not London where there was a CCTV on every corner. There were plenty of places where a man could hide, if he hadn't fled the county already. All the same, it made South uneasy that Bob's killer had not been arrested.

The burglary was a theft from a garden shed. Some power

tools and a transistor radio. It turned out that the home-owner hadn't been to the shed for more than a fortnight, which made it hard to pin down when it had happened, anyway. He took a few more notes, drank tea.

From there he drove to the Wiccomb caravan park.

It was a while since anyone had complained about Judy Farouk's dogs. They had learned not to.

He parked in the same place as they had before, but when he stepped out of the car, the dogs weren't barking at all, they were both lying down by the door of the caravan.

The man who had called the police lived in a static caravan close to Judy Farouk's. South got out and rapped on his door.

A thin, elderly man with papery skin and a dewdrop on his nose opened the door. He wore a brightly coloured hand-knitted tank top and complained, 'Don't let the heat out,' as South stood on his step. 'Shoes off,' he ordered. South sat on a small pink stool and pulled off his police boots.

The front room had nets in the windows. His large wife was sitting in an armchair with a Sudoko puzzle. She struggled up to put the kettle on as South walked in.

'You took your time, didn't you?' said the man.

'It was my day off yesterday,' said South. 'What's the problem? They don't seem to be making much noise now.' Which was odd in itself, he thought.

'Should have heard them yesterday,' said the man's wife. From their accents they were from the Midlands. One of the many couples who came south with their small pile of retirement money. She gave South his tea, then went to the window and peered through the curtains.

'They were hungry, see?' said the man. 'Now they're exhausted from all the yapping and barking.'

South went to the window next to the woman and looked through. Judy's static was pale yellow, with a small wooden deck built at one end. There were broad muddy semicircles of worn grass at the boundary of Judy's plot, where the dogs had struggled at the full lengths of their tethers.

'Starting to smell now too, all that dog do,' the thin man said.

'She's not been clearing it up?'

The woman snorted.

'What?' said South.

'She's gone, isn't she?' said the man. 'Just buggered off.'

South pulled the curtains further back. Her expensive-looking Audi was still there, parked in front of the caravan.

'Good riddance to bad rubbish. Hope she never comes back,' said the man.

'When?'

'Wednesday, I reckon.'

It was Wednesday he had brought Cupidi here. 'So they've been chained up outside since then?'

'Yes. Making a right bloody racket.'

By his leg, an automatic air freshener released a puff of something sweet and sickly.

'She's ruddy gone, finally,' said the woman.

'Ding-dong, the witch is dead,' said the man.

The woman giggled.

'What do you mean?' said South. 'You think something has happened to her?'

'You can hope though, can't you?'

Under the caravan, one of the dogs shifted, trying to get comfortable in the cold.

'Did anyone hear her leave?'

'Cars coming and going all the time. Nobody pays any attention.'

'There's been a string of druggies turning up. They knock on our door too. We had one this morning, didn't we? Young woman with her baby bawling her head off in the car. "Know where she's gone? I need to see her real urgent." Pathetic.'

South thought for a while. 'And who's been feeding the dogs?'

'No one, of course. Bloody monsters. Everyone here hates them.'

'So the dogs haven't been fed in, what, over forty-eight hours?'

The woman sucked at her teeth. 'Keeps them quiet though, doesn't it?' she said, giggling.

Back in the car, South called the RSPCA, then sat, waiting for them to arrive. Huddled together now, the dogs sat shivering in the lee of the caravan, whining quietly to themselves.

When the dogs had been collected, pelts matted with rainwater, tails between their legs, whimpering and snapping, South finally approached Judy's caravan. He knocked on the door, then tried the handle, then called her name. Locked. From one of the other residents, he borrowed a small stepladder, climbed it, then peered into Judy's front-room window.

The front room was empty. There was a small table lamp on, light shining through a pink fringed shade. Everything looked quiet and tidy, lace mats on the table, artificial flowers in a vase.

'You'd know it if she was here,' called the man in the tank top, standing at his door. 'She's gone. Hang out the flags, I say.'

South sat in his car for a minute, unsettled.

This week had been a succession of unexplained events. People don't just leave their expensive car and dogs behind.

He felt heavy-headed and anxious, as though his body was reacting physically in some way to the strangeness of it all. Maybe he was just coming down with something.

Starting up the car, he rolled forward and was looking to the left for oncoming vehicles when a sudden, raucous blaring made him put on the brakes. A massive articulated lorry roared past from the right, inches from his bonnet, driver still pressing on the horn as the vehicle shot down the road away to the north. The police car rocked in the lorry's wake.

South's heart jumped in his chest. If he'd been a foot further forward the lorry would have smashed straight into the car.

He had been sure he'd looked; but he couldn't have. Fumbling with the gearstick, he reversed the car back and sat in the small lane, sweat breaking through his skin. It took him another minute before he felt calm enough to drive again.

Later, on the journey home, he saw ahead of him an old black Rover 90. Normally he wouldn't have even noticed the car. Today it looked shiny and malign. Familiar.

It was driving at 40 m.p.h. along the clearway. As he passed it, South's hands tightened on the wheel and he felt his stomach turning somersaults, but when he looked left, all he saw was a woman of about seventy dressed in a pink lace hat, hands on the steering wheel. She turned and smiled at him.

What was wrong with him? It was just a car.

The cracked red leather was cold. The road wound up the hill into the heathland to the east of the estate.

Fat Elvis turned and said in a gentle voice, 'Don't worry, kiddo. We'll only keep ye a wee while.' Close to, he didn't look anything like Elvis. He had a big round nose thick with blackheads.

Heart pounding, Billy watched the lane ahead twist

up the hill, big hedgerows on either side. They drove a mile through the countryside until they reached a solitary red phone box that stood at a crossroads in the middle of nowhere. 'Wait there,' said Fat Elvis, and he got out and went to make a call.

'Am I in trouble?' said Billy.

'Jesus, no. What makes you think that?' said the one called Donny Fraser.

He wanted to make a dash for it. He knew the countryside around here. He came here on his own, most weekends. The hills beyond were where they said they'd spotted the snowy owl. He could run there; hide out. But instead he stayed, sitting in the car.

'OK,' shouted Fat Elvis, thumbs up, running back to the car. 'He'll meet us at the quarry.'

When they reached the top they turned right into the old quarry, which was now a picnic area. Supposedly. No one ever went there except to ignore the sign that said *No dumping by order*.

He imagined the news report – Boy's body found in car park. His mother watching it, weeping. 'How long will I be? My mum will be really worried if I'm late.'

'Not long,' said Fat Elvis, taking out a cigarette.

'Can I have one?' said Billy.

'No you bloody can't. It's bad for you.' Donny switched on the radio: 'Rivers of Babylon' by Boney M. A rubbish song. The sky was greying. Billy watched a wagtail in a puddle next to the car.

'I need the toilet.'

'Go on then.'

Billy hesitated, then got out of the car and walked towards the rocks at the edge of the quarry. He undid his flies, hands shaking. Both the men were looking at him.

'I can't if you're watching,' he called.

The men looked away. The quarry was a horseshoe. The only ways out would be the way they drove in or up the rocks, but they looked steep and slippery.

A car was approaching. What if he ran out and flagged it down before the men could catch him? But just as he was about to start running, the car swung into the picnic area, blocking his exit.

It was a black Rover 90, one of those old-fashioned, round, heavy cars his father hated. Right away, Billy recognised the man getting out it. His name was Mr McGrachy. A big, sick-looking man, with yellow skin and a face like crumpled laundry. When the Troubles first started, this man had often appeared at the house and he and Dad would go sit in the front room. Mum would usher Billy upstairs with a glass of lemonade and the two men would conduct long, whispery conversations.

Billy stood there, legs still shaking.

''Bout ye, Mr McGrachy,' called Elvis. 'We got the wee lad for ye. Over there. He was just having a Jimmy Riddle.'

'Hello, Billy.' When old man McGrachy smiled, his wrinkles multiplied. 'Jesus, you're a monster.'

It took Billy a second to realise that he was talking about how much he had grown since he had last seen him.

The car door closed with a heavy clump when McGrachy shut it. McGrachy had power. Billy knew that by the way the others straightened their backs, lowered their eyes, stubbed out their cigarettes.

'I want a little pow-wow,' said McGrachy.

Pow-wow. How old did he think Billy was? He was thirteen, God's sake.

'I was very very upset to hear about your da, ye know that?'

Billy stiffened. Aw Christ. Here it comes.

'Really upset. He was one of the coming men. One of the strong ones. One of the men who hold the line. You should be proud of him, young Billy.'

Billy nodded. With a click of the knees, McGrachy squatted down beside Billy, face close up so Billy could smell the fag breath. Could McGrachy see how much he was shaking?

'We were real shocked about his death, y'understand? Now I just want to ask ye a couple of questions, OK, sonny?'

Billy nodded again.

'Look at my ears, Billy. Would ye say they were big?'

Billy looked. They were huge, flappy things, with waxy lobes hanging down.

'I don't mind. Go on, tell me.'

Billy didn't know what to say. Jimmy Creedy's cousin Maureen McBride had once asked Billy if he thought she was fat. Billy had answered as truthfully as he could. It had been a mistake.

'They're big, ain't they?' said McGrachy.

'Pretty big,' conceded Billy, cautiously.

McGrachy laughed. 'And these ears hear an awful lot, too,' he said.

Aw Christ.

'Now then, my big ears heard that you were the one who found your daddy dead. Is that right?'

Billy opened his mouth to speak, but nothing came out.

'I'm sorry about that, Billy. Nobody should have to see that.'

Billy remembered his father, blood from his ruined forehead covering his eyeballs.

'And my big ears also hear that Sergeant Ferguson is sweet on your mother. Is that right?'

'Dunno.' But now McGrachy had said it he saw that it must be true. Sergeant Ferguson loved his mother. It was absurd. Why would anybody fancy his mother? Sure she was quite slim compared to the other mums round the estate, and she had nice hair, but . . .

Grimacing, McGrachy stood slowly, as if it hurt his legs to be bent for so long. 'So you've been seeing a lot of Sergeant Ferguson then?'

'Bit.'

'She could do much better than him, I'll tell you that. He's soft.'

Billy blinked. 'Fergie's all right,' he mumbled.

McGrachy grunted. 'So. What is Fergie saying about who killed your da?'

Billy considered a while.

'It's OK, laddie. No one's going to let on you told me. Us in the Volunteers are normally like that with the Constabulary.' He crossed his nicotine-stained fingers. 'But Fergie's a queer one. His mother is a Taig, you know that? He's a bit suspect, know what I mean?'

Billy said, 'No.'

Elvis giggled.

McGrachy said, 'So what is he saying, Billy?'

After sucking his upper lip a few seconds more, Billy announced, 'He says they're thinking it was one of the Volunteers killed my daddy.'

He saw McGrachy's eyes widen. 'Is that what he's saying?'

'Jesus. Why's he saying that?' Donny Fraser approached, standing on McGrachy's left.

''Cause of the gun he was shot with. It's one as has been used before,' said Billy.

'Is that right?'

And again, Billy nodded, emphatically this time.

'So they think it's one of us, killed him?' said Donny Fraser. 'That's mental. Why the fuck would we do that?'

In one simple movement, McGrachy swung round and punched Donny right in the middle of his face before he even knew what was happening. Amazing how fast he was, considering his age. Fraser took the full heft of the punch and tumbled straight backwards onto the wet gravel.

'Mind your language, you dumb gam. Show some respect, front of the lad.'

Donny Fraser lay on the ground, elbows in puddles. A little blood started to trickle from his nose.

'You broke my nose, I reckon.' Donny struggled to his feet.

'An' I'll do it again if ye like.'

'Sorry, Mr McGrachy.'

'It's not me you should be saying sorry to. It's the wee laddie here.'

Donny mumbled another apology. 'Sorry, Billy.' It was embarrassing.

McGrachy said, 'So they really think it was one of us Volunteers killed him? Did he say why? Why would one of our own do a thing like that?'

'The peelers are up to something, ask me. Trying to stir it up,' said Donny Fraser, dabbing his nose with a hanky.

'Maybe,' said McGrachy.

Fat Elvis spoke: 'But what if they're right? I don't trust that Portadown lot far as I can throw them. They're a bunch of psychos.'

'Not in front of the wee one,' said McGrachy. He was quiet for a minute. Behind him, a pair of crows tumbled in the wind.

'You are one of us, lad,' he said eventually. 'Like your dad. OK?'

'OK.'

'It's a war, you know?'

'Yes.' Billy thought he didn't want to be part of any war.

'And in a war, you have spies, don't you. Like James Bond, eh?'

Donny Fraser wiped his nose with the back of his hand and checked it for blood.

'That's what you are. Our spy. OK? Anything Ferguson tells your mother, you tell us, OK?'

'Jesus,' said Donny Fraser. 'The Portadown lot must think we're bunch a windie-lickers.'

McGrachy turned to him. 'Shut. Up. We don't know nothing. They may be a bit wild but they're on our side.' He turned to Billy and said, 'Good lad. Now you're one of us, right? Like your father.'

For an age, McGrachy stood there, hands in pockets. Donny Fraser and Elvis glanced at each other, unsure what to do.

'Do you want us to take the lad home now, Mr McGrachy?'

McGrachy took out another cigarette. 'No. You go home, lads. I'll do it,' said the big man.

Back down the hill they went in his Rover, McGrachy staring ahead, not talking for the first couple of miles. The man should have emptied his ashtray. It was full to bursting. Billy inspected the dials and the walnut fascia. The car had a radio too. He reached out and touched it. 'Like music?' asked the big man.

'Ay,' said Billy.

'Switch it on,' he said. Out came Nat King Cole.

'Great, hey? What a voice.' Billy hated Radio 2; the 'JY Prog'. Billy sat in the vast leather passenger seat, sliding from one side to the other as the car rounded the bends.

McGrachy stopped outside their house. He pulled out yet another ciggie, let out a big sigh, then lit it and blew a lungful of smoke. Billy wondered if it was OK for him to get out.

'Things are bad,' said McGrachy. 'Real bad.' He reached inside his jacket and pulled out a wallet. 'Here,' he said, holding a pound note.

Billy hesitated.

'Take it,' said the man. 'You've helped me today by being straight with me. Just like your dad. Chip off the old block, eh?'

Billy grabbed the note and pocketed it. His father would've said: 'Never take a man's money unless ye know why he's giving it ye.'

The man sighed again. 'How's your mother, Billy?'

'OK.'

'A nice woman, your mother.'

'Yes,' said Billy.

'Good-lookin' too. Quite a beauty.' McGrachy coughed phlegmily, then pulled out his hanky and wiped his mouth. 'I got somethin' to ask you . . . man to man, like.'

Billy fingered the pound note in his pocket.

McGrachy leaned slightly towards him. 'I'd like to pay her my respects. Is she ready to accept visitors?'

Billy blinked. 'I suppose,' he said. Loads of people had called round, the last few days. More than ever had when Dad was around.

'This is a terrible time, right now. There aren't enough good honest people around,' said McGrachy.

McGrachy looked over towards Billy and smiled. His teeth were even yellower than his eyes. 'I like ye, Billy. You're a good boy, ain't ye?'

Billy said nothing, just tried to smile back.

'Don't mind that idiot Donny Fraser.'

'OK.'

'I'm goin' to try to make all this up to you, Billy. I promise. Your generation deserves better than this.'

He wound down the window and flicked the ciggie out onto the pavement outside their house. 'Another thing. This little talk is between you and me, OK? Don't tell a soul.'

'OK,' said Billy.

'Not even your ma.'

Billy fidgeted.

'Remember my big ears will hear it if ye do.' He smiled so hard that even his wrinkles had wrinkles, then reached past him and opened the door for him to get out.

NINE

Two days later mud still lingered in the carpet. South was hoovering the hallway when the phone rang.

'What are your plans for the day?'

'It's Sunday, DS Cupidi.'

'Exactly, William. Only, I am going to work and Zoë doesn't have anything to do and she hasn't made any school friends yet . . .'

A voice in the background said, 'Mum. Shut up. God's sake.'

'You know you said how she was interested in going birdwatching?'

'Oh,' said South.

'Only if you're free, that's all,' said Cupidi. 'I really have to work. I wasn't planning to. We're extending the search for people matching the description of those homeless people you saw. Time's running out and every day counts.'

'You want me to be your babysitter?'

'No. She wants to do this.'

South paused. 'Really?'

'Of course she does. Don't you, Zoë?'

South wound up the lead to the vacuum cleaner and put it away under the stairs. South avoided going out with first-timers. You never managed to see very much if you spent your time pausing to identify every last bird. He wasn't sure if he even wanted to go out today. But the idea of going out with a teenage girl was even worse.

A steady drizzle fell as they sat in one of the hides on Burrowes Pit. She wore one of his raincoats with a pair of borrowed binoculars and a copy of the *Collins Bird Guide* open on her lap.

When she wrote, her tongue stuck a little way out of her mouth. He had given her a fresh police notebook and she was writing in it with a lilac biro.

'Shelduck. That's twelve,' Zoë said.

Waders and waterfowl were always a good place to start, especially when the light was so poor. They were bigger and the markings were more pronounced, which made them easier to identify. Even with that, for a teenager, he had to admit Cupidi's daughter was doing surprisingly well. She seemed to be genuinely interested.

'It's a cool bird,' she said.

'Yes. It is.'

'It would make a nice tattoo,' she said.

On a day like this he should normally be on his own somewhere, instead of sitting here in the hide, next to an elderly couple with a Thermos and sandwiches and biscuits, who just stared out of the lookout as they chomped and slurped. They didn't seem to be doing any actual bird spotting at all.

He scanned the huge pool but saw nothing that he wouldn't expect to see there. Birdwatching was like being a beat copper. You spent your days looking for anomalies. Things that were just a little different. An open window in an empty house; a man lingering too long by the edge of a platform. That's what got you excited.

'It freaks me out round here,' said Zoë. 'It's so dark at night. You ever seen *Saw*?'

The old couple fidgeted.

South changed the subject. 'What does your mum think about you getting tattoos?'

'Not keen.'

She lifted up the binoculars South had lent her. He had lent her boots too. They were two sizes too big, but she'd turned up in a pair of canvas sneakers.

'She said she left London to keep you out of trouble.'

Zoë scowled. 'That's so embarrassing.'

He was just trying to make conversation with a teenager; but of all people, he knew better than to open up the past. 'Don't talk about it. It's OK.'

'No. It was nothing to do with me.' The old man dropped his plastic teacup on the floor of the hide. It spilled onto the boards. 'Everyone wants to know why we moved down here and she's too chicken to say the real reason. It's not fair to blame me all the time.'

The old couple were packing up their lunch into a backpack.

'She's just chatting shit. It's lies. I should tell Social Services, reckon. Don't you think that's wrong?'

'Were you in trouble?'

She shook her head. 'Want to know the real reason we had to leave London?'

'No. It's none of my business,' said South.

'The real reason is she had an affair with her Detective Chief Inspector and he was bloody married.'

'You shouldn't be telling me this,' South said.

'She shouldn't be telling people that we left London 'cause I'm some kind of delinquent. Anyway, he said it was going to mess up his career if it came out. Awkward.'

Lowering the binoculars, Zoë started leafing through the bird book.

'And now I never hear the end of it. Her going on about how it was her that had to leave because she was a woman. She didn't have to have it off with him, did she?'

The old couple pushed past them to the door of the hide, the man grumbling as he left.

'Good riddance. They weren't even proper birdwatchers,' she said.

Her first time out and she was already judging others. She'd fit in fine; he smiled to himself.

'I hate the people round here,' Zoë said. 'You excepted.'

He smiled.

'I think Mum'd look real sexy with a tattoo. Don't you?'

Fortunately, before he had a chance to offer an answer, she pointed to a bird on the page and said, 'Golden plover.'

'Where?' South lifted up his binoculars, interested for the first time.

'By them other birds,' she said, pointing.

The lake was crowded with wildlife. It took a while for him to see where she meant. A wader was standing by the edge of some blackthorn bushes about thirty yards away. He focused his binoculars further into the distance.

'Where did you move here from, then?' she asked.

'Northern Ireland.'

'Wow. That's miles.'

Why had he told her that? He never told anybody where he'd come from.

'Is that what your accent is, then? Irish.'

'I tried hard enough to lose it when I was in school. The other kids took the mickey.'

'I know what you mean,' she said. 'I hate the other kids round here. They're vile.'

'Have you been in any more fights?'

She shook her head. 'I'm trying not to. For Mum's sake.'

'It wasn't like I tried to lose my accent. It's just at some point you have to fit in, don't you?'

'Why? I don't mean to. I've never wanted to fit in.'

'It's not a golden plover. It's a green sandpiper,' he said, getting the bird into focus.

'Oh,' she said, disappointed.

'No. It's good. As a matter of fact, this time of year, much less common,' he said.

'Really?'

'We'll tell them up at the observatory. They make a note of all the unusual birds. We'll tell them you saw it first, then.'

'Thirteen.' She grinned. She found the bird in the book and quietly read the page, then, tongue between her lips, she wrote the name in her notebook and underlined it twice. 'I'll catch you up, easy. She bring you here after your dad died?' she said.

'I suppose my mother wanted to start again,' he said.

'Same,' she said.

'Your father died?'

'No. I just meant my mum wants to start over.'

He was tempted to ask more about why; it was unlike him to want to pry into other people's stories. They were losing what little light there was already.

'What did your dad die of?' she asked.

He pretended not to hear. Focused on the sandpiper in his glasses, bobbing up and down by the side of the water.

By the end of the day, when her mother came to pick her up, Zoë had identified twenty-six birds, all named and neatly recorded in her book.

He went to work early on the Monday to finish the witness statement forms he'd failed to complete last week. They were experimenting with hot desking, which meant that you had to get there early if you wanted one of the computers that worked properly. By a little before 8.30 he'd completed the first, so he stopped, made himself a cup of tea and went to join the Monday morning briefing.

DS Cupidi was sitting on a desk talking to one of the young women constables. She stood up and came over to where South was standing at the back of the room. 'Thanks for yesterday,' she said. 'Bizarrely enough, she enjoyed herself, I think.'

'She was great,' he said.

'Really?'

'Any luck finding your homeless person?'

She shook her head.

'No. It's doing my head in. He seems to have vanished. It's weird. We're still waiting for a fingerprint or DNA match, though. Maybe that'll get things nailed down.' These things could take a long time, even in a murder inquiry. 'Did you take down Gill Rayner's number? I've been trying to call her but the constable must have taken the number down wrong. Number unobtainable.'

'No. I thought you had it.'

'I'll get someone in the Met to go and knock at her door,' said Cupidi. 'Maybe Zoë could come out with you another time, then?'

'I'd like that,' he said. 'It wasn't anywhere near as bad as I thought it would be.'

'Charming.' She went to fetch a coffee from the machine.

'Oi, oi,' said one of the constables, when Cupidi was out of earshot. 'She's got her eye on you, ask me.'

'Fuck off,' said South, joining the rows of seated officers. The briefing started. Cupidi updated everyone on the Rayner case, but there was nothing South didn't already know.

'Anything else going on?' asked the inspector.

'Chemists,' said one sergeant. 'Three of them in one weekend. Two in Ashford, one in Peasmarsh. Methadone tablets. Bottles of the stuff too. Temazepam. Diamorphine. All the usual.'

'Druggies,' said another copper.

'Obviously.'

'Is this a statistical anomaly or is something going on here?' said the inspector.

'Any CCTV?'

'Loads. Going through it now.'

'Anyone know of anyone new in the area?'

There was a groan. There were always new people in the area.

At the back of the room, South frowned, wrote the details in his notebook. 'Anybody heard anything about Judy Farouk?'

People turned in their chairs, looked at him.

'Only, she seems to have disappeared. She just vanished sometime last week; Wednesday, maybe. Left her dogs behind. I was thinking. Might be a connection? If they can't buy their drugs from her . . .'

People were already standing, putting on their jackets. 'Good point, Bill,' called the sergeant, above the noise. 'If one of you hopeless lot could turn drug dealer till she's back, it might keep the crime rate down for us.'

There was a laugh. South sat in the room until all the others had left. Nobody was sure why she had gone; nobody seemed that concerned. It was like the disappearance of summer cuckoos and nightingales; something far away in Africa was causing it to happen, but exactly what was obscure.

It was one of those long busy days when the hours flew past without anything much being achieved. Just before he left his desk a constable handed him a message. A woman had called, complaining that children had broken into the old Army Cadet Force hall in New Romney. He called, took down her address and promised to get one of the Community Officers to call on her.

Driving home in his own car, on an impulse, he took a detour to the east. Nayland's Farm was at the end of a long, straight single-track road that flooded in winter. Halfway down the road a lorry rattled towards him, headlights glaring and South had to reverse back into one of the road's muddy passing points. The lorry sped past, spattering his car in mud.

South began to regret the decision to come. He was hungry; he hadn't had time to eat a proper lunch. He could have been home by now cooking himself something, but he was almost there, so he drove on.

The farmyard was little more than a lorry park these days,

every inch of the old dairy now covered with trucks and trailers. A massive Scania truck had its cab tipped forward and its engine exposed. *Dacre's of Lydd, Kent*, it said on the cab door. The place smelt of old grease and engine oil. South picked his way through the tall vehicles, past a garage where a Land Rover sat on jacks above a dirty pit, towards a converted brick shed that served as the office.

Through the glass door he could see Christy Dacre, a weighty, pink-faced man in his early sixties, watching a small TV in the corner of the room. South knocked. Dacre beckoned him in, lifted the remote and switched off the TV.

'Sergeant South,' he said cautiously. 'On your own?'

'Just me.'

'Right.' He seemed to be taking this in, evaluating it. Finally he smiled. 'D'you like a tea? I was just about to have a cup. No?'

The yard outside was quiet. 'What do you know about Judy Farouk?'

'Judy who?' Either because the folds of fat on his face made it hard, or through lack of care, Dacre shaved badly. Tufts of untouched white hair lingered on his chin. His sleeveless shirt was unironed.

'You know who I mean, Christy.'

Dacre held up his hands, smiled again. 'Just kidding, Sergeant. Everyone round here knows that one. Doubtless wishes they didn't, know what I mean?'

They called it logistics these days, but Dacre had been

a lorry driver most of his life. In lean years, he kept the company afloat by bringing drugs across the Channel, stowed in his lorries. When two of his lorries had been caught at Folkestone loaded with heroin, Dacre had avoided prosecution by successfully insisting he'd known nothing about it. Two of his drivers had been jailed, younger men who had little to lose; the rumours were that Dacre had paid them or threatened them to keep their mouths shut about his involvement. The CPS had said there was not enough evidence to proceed with the prosecution.

'She has disappeared,' said South. 'I want to know why.'

'Disappeared? You must be terribly upset about that.'

'Devastated,' said South. 'What do you know about it?'

The expression on Dacre's face was like that of a child wrongly accused of dipping his finger in the jam. 'Why would I know anything about that, Sergeant?'

There was an orange plastic chair on the other side of the office. South picked it up, placed it as close as possible to Dacre's desk and sat down. 'I know you associate with her, Christy. You were photographed together last year by our lot when they were investigating your company.'

'Associate with her? What kind of terrible language is that, Sergeant? Are you associating with me right now?' He leaned forward, mock-serious. 'Is that what we're doing?'

'I'm just asking, Christy. I'm not accusing you of anything. If you did know something about where she's gone, I'd be grateful.'

Christy settled back into his chair again, shrugged. 'Why

are you even bothered? You say she has gone. I'd have thought you'd have been hanging out the bunting.'

'We're saving that for you, Christy.'

'Ouch.' Dacre frowned. 'You lot have me all wrong. Really. I'm just trying to make a living. I support my family. And it's hard enough these days out here.'

'What have you heard about Judy?'

He shook his head, raised his hands. 'Nothing. Swear to God. I'm the last man you should ask. Always half a beat behind the bar, me. You know that. Look around. Do I look like a successful bloody career criminal? That's my bloody problem.'

South didn't answer; he just held Dacre's even gaze until Dacre broke away to look down at his watch.

'Only, I got work to do,' said Dacre. South sighed. Framed and printed on canvas, there was a photograph of Dacre's wife and children on the wall. He had been ginger in his younger days: his children were all red-heads, all smiling brightly at the camera. In contrast to his smiling family, there was a sadness about Dacre that his bonhomie only made more obvious; it was as if he hadn't meant to end up like this.

'I'm just asking for a little help, Christy.'

'Sure. And I'm flattered you think I'm your man. But.' He looked at his watch again.

'What car do you drive, Christy?'

'Whatever's in the driveway, you know? I buy and sell.'

South took out his notebook and repeated the question. 'What car do you drive?'

'Why you want to know that?'

'I can find out easily enough.'

Dacre looked away. The roguish charm was running dry. 'Got a few.'

'What about a white SUV?'

'Might have done.'

'Not hard for me to find out, Christy.'

'Why ask me, then?'

South looked at his watch and wrote in his notebook, speaking the lines aloud for Dacre to hear. 'Mr Dacre was uncooperative and refused to confirm that he owned the vehicle.' It was petty, he knew, but he was beyond caring.

'The wife has one,' said Dacre. 'Nissan Pathfinder. Crock of shit, you know?' A final attempt at a small smile. South saw the tremble in his hand and wondered if it was age or anxiety.

'Thank you.' South stood.

'You done?'

On the way out, South peered into the garage. It smelt of thick oil and ground metal, just like the place his father worked in. Apart from the Land Rover, there was a motorbike chassis that had been stripped down. It had been placed on a frame. Somebody had been respraying it bright red. The can was there, lying on the ground next to it. The air still smelt of fresh paint.

There was a washing-line, strung across the back of the garage; pegged across it were jeans and T-shirts of varying sizes.

He turned, and Dacre was there, watching him from the office window.

South drove out into the dark lane, dissatisfied. The company of old criminals always left him depressed. They were always the same; used up and weary of the life but still as evasive and intransigent as they had been the first time they had been nicked. They made him feel that much of his job was utterly pointless.

He drove back home and made himself pasta and ate it too quickly. Around nine o'clock, he finally picked up the phone. It was Zoë who answered. 'Cupidi residence.'

'Classy.'

'I thought so.'

'Is your mum there? It's William South.'

'I know. No. She's working.'

'This late?'

'I'm a latchkey kid. I've turned delinquent.'

'Probably,' he said. 'Never mind, I'll call her later.'

'I can pass a message if you like.'

He paused. 'I was going to invite her for dinner.'

'Dinner? What are you doing that for?'

'Being neighbourly, that's all.'

'Just her?'

'Yes.'

'Do you actually fancy my mother or something?'

'I was being friendly. Something you might consider working on, Zoë.'

'I am bloody friendly. Not my fault if the girls at school are all wankers.'

'And there's some work I want to discuss.'

'Very friendly of you,' she said.

'Will you pass the message, then?'

'Why don't you fancy her? What's wrong with her?'

'Goodnight, Zoë,' he said, and put down the phone. Still in a sour mood, he remembered the smell of fresh paint from the garage. He showered before he went to bed, but the smell of it still seemed to cling to him.

At school the next day, they were doing river deltas.

'Homework in a pile on my desk. Now,' said Mr Francesci, whose sleeves were always lightly dusted with chalk.

'What's the point of studying Egypt, sir?' said Rusty Chandler. 'It's miles away.'

'Don't try and change the subject, Chandler. Have you done your homework?'

'No, sir. My dad said I had to help him fixing the car last night so I didn't have time.'

Mr Francesci was one of the strict ones. 'Hand it in to me in the staff room, first thing tomorrow. Plus five hundred lines: "Whatever my father says, I must not forget to do my homework".'

Rusty groaned.

'What about you, McGowan?'

'Forgot, sir.'

Mr Francesci sighed, paused for a second, then said, 'Well, don't forget next time, OK?'

'Yes, sir.'

There was another groan, this time with an edge of menace to it. 'Don't McGowan get lines too?'

It was starting to really annoy the other boys, how much he was getting away with.

After school, Sergeant Ferguson was outside waiting, smoking a cigarette, trousers flapping at his ankles and cap slightly crocked on his head. He gave Billy a little wave as they came out of the main building.

'Oh Jesus,' said Billy.

'Crap,' said Rusty Chandler. 'He's gonna nick us.'

'Us. Why should he do that?'

'Because of the paint.'

The can of Flamenco Red spray-paint that now lay under his bed.

He looked at his friend. He liked Rusty, but he'd never have called him smart. His brother Stampy had all the brains. 'I don't think he'd be bothered about that, Rusty.'

'Dunno. Your dad was, I heard.'

'Besides, it was what your brother did. I didn't do it.'

'You wouldn't peach on Stampy, would you?'

'Not in a billion years,' said Billy. 'Cross my heart.'

'We were there when my brother did it though. You think he's found out it's us?'

'Know what? I really don't think it's about that, Rusty.'

'You sure?' he asked.

'Pretty certain.'

Rusty looked relieved. 'I'll be off then,' he said, and he left Billy alone on the playground tarmac. Ferguson didn't even glance at Rusty. It was Billy he was after.

'I was thinking,' Fergie said, as Billy emerged from the gate. 'You fancy a milkshake?'

'A milkshake?'

Billy wouldn't have called Fergie a handsome man with his thin face and long legs in his big police trousers but he was better than McGrachy at least. As they walked from the school down the road into the centre of town, he tried to imagine how things would have been if Fergie had been his dad.

The whole town was looking worse than ever with all the checkpoints and breeze-block sentry huts. The people who had owned shops next to the checkpoints had cleared out. It wasn't safe, so close to the army. Empty for months now, the buildings around the checkpoints were dark.

Sergeant Ferguson pushed open the door of the Manor Hotel. Billy lingered.

'Come on, it's OK. I'm buying.'

In the restaurant, a young woman in a black skirt and white pinny sat them at a table by the window and licked her pencil.

'What flavours have you got?'

'Chocolate, vanilla and strawberry.'

'I'll have chocolate,' said Fergie. 'What about you?'

Billy and Sergeant Ferguson were the only customers in the restaurant, sitting among the places that were already set for dinner. The milkshakes arrived in tall thick glasses, two straws each.

They sat in silence a while, sucking, looking out of the window. The cold made Billy's head ache, but was worth it. The town square beyond was quiet and grey. A pair of motorbikes paused at the lights.

'You heard any more about the snowy owl?'

'Nothing, no,' said Billy.

'Me neither. Maybe it was just a rumour.'

'I was thinking of going up to Carn Mountain one day to see if I could see her,' said Billy. 'Get up real early.'

'I've been driving up that way myself to take a look. I can take you if you like?'

'No. I'm OK.'

Ferguson smiled. 'Don't want an old fucker like me around to share in the glory if you do see it?'

Billy blushed. 'It's not that.'

'I know. It's your thing. Not mine. I get that.'

Billy was unused to a man understanding him so well; the birds were his and his alone. Not his friends'; not his father's; just his.

'So. I heard some fellows picked you up in a car yesterday,' Ferguson said eventually.

Billy tensed, but said nothing. *Don't tell a soul*, McGrachy had said. He just sucked down to the bottom of his glass, until his straw started to make that slurping noise. How did Fergie know about yesterday? In this town, everyone knew everyone else's business.

Ferguson emptied his glass and did the same, slurping at the half-inch that was left. Billy giggled.

'I just love that sound,' said Ferguson. He did it again. 'These fellows, they told you not to say anything, I'll guess.'

Billy sucked harder.

'Did they threaten you?'

By the door, the waitress was quietly biting her nails, bored.

'God, Billy. They did, didn't they?'

Still Billy said nothing.

'I'm your friend. Not your enemy. If you keep it to yourself, there's nothing I can do to help you. Please, Billy.'

The waitress switched fingers. Chewed on her other hand.

'It's OK, Billy. Tell you what. You don't have to say anything,' said Ferguson. 'Nothing at all. Just stay still. Keep your lips buttoned up. Anything I say that's true, you don't say a word, OK?'

Billy nodded, cautiously.

'You understand how this works? Stay quiet as a mouse. That way you can keep your promise. And if they come back and say, did you talk to the police, you can say not a bloody word, and you won't be fibbing.'

Billy thought of McGrachy's big ears.

'But if I say something that's not true, you have to make

that noise with your straw, OK?' He picked up his glass and sucked, to demonstrate.

Billy sucked his straw again too, experimentally. It was the next best thing to being told it was OK to fart in public. He giggled again, out loud this time. The waitress looked at the pair of them. 'You OK?' she asked.

'Fine.' Ferguson turned back to Billy. 'I'm starting now, OK? Get ready with your straw.'

Billy leaned over his glass.

'It was McGrachy's men that picked you up yesterday, wasn't it?'

No sucking.

'And McGrachy was there too, then?'

Still no sucking.

Ferguson nodded. 'Right then. Good. Understood. And he talked about your dad, then, I expect?'

Billy stayed there, cheeks all primed to make a loud noise, but he didn't. Everything Ferguson had said so far was true.

'He knows who killed your dad, though, doesn't he?'

Billy sucked loudly.

Ferguson raised his eyebrows. 'He doesn't? So he wasn't there to make sure you kept your mouth shut?'

Billy sucked but this time only air went up the straw. Sergeant Ferguson tipped the last dribble of his own milk-shake into Billy's glass to give him something to work on.

'So I get it. He was asking you who killed your dad?'

Another suck. 'Sorry,' said Billy, letting the straw fall from his lips. 'Didn't mean to do that. Yes. That's what he was asking.' He put his hand over his mouth. He hadn't meant to speak.

'Jesus, Billy. You have any idea what this means?'

Billy picked up the straw again and slurped.

'No. I don't expect you would.'

Ferguson took out a packet of cigarettes and lit one. He leaned forward across the table and spoke quietly, seriously, man-to-man. 'A world of trouble, that's what it means. Protestants fighting Republicans is one thing. We've been getting used to that. But Protestants fighting each other is another. And McGrachy himself doesn't know who's behind all this? Does your mother have friends anywhere away from here?'

Billy thought for a while. 'We used to go to stay with her schoolfriend in Warrenpoint, only they stopped talking after she had a row with my dad.'

'No. Somewhere further than that.'

'Away from here?' Billy said.

'This place is finished,' says Ferguson. 'Until all the Troubles are done. It's no place for a lad, growing up. The barbarians are at the gates. You stay here and it'll suck you in. Has your mother got money?'

The question surprised Billy. 'Reckon.'

'Enough to move somewhere?'

'You mean, go somewhere else to live?'

This was his world. This grey town was all he had ever known.

'Would you need a lot of money for that?'

Fergie didn't get the chance to answer. A shadow fell on the tablecloth. Then, *bang bang bang*.

Billy jerked his head up and saw the man outside the window who had just thumped on the glass with the flat of his hands; he was dressed in an army surplus jacket. It was the one from the car who was called Donny. Startled, Billy jumped back in his chair and knocked his empty milkshake glass onto the floor.

'Heya, Billy,' shouted Donny, grinning. 'Heya, Sergeant Ferguson,' he called through the glass.

'Jesus,' said Ferguson.

Donny looked from one to the other meaningfully. He pointed two fingers of one hand at his eyes, then at the pair of them. 'I seen ye, Billy McGowan,' he said. 'Right? I. Seen. You.'

And then he strode off down the street, swinging his arms like he owned the place.

Billy looked down. The milkshake glass was broken, its base snapped off.

'I'll pay for it,' Ferguson told the waitress, who was squatting down to pick up the pieces.

'Doesn't matter,' said the girl.

Ferguson looked at Billy, pale in his chair.

'Was he one of the fellows in the car, Billy?'

Billy said nothing.

'I'll protect you, Billy. Don't you worry. I'll protect you.' He put his hand on Billy's shoulder. 'You and your ma. I promise. I'll do anything it takes.'

Billy felt trapped. By not talking, he was answering Fergie's question. He was shopping Donny, either way.

Ferguson said, 'I know him. He's a builder on the council. And he's UVF too. Isn't he?'

Still Billy said nothing.

Ferguson paid the bill. 'I'll walk you home if you like,' he said.

Billy shook his head vigorously.

His mum woke him, switching on the light.

He blinked in the painful glare.

'I heard you calling out for me.'

'I was?' He looked around him. The room was normal. Just as it should be; his birds all around the walls.

'You were having a nightmare.' She was dressed in her blue nylon nightie, hair down.

'Sorry, Mum.'

'It's not your fault,' she said, and she walked to his bed, knelt down and kissed him on the forehead. Though he was too old to be kissed by his mum, he wouldn't have minded, but he didn't deserve this kindness.

'You and me, Billy,' she said. 'You and me.'

She stood and returned to the doorway. When she had switched off the light again she turned, about to go, then stopped and asked him, 'What was the dream about?'

He turned away to face the wall. 'Nothing. I don't remember.'

'Go back to sleep then, little one,' she said, and though

he was hardly little any more, secretly he liked it when she called him that.

In his nightmare, he was in a dark wood. And the trees all seemed to have faces in them. There were eyes and open mouths, lurking in the curves and crevices of the bark. And as he stared at them, he realised that one of the trees was his father.

The eyes blink open. And as he watches, a hole appears in the face's forehead and blood starts to gush out of the hole in the bark. And Billy wants to run away but he can't. And his tree-father starts shouting, 'Which of your degenerate little fucken friends did this?'

That's when he screamed for his mummy.

'It's not your fault,' Mum said again.

But it was. It was all his fault.

TEN

He sat up in bed suddenly. Dreaming of his father was something he had not done for years.

He was covered in sweat too. Was he coming down with something? He wondered where the thermometer was; he couldn't remember the last time he'd had a day off sick. But in the end he decided that would be worse; at home, he'd just be brooding about Bob Rayner.

He spent the morning at the station, finally finishing the last of the MG11s he had to complete and was grateful when the duty sergeant begged his help to follow up on a brawl there had been last night in a pub in Ashford, even though it was outside of his area. 'I wouldn't ask, but I'm desperate.'

For an hour and a half he took witness statements from the bar staff.

That afternoon, dropping into the Over 60s club in Lydd to leave some leaflets about burglary, he got a call from control; an elderly man with Alzheimer's was missing from one of the nursing homes in Littlestone. By the time he arrived there the man had been spotted sitting in a bus shelter. South drove a nurse – a young Filipina woman who hardly spoke English – out to pick him up.

The man said, 'I'm not being arrested, am I?'

'No.'

'But she is, isn't she?' he said, pointing at the nurse.

'That's right,' said South. 'She's a wrong 'un. Will you help me take her in?'

The nurse didn't seem to think it was funny.

It was simple police work. The kind he liked; the kind that did good. After that he had half an hour free before his shift ended; not long enough to go and write anything up. So he drove to Wiccomb caravan site. He parked twenty yards from Judy Farouk's caravan and sat in the car, watching.

The days were getting shorter. It would be winter soon. In other mobile homes, TVs and lights came on. The car was still there; Judy's caravan remained dark.

He was about to call it a day and drive home when his mobile rang. It was the woman he'd spoken to yesterday about the break-in at the old Army Cadet Force hall. 'Your policeman didn't come,' she complained.

He sighed, looked at his watch. 'OK. I'll drive over there now.' He would be late home.

The Cadet Force hall had been disused for a few months now. White paint was already peeling from the walls. The front doors had been covered by a metal grille to prevent break-ins and the building was surrounded by a wire fence.

The grass around it was choked with ragwort. He parked by the galvanised metal gate and walked up to it; it was secured with a bicycle lock.

He checked his notebook. The person who had complained about the children lived in the house opposite. He waited for a gap in the traffic, then crossed over.

The woman who opened the door was his age but almost totally bald; small patches of pale hairs sprouted from her scalp. He wondered if it was cancer.

Hoping she hadn't noticed him looking at the top of her head, he said, 'I came about the break-in at the hall.'

'You better come in then,' she said. 'Wipe your feet.'

She led him into the living room, a small room crammed with furry animals: two pandas and a tiger sat on the best armchair, a row of meerkats lined the window ledge and there was a family of lemurs on the radiator.

'Do you know who the children are? I could have a word with their parents if you like.'

'I've not actually seen them.'

'Them?'

'More than likely, kids from the village. They don't go to school or nothing. They're always hanging around.'

Several refugee families had been housed in a local bed-and-breakfast over the last twelve months; they were mostly Somalis, but a large Syrian family had arrived more recently. The landlord had been happy enough with the business but locals had complained about children with nothing to do playing so close to this busy road. Hostility round here wasn't as bad as it was in the towns, where fights between locals and immigrants or between groups of new arrivals were a regular occurrence, but he was keeping an eye on it.

'You saw them breaking in?'

'No. But I saw them in there.'

South blinked and tried to understand what she was saying. 'You say it's children, but you haven't seen them?'

She backtracked. 'It's just an intelligent guess. I mean, I've nothing against those kids.'

'So you saw people in the hall?'

'I saw them in there. The night I first called. Only, no one got back. They haven't been back since.'

He took his notebook out and checked the date. 'When was this?'

'Almost a week ago. Last Wednesday, I think. I didn't think you were bothered.'

'Sorry. For some reason I was only passed your call yesterday. So what exactly did you see?'

'I'm telling you. I saw the kids playing in there. You could hear them banging about. They had a torch. You could see it shining through the windows.'

'Did you go and talk to them?'

'I wouldn't. I don't go outside. I've got agoraphobia.'

He walked to her window and peered through the curtains. 'Thieves stripping the place, maybe?'

'Nothing in there,' she said. 'The army took everything. Even the light fittings.'

'Who has the key?'

'The army.'

It was dark now. Low cloud hung over the road. 'I'd better go take a look,' he said.

He went back outside and took his torch from the glove compartment and rattled the gate. The chain was rusty and didn't look like anyone had shifted it in months.

Leaving his cap inside the car, he put on a pair of gloves and went to climb over the gate. There wasn't anywhere obvious on the metalwork to get any purchase, so he moved towards the side, putting the toe of his shoe onto one of the hinges and lifting himself up on that.

At the top, he paused, one leg on either side. A speeding car came past, lights on full beam. In their sudden light, he noticed a mobile phone mast behind the shed. He frowned. A phone mast would need maintenance. There must be some other access road to the building from the rear. He could have saved himself the bother of climbing in this way but it was too late now; he was already most of the way over.

Swinging his other leg over, his trousers snagged on a metal burr on the gate as his weight carried him down.

He landed awkwardly on the ground, on all fours. Brushing his hands clean he looked down at his trousers and saw his left leg was ripped from the knee downwards.

'Bugger.'

He switched on the torch and shone it on the front doors. They were firmly secured by the grille he had seen from the road, so he made his way down the overgrown pathway to the right of the building.

At ground level, the first windows he came to were covered by old curtains he couldn't see through. Spiderwebs covered the glass.

He went further back, away from the road, and found another window, shining his torch inside.

At first he thought it was rags, dangling from one of the cross-beams below the roof. Some old curtain perhaps, abandoned and rotting.

And then he wiped the glass with the elbow of his jacket and peered in again. As a face emerged from the shape he had taken for rags, he stepped back, stumbling on loose bricks and rubble. A body, revolving slowly.

He had found dead bodies like this before; all coppers did. It was part of the job, but it was always a shock.

At the back of the hall, the back door had been broken open. Fresh splinters on the jamb. He stepped inside. A cool wind blew through open skylights in the ceiling.

He shone the torch. A wooden stepladder was standing in the middle of the room, with a pigeon perched at the top of it, one sleepy eye gazing back at South.

Hanging close to the ladder on a rope improvised from what looked like his own trousers was the body, rotating slowly. His bare legs were pale; his feet dark and purple. The dead man's blood had pooled downwards, bloating and discolouring them.

South shone his torch at the man's head as the body spun.

The dark face turned away.

As the face inched back into view, tilted upwards by the noose beneath the chin, he got a better look. It was bloodless; flesh had sunk onto the bone beneath. The eyes showed white.

There was something hauntingly familiar about him, but South couldn't figure out what. Had he seen him somewhere before? The body rotated away again.

He knew many of the vagrants around here, but the more he thought about it, the more he felt sure this wasn't one of the men he had found sleeping in the huts, or in porches.

The pigeon exploded into flight, noisily, wings slapping.

The walls of the hall were flashing blue. The hairless woman was at her bedroom window again, looking down at the cars and vans and the ambulance.

South walked from his car through the gates which had been busted open now, towards the back of the hall again. The forensics teams were busy unloading the aluminium cases that held their equipment and carrying them down the track towards the open door.

DS Cupidi was on the phone. 'There's money in the tin. Order a pizza,' she was saying. 'What do you mean the tin is empty? What about pasta? There must be pasta in the cupboard.'

One of the detective constables who had been at South's house said, 'Well. That's that then.'

They were standing outside the hall peering in, while

the Crime Scene manager did his work. They had brought lamps which they'd placed around the floor. The dead man's shadow swung on the walls, now, large and sorrowful. Cupidi joined them looking in at the men and women doing their work.

The Crime Scene manager said, 'If you'd prefer to go and look after your daughter? It's all wrapped up here. Job done.'

'No. I should be here.' She shone her torch up at the dead man.

'Well. So that's why we couldn't find the bastard,' the constable said.

Cupidi's torch moved down towards the floor. 'Are those your friend's binoculars?'

South hadn't noticed them before. Sitting at the bottom of the ladder was a small plastic bag, an empty bottle of vodka, and a pair of black binoculars.

'Looks like it,' said South.

'He never even sold them,' said Cupidi. 'What a useless stupid thing to do. Stupid, stupid, stupid. Well that simplifies matters, doesn't it? This stupid arse killed Mr Rayner and then came here and killed himself. Murder–suicide.'

They stood aside for a second as a technician in a sterile suit made his way into the hallway with a case of equipment.

South was conscious of Cupidi looking at him. Eventually she asked, 'Are you OK, William?'

The constable laughed and said, 'Of course he is. Bill South's used to this kind of thing, isn't he? And worse.'

'Was he one of the ones you'd seen on the beach?' asked Cupidi.

'I'm not sure,' said South.

'Shame. It would have been good to have a witness putting him at the scene.'

'Got his wallet,' shouted a blue-gloved copper, holding up a small canvas rectangle.

'ID?' said Cupidi.

The copper held the wallet open. It was empty, save for a couple of pieces of paper that dropped out onto the dusty floor. 'Medical card,' said the copper. 'Name . . .' The copper squinted in his torchlight. 'Donald John Fraser. Date of birth . . . I can't read it. 1957, I think.'

'First the uncontrollable rage and the sense of feeling trapped by what you've done. The knowledge that you've gone too far. Then the self-pity,' said Cupidi. 'Then the act itself. I've come across it before.'

The name was jangling in South's head. The body swung round once more to face them, just as one of the technicians shone a torch directly up at it.

'What was that name again?' he called out to the copper with the medical card.

'What's wrong, William?'

'Donald James Fraser. With an *s*,' said the copper.

South felt cold. And then a rush of nausea. The dead man waiting to be cut down and bagged was a ghost. The last time he had seen him, South had been thirteen years old.

★   ★   ★

She came to him again as he was getting back into the police car. There was no need for him to be here, she was saying. He should go home.

'You look like shit,' she said, leaning towards him. 'Are you going to be sick again?'

'No. I'm fine.'

'Delayed shock?'

'I'm not normally like this,' he said.

She frowned at him. 'Is there anyone who you can stay with tonight?' she said.

'I'll be OK.'

She was peering into his face. 'No. I'm not sure you will.'

He nodded. 'It shook me up,' he said. 'That's all.'

'Nothing to be ashamed of,' she said. 'What about a drink, when you're done here?'

The other option was going back to his empty house. 'You sure you should be seen asking another copper out?'

She looked at him quizzically for a second. 'Did Zoë say something to you?'

'No,' he lied.

'I just don't think you should be on your own tonight. I'm concerned about you, that's all.'

She was right. He didn't want to be alone.

'I'll be done here in an hour. Come back to mine. Have a takeaway. I've got some wine. Just talk about it. That's all. It'll help.'

He thought for a while. 'OK. Maybe I should.'

She gave him a small smile. 'You head off there now. I'll

catch you up.' Then she reached in her purse and pulled out a tenner, and said, as if it was an afterthought. 'And could you order a Chinese or something for Zoë? She's there on her own. There's wine in the fridge. Tell her I'll be there soon.'

'You want me to go and feed your daughter?'

And before she could answer, she had turned and was heading back towards the hall. He looked at the ten-pound note and wondered if he should just go home.

Head aching, he drove back to the police station, swapped the police car for his own, ordered pizzas from Papa John's and then drove the ten minutes back out towards the Cupidis' house.

Zoë was at the door. 'What did you order?'

'One pepperoni, one chicken.'

'I don't eat meat. I'm a vegetarian.'

'Right,' said South. 'Take the chicken off then.'

'Doesn't matter,' she said, letting him into the house. She had a laptop on the kitchen table and was watching some programme on it. 'What's wrong with your trousers?'

'I ripped them, getting over a gate.'

After the cold dark scene he'd just come from, this kitchen seemed so ordinary, so domestic, so brightly lit. He was grateful for it.

'School OK?'

'Peak,' she said, scowling, and went back to watching her programme.

'That means bad?'

'Peak,' she said again. When the pizzas arrived, she closed down the computer, opened one of the boxes and sat quietly picking off the meat.

He picked up a piece of pepperoni pizza and almost took a bite. Then he put the pizza slice down and stared at it.

'Not hungry?'

Cupidi had said there was wine in the fridge, he thought.

'Not really, no.'

He couldn't stop thinking about Donny Fraser, half naked, slowly turning in the dark hall.

'So why did my mum ask you round?' she said, between bites.

'It's something to do with work.'

'Sure it is,' she said.

'It's work. That's all.'

'That never stopped her in the past.'

'Don't,' he said, quietly. 'Please.'

'Sorry. It's my brat act. I didn't mean it.'

South closed the lid of his pizza box and watched Zoë eating. In his mind, Donny Fraser had always been around twenty. South had never really imagined him becoming so decrepit, so used up. Death made you look older, but that man had looked ancient, worn and brutalised by whatever life he had led since South had last seen him.

Zoë was already on a second piece of pizza, removing the meat. 'Can I come birdwatching again with you sometime?' she said, mouth full.

'I'm sorry?'

'Out at the bird sanctuary. Can you take me again?'

'I suppose so. Did you enjoy it?'

'Did you think I didn't?'

'I just didn't think that's what teenage girls did these days.'

She shrugged. 'They probably don't. What made you like birds?'

'I was going through a hard time. I found them less complicated than humans, I suppose.'

'Same,' she said.

'I really doubt it.'

The sound of keys in the front door. 'That's Mum,' said Zoë, wiping sauce from her mouth.

Alex Cupidi came in, put down her handbag and looked from one to the other.

'You OK, Mum?' said Zoë.

She kissed her daughter on the top of her head. 'How's the pizza?'

'Meaty.'

'Sorry. I forgot to tell him.'

'I know.'

She pulled up one of the chairs at the kitchen table. 'Have you got homework to do?'

'Done it,' said Zoë.

'I just need to talk to William.'

Zoë looked from South back to her mother again.

'In private.'

'I haven't finished eating.'

'Please?' As Zoë headed upstairs Cupidi went to the fridge and pulled out a bottle of white wine. It was half full. 'You need a drink? I do.' She placed two glasses on the table.

'Tell me, William. How old were you when you joined the force?'

'Twenty-eight,' he said. 'I'd tried a few things, but this is what stuck.'

'What made you join up?'

'I'd known a copper when I was a kid. A friend of my mum's. The older I got, the more I admired him, I suppose. So I thought I'd give it a try.'

She pulled the old cork from the bottle. 'Remember the first time you saw a dead body?'

'An old man. Died in his bed. Nobody noticed him for a week. Milkman called it in.'

'You've seen quite a few, over the years, I suppose.'

He nodded.

'You always throw up?'

She didn't miss a thing, he thought.

'What was it about that man? That man in particular?'

'You could see, then?'

'When you heard the name. It's like you went rigid. It's OK. I don't think anyone else noticed.'

He looked down at the table. 'Last time I saw him was nearly forty years ago. It was a bit of a shock.'

'Forty years?'

'Yes.'

'So you knew him?'

'It's a long story.'

'I thought it might be.' She poured him a huge glass. 'Tell,' she said, pouring another for herself.

He took a gulp from the top of the glass. 'Can this be between you and me?'

She looked at him. 'Why?'

'It's personal.'

She felt in her bag for her cigarettes. 'You know I can't promise that until I've heard what you've had to say,' she said.

He took a deep breath. 'Donny Fraser was the man convicted of killing my father.'

Her eyes widened. 'Christ.' She took a gulp of her wine. 'I didn't know your father was murdered.'

'I don't tell people.'

'My God. No wonder.'

He pushed the box of pizza away. 'To be honest, I'm not really hungry,' he said.

'When did this happen?'

'In '78,' he said. 'In the Troubles. My dad was in the paramilitaries. Lots of men round our way were. Donny Fraser was too. Same unit.'

In a single movement, she got up and walked around the table and put her arms around him. 'You poor boy,' she said. 'You poor, poor boy.'

He raised his hand and squeezed hers.

'So he has a history of violence. Just like I said.'

He put his hand back down. 'I don't really like to talk about it,' he said.

'Sorry.' She drew back, too.

'They tried him, put him in jail. They wrote to us to let us know when he was released. That's the last I heard about him.'

'It'll all be on the news, I suppose,' she said.

'I hadn't thought of that.' On tomorrow's news bulletins they would be talking about a murderer who had been a terrorist in Ireland, during the bad days. They would mention his father's name. It was all coming back again.

She refilled his glass. 'I wonder what he's been doing all this time, then?'

'Me too,' he said.

'Mind if I smoke?' She stood and opened the kitchen door. 'Zoë doesn't like it,' she said.

They stood outside in the back garden. A mean square of grass with a new wooden fence on three sides.

Even in the light of this new estate, there were stars. Cassiopeia was right above them, a big W in the night sky.

'You left Ireland after your father was killed, then?'

'And never went back,' he said, looking upwards. 'Mum got a job on the council. We had a quiet life. She liked it here. Married again. A good man this time. He took us in, treated me like his own son. It's his house I live in now. I loved it here. Still do. I was happy.'

'You've lived here since you were a boy?'

'Thirteen,' said South, waving her smoke away.

172

She went back inside and returned with another bottle of wine. They had another glass. Then another. 'What was Donald Fraser doing around here? Was he looking for you?'

'I don't know. Maybe it's just coincidence.'

'Maybe,' she said.

What if he had been, though? thought South. He shivered briefly in the cold.

'What about Bob's sister?' South asked, leaning back against the wall of the house. 'Have you found her yet?'

Upstairs the bathroom light came on. Zoë was brushing her teeth. 'You know what?' said Cupidi. 'Bob Rayner didn't have a sister.'

South looked at her in the gloom. 'But we met her.'

'We met a woman. A woman who said she was his sister. When it turned out that the address she had given us was wrong, I looked around for a Gill Rayner, checked all the usual records. Common enough name, but none of them turned out to be her. So naturally I wondered if Rayner was just her maiden name. Checked for any marriage licences. Birth certificates. Nothing. Then I went and checked Robert Rayner's records. He had an older brother who committed suicide in his twenties, but no sister.'

'That's bloody weird.'

'Isn't it?'

'What about his phone records? He must have called her. They met every fortnight.'

'I thought of that. We've checked his mobile and his

landline. Everyone is accounted for. No sign of her. You're on there a lot. You spoke most days.'

'Yes,' he said. 'We did.'

She smoked more cigarettes in the darkness. The night was still, the first frost of the year starting to settle. If he hadn't been in a dark mood before, the revelation about Bob's sister made the weight heavier. He had never lied to Bob; but Bob had lied to him. Even Bob hadn't trusted him, in the end.

'Why would someone pretend to be his sister?' he said.

'People have secrets. Maybe she was his lover. Maybe they were having an affair.'

'Did you find out anything about those dressings? In the bin outside?'

'Those?' She shook her head. 'What made you think of that?'

He shrugged. 'I just thought it was odd, that's all.'

'We asked every branch of Boots in the South East if they remembered a man coming in and buying twenty packs of dressings but it didn't turn up anything. I don't think it was connected.'

He nodded. She said, eventually, 'I'm getting cold, aren't you?'

'I should probably go,' he said. 'I'll call a taxi.'

'Don't be daft. There's a spare room.' She reached out and took his arm and led him back inside. Then sat him down and poured the last of the second bottle of wine into their glasses.

'You must be pleased,' he said. 'First case, all wrapped up.'

If she heard a bitterness in his voice, she pretended not to notice it. 'I wouldn't say pleased. A bit more secure, perhaps. I don't know.'

He ran his finger around the rim of his glass. Then he looked up. 'What if he didn't do it?'

'What?'

It had been niggling at him since he'd found Donny's body. 'What if Donny Fraser didn't kill Bob?'

She looked at him, puzzled. 'We don't know if he did yet for sure. But we will do if we match his prints to the murder weapon. And I'll bet you they do.'

'But what if he didn't do it?'

'They told me you've never worked on a murder, William.'

'That's right. I never have.'

She picked up a cold slice of pizza and picked off a square of cheese. 'Sometimes I don't think we understand the effect of crime on victims enough,' she said. 'If it's your child murdered, or your father, you see the world differently. But the evidence is all there.'

'That's what I thought too,' he said. 'The evidence is all there.'

'You should be pleased. The man who killed your father finally got what was coming to him. And he killed himself. That's all.'

He stood up and poured some tap water into his glass. 'Thing is, I don't think he committed suicide.'

'Jesus, William. You saw him there. Why are you finding this so hard? Maybe you should apply for some leave.'

'Right. I should go to bed.'

She put the pizza boxes outside in the recycling box and then showed him upstairs to the spare room. It was small. There was a desk in it.

'Do you want me to put a stitch in those trousers?' she said, handing him a towel. 'I'll do it now, if you like.'

'You don't have to. I can do it,' he said. She turned to go. 'One thing,' he said. 'The woman opposite called in a disturbance. That's why I was checking the place out. She thought it was kids in there.'

'By the look of it, Fraser had broken in to find a place to doss. She probably heard him.'

'But she saw torchlight inside the hall.' Cupidi stopped smiling at him. 'Did you find a torch?' he asked.

'No.' She frowned. 'We didn't. But we weren't looking for one.'

'No. I didn't see one either. I looked for it.'

'Even if there wasn't one there, that doesn't actually prove anything,' she said. 'He could have had a torch in there before he killed himself, but lost it. He was a drunk. It could be somewhere we haven't found yet. Or maybe some kids with a torch did break in, saw him hanging there and were too shit-scared by what they'd seen to tell anyone.'

'Could be,' said South. 'I should sleep.'

'You look done in,' she said.

'I am,' he said. 'I really am.'

The bed was small. It was a long time since he had not slept in a house on his own.

—✈—

By Saturday morning everyone was talking about how Sergeant Ferguson had pulled Donny into the station for questioning.

In Armstrong's the butchers, the young Mr Armstrong said, 'I heard it's something to do with your husband, Mrs M.'

Billy's mum pulled Billy out of the shop behind her. 'Common gossip,' she said. 'I don't want to dignify them with my business.' Even if it was only going to be half a dozen pork sausages and some bacon scraps.

As they walked home, Billy sensed that people were staring at them again, like they had done after his dad had been killed. That night they only had mashed potato and spaghetti hoops for tea, because mum had left the sausages behind in the shop.

On Sunday morning, he went into his mother's bedroom and lay next to her in bed. He had taken to doing this on weekends; his dad wasn't there any more to say that he was too old for that.

'What if we repainted the whole house, Billy? Painted it some wild colour maybe. Like purple. Or red. Or pink. Or orange. No. Not orange.'

'Not pink. Purple,' said Billy.

'Just imagine the neighbours' faces. That would be something, wouldn't it? God. They'd start talking then.'

Billy pulled the sheets tighter around him, thought of Donny banging on the window and said, 'Do I have to go to school tomorrow?'

'We'll see.' And she leaned over and kissed him on the forehead.

'I was thinking . . .' He hesitated. 'What if we just went to live somewhere else?' When he said it, it seemed like an outrageous thing to say; he had never lived anywhere else. Now it seemed a good idea.

His mum, still in her pink dressing gown, with a cigarette in her mouth, looked at him. 'Leave here?'

'Yes.'

'But all your relatives are here.'

'Just Dad's family,' he said.

She tugged on the cigarette, thoughtfully. 'That's an idea,' she said, grinning.

'How soon could we go?' he asked, and realised as he said it that he was going too fast.

She frowned. 'Is something worrying you, Billy?' she asked, but he didn't have to answer, because just then the doorbell rang.

'Jesus. Who's that at this time on a Sunday morning?' She got out of bed, ciggie in hand, and lifted the curtain from the window.

'My God.' She let the curtain drop like it was on fire.

'It's Joe McGrachy. I think he saw me. What the hell's that bastard doing, round here this time of the morning?'

'It's almost eleven, Mum.'

'Is it? Jesus Christ.' The doorbell sounded again.

'Get dressed quick, Billy. Go and answer it. Make him a cup of tea or something. Offer him a cigarette. Tell him I'll be down in a minute.'

Jesus. Mr bloody McGrachy. What was he after now? Heart going fast. Billy went to his room and threw on his trousers and shirt.

McGrachy was standing outside the front door in his black Sunday coat and suit, holding a bunch of roses and smiling. 'Is your mother in?' he said. 'I've come to pay my respects.'

'She'll be down in a minute,' Billy said, his voice too high. 'She says would you like a cup of tea?'

McGrachy shucked off his black coat, moving the flowers from one hand to the other. Billy took it, thick, heavy and reeking of nicotine, and hung it on the back of the kitchen door. As Billy led him into the living room, McGrachy lowered his voice. 'I been thinking about ye, Billy.'

Here we go.

'You heard what's going on with Donny Fraser?'

'A bit,' said Billy.

'That fucker Ferguson pulled him in. He's been asking him all sorts of questions. Why?'

'I didn't say nothing, Mr McGrachy.'

McGrachy leaned forward so his face was just a few inches away. 'Donny said he saw you with Ferguson.'

'He wanted to talk to me. Honest to God. I didn't say nothing.'

McGrachy paused, stood up straight again. 'Course ye didn't, lad. But why is he thinking Donny is anything to do with this?'

'Is that you, Mr McGrachy?' called his mother down the stairs.

'That's right, Mrs McGowan.' McGrachy lowered his voice. 'Has Donny been up to something?'

'No. I mean. I don't know.'

'Your ma and Sergeant Ferguson are close, aren't they?'

'Not close,' said Billy. 'Not really.'

'I'll be down in just a sec,' his mother shouted.

'Did you tell your mother about what happened?'

'Never. Cross my heart.'

McGrachy nodded. 'Thing is, Ferguson was asking Donny about the gun that killed your father. Why would he think my men have anything to do with that?'

'Don't know, Mr McGrachy,' said Billy. 'Would you like tea?'

'There's something going on here I don't know,' whispered McGrachy. 'And I don't like not knowing things. Be my ears, Sonny Jim. OK? Listen out for me, lad. You'll hear things even my big ears can't.'

Billy went into the kitchen, trembling, and put the kettle on, leaving McGrachy standing there, flowers still in hand. He made the tea extra strong, squeezing the bag dry into the cup just as his father had liked it, and brought it out on a tray with the sugar.

'Have a seat, Mr McGrachy,' said Billy.

'Man of the house, now, eh?' said McGrachy.

Billy sat down on the small chair opposite McGrachy, and they both listened to his mother bustling about upstairs.

What Billy found funny was the way McGrachy shot up like a rocket the moment his mother finally entered the room, dressed in a miniskirt and a pullover that looked too tight.

'Hello, Mary. I brought these for ye,' he said, embarrassed, holding out the flowers. He was not a man who was comfortable with these things.

She looked at them. 'And?' she said, not taking them.

The Sunday suit said he must have come here straight from church. 'I thought you'd like them,' McGrachy said, hesitantly.

Billy was amazed at the power of a woman over a man like this. There was nobody in the town, Protestant or Catholic, who wasn't a bit scared of McGrachy, and here he was, standing and holding out a bunch of flowers to his mother, anxious that she wouldn't take them off him.

'It's been a while since the funeral,' he said. 'I wanted to ask how you were keeping.'

'We're fine, aren't we, Billy?' she said.

'My arm is getting tired from holding these flowers,' he said.

She took them finally and handed them straight to Billy. 'Put these in the big jug, will you, Billy?'

Billy left the two of them in the front room. Returning with the jug, he paused outside the door to listen.

'I'm a widower, Mary,' McGrachy was saying. 'I know I'm a little older than you, but I have savings and a decent house of my own. I know you're going to be a little short now. I'd be happy to lend some money. Just ask. Will you promise me that you'll ask if you ever need it?'

'Thank you, Mr McGrachy. That's very generous.'

Billy coughed and entered.

'They look nice. Thank you, Billy.' Billy put the vase down on the sideboard.

'Maybe the pictures, then? We could go to Belfast in the Rover,' McGrachy said. 'There's a new Burt Reynolds.'

'I don't think so,' said his mother.

Mr McGrachy looked shocked. 'I thought you'd like that, Mary. You must be lonely, here on your own.'

'Billy. Run upstairs and play in your room,' said his mother.

'I'm sorry if I asked too soon. You must be grieving still.'

By the time he returned back on tiptoes to the bottom of the stairs, McGrachy was saying, 'It was me that got you and your late husband this house from the council, Mary. Remember that, don't ye?'

'The answer is still no, I'm afraid, Mr McGrachy.'

He was scared for his mother; McGrachy was not the

kind of man to stand for this. He wanted to go and tell her to just pretend to like him at least.

'Your husband loved you, Mary. He talked about you all the time.'

'Well there's something. He talked about you a lot too. He thought you were great. And the rest of your lot. He thought that made him a big man. And look at him now.'

There was an uncomfortable pause. He heard them moving. Now his mother was opening the front door.

'I understand your bitterness, Mary, of course I do. But I'm here to help. One more thing, Mary, I want to ask. Your husband had something of ours.'

'Wouldn't know.'

'I need it back.'

'I don't know what you're talking about, Mr McGrachy.'

'Something we had issued him with. On behalf of the Volunteer Force. He'd have kept it hidden somewhere, I guess. I expect you'll know all his little secrets.'

'Why would I know anything about it? He never discussed his business with me.' She would have been standing there, arms crossed, waiting for him to leave.

'I would appreciate it if you could find it, Mary.'

'I'm sorry, Mr McGrachy.'

'I need to know where it is, Mary,' McGrachy was whispering again.

'I would appreciate it if you went now.'

'I'll be back if I don't hear.'

'Goodbye, Mr McGrachy,' his mother said.

'Well, I'd earnestly appreciate it if you would start looking for it, Mary.'

Billy crouched on the stairs, barely breathing, hoping his mother couldn't hear him. Only when McGrachy's car drove away did he dare fill his lungs.

He emerged from the bottom of the stairs, moving as if he'd just run down them. 'You OK, Mum?'

'Fine,' she said, wiping her eyes on the sleeve of her pullover, even though all the time she made it sound like she hadn't been frightened.

'Where do you think we could go?' said his mother. 'What about Rome? I always fancied Italy. "Three Coins in a Fountain".'

Sunday evenings there was nothing on the telly if you didn't want to watch *Songs of Praise*. They were both lying on their backs on the living-room floor.

'Not Italy. We don't speak the lingo.'

'Jamaica.'

'What would you do?' The furthest they'd ever been was on holidays to Portrush.

'I will open a bar on the beach and make a fortune. Or maybe Paris. I could be an artist.'

'You've never painted a picture in your life, Mum.'

'You don't know. I could be a great artist. Do you think there are still artists in Paris?'

They had a packet of crisps and a bottle of red lemonade each. Mum had put some vodka in hers.

He wondered, was this just a game, like when he was a kid and she used to make up stories? Or did she really mean it? If they could get away from here, maybe everything stupid he had done would be forgotten. 'Are you being serious, Mum?' said Billy anxiously.

'Serious as a broken bone,' she said.

'Good,' he said. 'So am I.' It would mean leaving his friends too. He was scared he would never make new ones.

After a while, Billy said, 'America, Mum. Can't we go and live in America?'

They would speak English there, at least. She sat up on the carpet and took one of her crisps from the packet, and before putting it in her mouth, said, 'I don't like the accent. Or the cars.'

He thought of his dad, working in the garage on his Pontiacs and Cadillacs. 'No. How much money would we need, to leave, Mum?'

'Quite a bit,' she said.

'So we have some?'

'Some.'

'How much have we got?'

'Not a lot.'

And they lay on their backs, looking up at the ceiling.

'Well if you're not going to school today, you'll have to help me pack away your father's things.'

Pack away his father's things? He had never thought that they'd have had to do that.

She took his father's cap off the back of the kitchen door, and chucked his walking stick out of the back door. 'Good riddance to the bloody thing.'

Billy had not liked that stick much either.

He watched as she threw open the doors to his father's wardrobe and started pulling out his suits, laying them on his bed. In the pockets of his suits they found two pound notes, a toffee and a few bus tickets. Billy was disappointed. The contents of his father's pockets should have been more interesting.

'Maybe I should keep his best suit for you,' Mum said. 'For when you're the big man.'

He imagined wearing it, collar turned up like he was a punk rocker. Last week Rusty Chandler's older brother Stampy came back from Belfast with a suit that had five-inch lapels. It was bloody extreme. Billy looked at the jacket and pulled a face.

'Perhaps not, then.'

Billy's mother packed the clothes in a large suitcase and Billy sat on the lid while she strapped one of Dad's belts around it.

'Take it down for me, will you, lovely. I'm just a poor weak woman.'

So he lifted it and started dragging it to the landing and he was just at the top of the stairs, when something caught his foot.

He felt himself slowly tripping forwards. In an attempt to regain his balance he let go of the case, but he was already out over the top of the stairs, falling head first, crashing to the bottom, his load following behind.

His mother screamed.

On the floor, Billy lay dazed, soft, hazy whiteness all around him. Had something happened to his eyes? Had he gone blind? He raised his fingers to his face to check.

'Aaaah!' With a yelp he jumped up. The case had sprung open, sending clothes everywhere; a pair of his dad's old underpants had landed on his head. Big, pale floppy things. Jumping up and down, he flung the dead man's underwear away from him.

Seated on the kitchen stool, Mum held him on her knee and stroked his head like she had done when he was a little boy, though he was far too big for that. 'You must have caught your foot on that loose carpet. I was always after him to fix that. Looks like he's gotten out of that one, anyway.'

'Is it swelling up?'

'Like a ping-pong ball,' she said. 'The arsehole is still taking a whack at us from the grave, eh?'

For some reason that was funny and they were both laughing as the doorbell rang. Neither of them moved.

'Pretend we're not in.' She winked. And she hugged him even closer, smiling.

'I'm just calling to see if you're OK, Mary. Open the door.'

She unfolded her arms, and stood, putting Billy back on his feet, then went to the kitchen door and called, 'Go away, Fergie. I don't need your help.'

The neighbours would be watching. It would get back to McGrachy again that Ferguson had been here.

'Mary. I'm not going until I find out if you're all right.'

'It's not helping. Just go. Please.'

They could hear him standing a while, feet on the back-door metal door scraper. They could see him too, a dark shape through the patterned glass. Mum went to the hall-way, picked up a pile of shirts that had been thrown out of the suitcase and started folding them again.

He left his mother to the clothes and went back up to his room where he was supposed to be doing the homework he had never handed in last week. On the way up, from the landing window, Billy watched Fergie trudge back to his car, feeling sorry for him. It was sort of embarrassing that a policeman liked his mother this much, but Fergie was OK.

Billy was there five minutes, kneeling by his bed with his homework open on the blankets, when his mother called, 'Billy. Can you come down? Without tripping this time.'

She wanted him to take the clothes out. The Sally Army would be picking them up that afternoon.

There was a suitcase and a cardboard box. He picked up the box first.

Outside, when he looked up, he saw that Ferguson had not driven off. He was still there in his police car, head down. Billy squinted. *Go away, Fergie. Leave us alone.* Fergie sat, writing something.

Billy went back inside the house, saying nothing, and

lifted the suitcase. Was this all his father had owned? It didn't seem like much.

Ferguson was sucking the end of his biro. He didn't even look up.

An hour or so later Billy came back downstairs. He had been drawing birds instead of doing his homework. When he opened the front door to see if Fergie was still there, he saw that the box and suitcase had gone, but there was now a piece of paper folded in half.

On the outside it said: *Mrs Mary McGowan*. Thinking it was probably a thank-you note from the Salvation Army, he opened it.

Dear M.

Things are a little hairy now, I know. There are a lot of rumours flying around. But everything will be all right.

The writing was neat; even letters, all nicely upright.

I've been trying to say this to your face, but I never could figure out how to do it. You don't have to tell me what happened. But trust me. I will protect you WHATEVER you did and WHATEVER has happened and WHATEVER is going to happen too. Please remember that.

Your loyal friend,

John Ferguson

I love you. Always did.

He read those last words with puzzlement. To a boy of his age, love was mysterious, especially when applied to his mother. Love was something that sent grown-ups nuts. It was scary.

'Come and help me wash up.'

Fergie and Mr McGrachy? Both of them. God's sake.

'What are you doing out there, Billy?' called his mother from the kitchen.

And, not wanting to be caught reading it, he scrumpled the note up and stuffed it into his pocket.

'Was that a note?'

'No. Just my homework.'

'You're a good boy,' she said, and she handed him a drying-up cloth.

Donny finally caught him on Tuesday, on the way back from school.

He had been expecting it. Billy had just crossed River Street when out of nowhere, a fist clouted him on the side of his head.

Sitting on the pavement, Billy looked up.

In flared jeans and dark glasses, Donny stood above him. He must have been there in the alleyway, waiting for him.

'I seen you and that copper Ferguson.'

'I didn't say nothing.'

Grabbing his shirt collar, he yanked Billy to his feet.

'You're hurting me.'

'Yes,' he said.

Tugging on the shirt, he pulled Billy into the small alley that led down to the path alongside the river, behind the workshops. No one could see you from here.

'Well how come, after you talked to him, he pulled me in and started asking me about some gun?'

'Can't breathe,' whispered Billy.

'There's people saying I killed your father now. Jesus, Billy. What sort of fucken stuff have you been spreading about me?'

He released Billy's collar. The path was dark, overhung with brown bramble stems that had never been cut back. Behind the weeds, there were red-painted words on the brick wall: 'FUCK', 'SHIT' and 'CUNT'.

Billy had a vision of himself, lying still in the cold river water. 'You can't touch me. Mr McGrachy said so.'

'That right?'

'I'll tell Mr McGrachy on you.'

'I don't see McGrachy running to help you now. Is it right your mammy is courting Fergie?'

'No. She's not. She can't stand him. She's always telling him to leave us alone.'

'We seen him hanging round your house, Billy. So tell me. What did you say to Sergeant Ferguson?'

'Nothing.'

He grabbed Billy again and dragged him down the path to where there was a gap in the trees. Billy tried to scream, fingers clawing at his collar, but only a squeak came out.

Donny said, 'I don't want to do this, Billy. I like ye. I just want the truth.'

Billy was like a baby rabbit when hawks dive, unable to move his own limbs for fear. Donny kicked Billy's left leg hard so that Billy went down on one knee, Donny still clutching him by the neck. He yanked him down towards flowing water.

'You'll tell me, Billy.'

And before he knew it, Billy's head was being pushed underneath the cold water. He tried to arch his back against Donny's weight, but Donny was too strong for him.

It was only a few inches deep at the edge of the river, but the front of his face was being forced down into it. The water was murky brown and perishingly cold. It invaded his nose and mouth as he tried to scream. He sucked it in instead of air and his lungs convulsed.

Panic now. He wriggled and slithered but could not get free; he was going to die.

And then Donny pulled him out.

Spluttering and coughing, covered in brown mud.

'Well?'

The coughing wouldn't stop. His lungs hurt from the water.

'All I said . . .' Billy croaked. Water dripped from his wet hair.

'What? I can't hear you.'

'All I said was that some people wanted to ask me

questions about my dad. Swear to God I never told him nothing about a gun.'

Donny nodded. 'You better not be fibbing. I tell you, Billy. That fucking Ferguson is a menace. You know? I thought I was going to be put away for murder, for a second.' He pulled out a cigarette and lit it. 'I don't mind saying I was pretty fucken scared. Nobody's telling me anything any more. It's nuts round here. What about you? You going to be OK?'

Billy nodded.

He offered Billy a drag on his cigarette.

'Something weird is going on. Even McGrachy is treating me strange, now. He won't talk to me. Like even he thinks I done something. I had to be sure you didn't try and dob me to Ferguson.'

'I know.'

''Cause I never did nothing to harm ye.'

Billy nodded.

'No hard feelings?'

'You're OK.'

'Good lad.'

Billy handed back the cigarette.

'Your dad was a strong man,' said Donny, taking a drag. 'I looked up to him. We all did, us lads. I'm the last man that would have killed him. When all this started, when the Taigs started all the Brits Out shit, he took a stand. He wasn't afraid to fight back. I thought he was cool, you know. His sideburns and his cars. Really fucken cool. McGrachy's an old fucker, but I wanted to be like your dad, you know?'

'Right,' said Billy.

'But it's serious now. People are killing each other every day. And your dad's dead. And every day I'm wondering if I'm next.' He took another deep suck. 'Some days I wake up and I think the whole thing is a fucken mistake. I just want to go off and have a pint and smoke some dope, know what that is?'

Billy nodded.

'I'm all peace and love, truth to tell. But I can't now, know what I mean? Leave it to me, I wouldn't harm a fly. Even a Taig fly. I haven't killed anybody yet, swear to God. And I'm scared of the day I'm going to do that. Honest, I am.'

He turned and headed up the narrow alley, back up to the pavement.

Billy stood shivering, snivelling. There was blood dripping onto his school shirt from something in the water that must have cut his head. Broken glass or an old tin can, maybe.

All the way home people stared.

ELEVEN

His head hurt and his mouth was dry.

He remembered the body swinging. He remembered the wine.

He was in underpants, lying in a sleeping bag on the bed in a room so small that his feet were beneath a desk. He sat up and banged his head on a bookshelf above his head.

A book tumbled down. *Basic Concepts in Criminology*. He stood slowly and replaced it on the shelf between a 2010 copy of *Blackstone's Operational Manual* and *Tactical Counter-Terrorism*. Cupidi was the sort of copper who read the books you were supposed to read.

The bed he had slept on was a chair that they had, with some difficulty, unfolded last night. He remembered limbs touching awkward limbs as they had both struggled to tuck the foot of the bed under Cupidi's desk.

His clothes were folded over the back of an office chair. Only when he was pulling his trousers back on did he remember the rip. He looked down at his leg. Pale hairy flesh showed above his shoe.

★   ★   ★

Downstairs, Zoë was spreading margarine on sandwiches.

'What time is it?' he asked.

'Seven. Shit. I'm going to be late. The bus round here takes forever. It's like the five miles from nowhere, this place. I hate school.'

'Where's your mother?'

'Gone. Work. Want a sarnie?' she said.

'Already? What time did she go?'

'Don't know. I don't think she actually sleeps. She's a vampire. There's tea,' she said, putting the margarine back in the fridge. When she turned round she saw his legs and started laughing. 'You can't go out like that.'

He looked down at his leg. 'I'll be fine,' he said.

She wrapped the sandwiches in a carrier bag and stuffed them into her backpack. 'You going birdwatching this weekend?'

'Yes.'

'Can I come?'

He stared at her. She had no idea of the weight hanging over him right now. Why should she? 'There's a youth group. You should join them,' he said.

She looked stung. 'I don't want to be in a bloody youth group.'

She left via the back door, slamming it behind her in anger.

At around eight, he pulled up at the Cadet Force hall. A mist hung over the flat land. Though there was still police tape across the doors, there was no sign of any policemen there. Which probably meant they weren't treating it as an important crime scene. Just a suicide.

He looked at his watch. He would need to go home. He would be late on the morning rota, but he needed a change of clothes, plus he hadn't even brushed his teeth.

The gates were still open. He backed his car up a little, then drove it slowly inside the fence. A small lane ran alongside the hall, then curved away towards the right, where he had seen the mobile phone mast.

At the steel legs of the mast, the pitted tarmac ran out and the lane became a muddy track, heading north, parallel to the main road. South got out and squatted down in front of the car. There was a hint of tyre marks heading along the track. Probably someone from one of the telecoms companies. Rain had made the ruts indistinct.

Leaving the car, he turned and walked back to the hall's rear door, out of which Fraser's corpse would have been wheeled last night. There was an untidy pile of Chinese takeaway trays left at the doorway. The body-baggers and forensic team would have worked here until late. He lifted the single strand of police tape that had been put across the door and entered the hall.

Walking slowly around the empty room, his feet crunched on broken glass, echoing on the hard bare walls. The wooden stepladder was still there, lying on its side now though.

There were many more homeless people around here

than there had been when he first started the job. He was used to finding their lairs.

Lying against the wall was a single blue polythene bag. Squatting by it, he hooked one finger and raised the bag. A nylon pullover. He sniffed at the top of the bag and smelt woodsmoke and old nicotine. It would have been Fraser's, he guessed. Because they weren't treating the scene as anything but a suicide, the forensics team had not bothered with it.

He stood and looked around. Then walked the rectangle of the hall, stepping over broken glass and splinters of wood.

It did not feel right. Was that because of his own history with the man? Or because, to him, this didn't look like where a homeless man had chosen to kill himself?

Apart from the single pullover, there were no signs of blankets or improvised pillows; there were no blackened sticks of old fires. It did not look like Fraser had even slept here. There were no other possessions. Homeless people carried their lives in plastic bags. There should be more than just a single item of clothing. Tellingly, no empty bottles; and no signs of defecation.

He was searching a side room when he heard a car pull up into the back lane, then footsteps. Someone was walking up the side of the hallway. He ducked behind the wall, out of sight. There was no longer any door to hide behind; it had been removed from its hinges.

He listened. Now whoever it was was coming in through the open door.

South was quiet. The footsteps moved to the middle of the room and stopped. South peered out of the empty doorway. A young man with cropped black hair and a green bomber jacket had entered the hall and was looking up at the rafter from which Fraser had hung.

After inspecting it for a minute or so, the man lowered his head to look around him, hands in the pockets of his jacket. Just as South had done a minute ago, the man started to walk slowly around the room, as if looking for something. The man was definitely younger; though South was fit, he always liked the odds to be clearly on his side. And though he had his uniform on, South's stab vest and baton were in his police car boot. South pressed himself back against the wall.

The footsteps were moving again. As quietly as he could, South edged back towards the doorway to see what the man was doing. Brushing the wall, he knocked loose plaster. It fell to the floor.

'Who's there?' shouted the man.

Shit. South stepped out. 'Police,' he shouted. 'Don't move.'

'Christ in a bucket. You gave me a shock. What the hell are you doing here?'

'I was going to ask the same.'

And when the man pulled his hands out of his bomber jacket, South saw he had a pair of blue cleanroom gloves on.

'You're SOCO?' said South.

'DS Cupidi said there was no one on duty here,' said the Scene of Crime Officer. 'Jesus. You almost gave me heart failure.'

'Cupidi sent you?'

'What are you doing here, officer, didn't you see the tape?'

'I'm the officer who found the body.'

'You have no bloody right to be inside here, dressed like that,' said the SOCO, looking him up and down.

'I assumed you were no longer treating it as a scene of crime. There was no one here.'

'Well maybe we are.'

South stepped out of the doorway. 'Why did she tell you to come?'

'Cupidi? She called me this morning and asked me to take a look to see if there was anything to confirm a suspicion of foul play. Just to make sure we did everything to rule it out.'

'She did? And?'

'Give me a bastard chance. Just got here.' He looked down at South's trousers and said, 'Is that what passes for regulation uniform these days?'

The officer had started moving around the room again. When he saw the bag he picked it up and, just as South had, sniffed it. Then he upended it and tipped out the jumper.

'Anything in that room?' he asked.

'Not that I saw.'

'Like looking for a contact lens in the snow.' The man looked around. 'Nightmare, really. I mean, for one, this is not exactly the kind of place where you could tell whether there's been a struggle or not, is it? Or signs of forced entry.' He leaned down and picked up a piece of broken glass, then dropped it again. 'Ask me, not much point in wasting my time treating this as a murder scene until the results of the autopsy. And I bet they'll say suicide.'

South said, 'So you don't notice anything odd?'

'No.' The man stopped. 'What?'

'If he was dossing here, wouldn't you expect to find something more than just a jumper in a bag?'

'That's because maybe he wasn't dossing here, was he? Maybe he just came here to top himself,' said the Scene of Crime man, unimpressed.

South left him to his work and made his way back to his car. Scenes of Crime men were trained to look at what was there, South told himself, not what wasn't.

Changing his clothes made him even later than he would have been for the morning briefing. The sergeant in charge raised an eyebrow as South appeared at the back of the parade room, but didn't say anything.

It was almost over. The sergeant was mumbling through his list: police cars parking inappropriately outside the take-away; a rambler attacked by a Staffordshire terrier, and, of course, the body found in the old Cadet Force hall.

'No signs of anything suspicious, but CID have asked us to keep our ears peeled.'

There was a weary snigger.

'We have reason to believe the deceased was the person who killed Robert Rayner but investigations are ongoing.'

South's head was fuzzy. The day had started all wrong; Cupidi had, at least, taken seriously his suggestion that it might not have been a suicide. She must have if she had sent the Scene of Crime Officer back to the hall and briefed the shift sergeant.

'Anything else?'

South knew there was something he'd been meaning to raise but he couldn't remember what. He needed tea. Between heading home to change and driving to the station there had not been time for a cup.

'Right then,' said the sergeant, picking up his notes. His lips looked pink and sore.

South remembered what he had wanted to ask. 'What about the chemist shops? Anything else there? Any other break-ins?'

The men were already pushing out of the double doors behind him, eager to get away. 'Not as far as I know,' the sergeant said. 'Not for a couple of days. It seems to have calmed down a bit on that front, at least. Got any ideas on that?'

As the sergeant approached, he lifted a small white stick to his mouth. South realised his lips were badly chapped. The raw season was starting, the north wind coming across the weald.

'Judy Farouk disappeared a week back. And the break-ins started after she'd gone. My guess was that all the users were desperate after she'd gone.'

'Well, they stopped now, at least.'

'Only Judy isn't back. Not at her caravan, at least.'

'Maybe she's just moved the operation somewhere else. My guess, anyway. Tired of coppers like you knocking on her door.'

'Maybe,' said South.

In the hallway, he made tea from the machine and was so desperate for it he burned his tongue on the first sip.

The morning was the first chance he'd had to update his notebook, so he found an empty desk in the back office and wrote up everything he could remember from yesterday afternoon. '*Donny Fraser*', he wrote. Underlined the name three times. Added a question mark.

The office was quiet, which was good.

At the desk next to him, a woman constable South knew vaguely was scrolling through Facebook pages.

'You don't have an aspirin, do you?' he asked her.

'Not aspirin,' she said, eyes glued to the screen. South tried to remember her name, but couldn't.

'What are you doing?' he asked.

'Cyber-bullying,' she said. 'Some kids from the High School. Posting photos online. Revenge porn. I got Feminax.' She reached down and lifted up her handbag and pulled out a packet.

South took it, hesitated. The box was pink. 'Faster relief for period pain?'

The woman laughed. She had ginger hair and a round, friendly face. She was pretty, he realised, even with a strawberry birthmark on her cheek. 'It won't turn you into a nancy,' she said. 'It's just ibuprofen.'

He returned to his notebooks. Flicking back through the earlier pages, he saw the number plate he'd noted down. There was no computer on his desk, so he turned to the woman constable and said, 'You got the PNC on that thing? Can you look up a car number plate for me?'

He held out his notebook for her to read. 'Is that a P? Your writing is atrocious.' She keyed in her password, then the number. Within a minute she was writing something down on a Post-it note. 'Red Smart car registered to a Mr Steven Kriwazek, Durham. No outstanding notices.'

'That's funny. Because I saw it on a white four-wheel-drive down in Lydd.'

'Sure about the number?'

'A hundred per cent.'

He pressed one of her pills out of its bubble and gulped it down with the last of his tea.

'Fake plates,' she said.

He nodded.

The door to the back office swung open. 'There you are,' said DS Cupidi. 'I've been trying to call you.'

South picked his phone out of his pocket. It was on silent, he realised.

Cupidi was standing, arms crossed, looking angry. 'What were you doing at the Cadet Force hall?'

'I was just passing by.'

'Really? I had SOCO on the phone complaining that you were tramping around the crime scene.'

'Actually, your officer didn't seem to be that interested in whether it was a crime scene or not.'

'You can't do that, William. You're not even on the case any more. If . . .' She looked at the woman officer. 'After what you told me last night, I can't have you anywhere near this investigation. You would compromise it. Do you understand why?'

The younger woman concentrated on her screen, pretending not to listen.

'I didn't even know you were taking that seriously,' said South. 'There wasn't anyone at the hall when I arrived. The place was deserted. Anyone could have got in.'

'I sent someone there first thing this bloody morning. And you need to stay away. OK? Well away. For operational reasons. I can't afford to have this mixed up with the fact that I'm your friend. I've had enough crap with that already in my career. As my daughter seems to have told you.'

'So you are taking it seriously, then? What I said. About it not being a suicide?'

She picked up the box of pills next to his desk. 'Your time of the month, William?'

'Headache. Drank too much of your wine.'

'Lightweight,' she said. She sighed. 'Do you want to

know what I found out about Donald Fraser?' she asked, holding out a folder.

He hesitated, then said, 'OK.'

'Can we have a minute, Constable?' Cupidi said to the WPC.

'Don't mind me,' said the young woman.

'In private, actually,' said Cupidi.

Pushing her chair back noisily, the woman huffed, then left the room without another word.

'As you said, he was arrested for murder in 1978,' said Cupidi when she'd gone. 'For the murder of William "Billy" McGowan.'

'My father,' said South.

'Right,' Cupidi said quietly. 'Fraser was convicted, and released in 1991 on licence, before the Good Friday Agreement.'

'I know. They wrote to us and told us that. What about afterwards?'

'What do you mean?'

'Had he been an alkie all this time?' South asked. 'Since he got out?'

'It looks like it. When he came out of The Maze, he was put in a hostel for a while and then he was given a council flat in Belfast. Evicted three years later for non-payment of rent and abusing the property. Then he turned up in Aberdeen, London, Birmingham, Wales . . . pretty much everywhere. But he's been arrested for something pretty much every year since then.'

'Burglary?'

'Once or twice.'

'What about assault?'

'Actually . . . no. I looked for that. Begging, antisocial behaviour, breaking and entering, possession. No violence. Not since your father. Not until now.'

'Nothing like what he's supposed to have done to Bob?'

She frowned. 'He was an alcoholic. An addict. All addicts behave irrationally to feed their addiction. I'd guess he was getting pretty close to the bottom.'

'What if it wasn't him that killed Bob?' he said.

She picked at a nail, where the polish was cracked. 'Last night you said you didn't think he killed himself. Now you don't think he killed Bob, either?'

'I'm just saying, what if?'

'Know what? His prints have been matched to ones on the broken bottle you found. One hundred per cent accuracy. There aren't any distinct prints on the axe handle but I bet you good money we'll get a DNA match back this afternoon. And the hair on it is almost certainly Rayner's. We'll have that confirmed in a day or two as well.' She sat on his desk. 'Are you sure you're all right? This is the man who killed your father. He one hundred per cent fits the profile. If it was me, I'd be pleased, at least. I mean, I know it's been a shock, but . . .'

South hesitated. 'It doesn't feel right, that's all.'

She paused. Frowned. 'Do you know something you're not telling me, William?'

He looked away. She was not stupid, he thought. She could tell he was holding something back. He had never told anyone the truth about what happened to his father. It wouldn't be easy to start now. 'What do you mean?' he said.

'Bob Rayner.'

'What?'

'Do you know something about Bob that you haven't told me?'

Now it was his turn to look puzzled. 'What are you on about?'

'Do you swear?'

'Yes,' he said. 'What's wrong? Tell me.'

'Because it turns out not only does Robert Rayner's sister not exist, as I was saying, but pretty much everything about your pal Robert Rayner is a fabrication.'

'Sorry?'

'One. The school he supposedly taught at have never heard of him. Two. Actually, I can't find any record of him teaching anywhere, in fact. Yes, he exists. He has a National Insurance number and a birth certificate. He was all paid up in tax and NI, but God knows how because there's no record of him having worked anywhere at all since 1997.'

South took a while to take this in. He had been a friend; he had trusted him.

He asked, 'Where was his income coming from then? He must have been pretty well-off to buy that cottage. They cost a fortune these days.'

'That's it. His bank account had regular sums being

deposited into it from a private account in Switzerland. What sort of schoolteacher has a private account in Switzerland?'

'Somebody was paying him via a Swiss bank account?'

'I think he was paying himself. The account was in the name of Mrs Rayner. Who doesn't appear to exist. Bloody hell. And say you had no idea at all about this?'

'Nothing. I promise. He just didn't talk about anything.'

'I thought you were supposed to be the observant one?'

'He lied to me,' said South.

'It looks like it. How does that make you feel?'

'Angry, I suppose.' Though he had no right to be.

Cupidi's shoulders were down. 'And because he was your mate I just assumed he was straight. I shouldn't have assumed anything.'

'He had me fooled, too,' said South.

She sat on the desk next to him. 'I'm sorry. It's not your fault.'

South stood, paced up and down the small room. 'I just wasn't expecting it, that's all. But you're agreeing with me now. You think there's more to this, too.'

'I don't know,' she said. 'I don't see what it has to do with Donald Fraser.'

'Did you tell any of this to McAdam?' Her boss, the Detective Inspector.

'Of course I did.'

'What did he say?'

She picked up the folder, looked at her watch. 'He was

interested, but he doesn't think any of this is relevant. We have a suspect with a previous history of murder. We have evidence that places him at the scene of the crime. That's all we need. He says I don't need to spend any more time on it right now.'

'What do you think?' said South.

'I think I need to get on with my caseload,' she said, standing. 'Keep my head down. But please, William. Keep your nose out of this. If there is more to this than meets the eye, it won't help if you're involved. Not with your history with Donald Fraser. It will only make things harder.' And she went, leaving the door open behind her.

South sat back in his chair, hoping the painkillers would start to take effect soon.

'Ooh. You were round at her house last night, then?' said the WPC, after she'd returned to her chores at the computer.

'Fuck off,' said South.

'Charmer.'

'Don't go gossiping. It was nothing like that. I swear. I had something pretty bad happen to me last night and she was there for me. She just held my hand.'

'Message received.'

South looked at the registration number in his notebook again.

'Can you do me something else? Can you access the Automatic Number Plate thing on that machine?'

'I've got my own work to do.'

'What? Looking at Facebook?'

'Give it here. If you fuck off and leave me alone I might see if there's time to do it in my lunch break. If I feel like it.' She winked at him. And for a second he thought she was flirting with him; but then he realised that it was just a pretty young woman teasing a man twice her age.

'Tell Fergie who did it to you.'

'I can't.' It was the day after Donny Fraser beat him up. They were in the front room again.

'Yes you can,' Mum was saying. 'You have to. For me. If somebody's been hurting you, I have to know who it is.'

She had seen the blood on his shirt. She knew something was going on.

Ferguson, too, sat there, like he knew everything. Billy couldn't ever remember seeing Sergeant Ferguson out of uniform before. He was wearing an Aran cardigan and brown cords, as if he was trying to look like a normal person on a Saturday. There were leather tassels on his shoes, too; it all made him look like he'd walked out of a knitting catalogue.

His mother had cried when Billy had come home yesterday; big splodges of mascara on her cheeks.

'That's it. I'm leaving this place,' she was saying now. 'My mind's made up.'

'I know why you need to go,' said Ferguson, quietly. And

he looked first at Mary, then at him. 'I can help. But we've got to tidy up a few things first.'

'Will you get whoever did this to him? He won't say.'

'I know who did it,' said Ferguson. And for a second Billy wondered if he meant he knew who had beaten him up or who had killed his father and his heart stopped. 'I just need a wee word with the lad.'

Mum said, 'I just want to go now. Only we can't leave this dump unless the bank agrees to the loan.'

'Leave us alone a minute, will you, Mary? I need to talk to the lad in private.'

His mother hesitated. 'I don't know.'

Ferguson said, 'Please. Please trust me. I only want to do you good. Swear to God.'

Billy said, 'I don't want to talk to you. Why should I? I got nothing to say.'

'Can't you talk to him in front of me? Aren't you supposed to do that?'

He looked straight at Billy, all serious. 'I'm not talking to him as a policeman, Mary. I'm talking to him because I'm your friend. The only real one you have.'

He knows, thought Billy. *He knows what I did. He knows about the gun. He knows everything.*

'You're looking really strange, Fergie,' Mum was saying. 'Is something wrong?'

'You know why. I care about you.'

Billy stood.

'Where are you going, Billy?'

'Bog,' he said.

'It's called a toilet,' said his mother.

'I need to go,' he said.

'I'll just be a minute. Will you leave the two of us together?'

'OK then. I'll be in the kitchen,' she said.

When she'd shut the door behind her, Fergie said, 'I heard McGrachy was looking for something.'

'I was upstairs. I didn't hear anything.'

Fergie knelt down, close to Billy. 'I'm about to do something terrible, Billy. Something I don't want to do. You can help me out here.'

That was it. He would be arrested now.

'Where did your daddy keep his gun, Billy?'

See? Fergie had worked it all out.

'I got to go. I'm busting,' he said, and leaped up and ran up the stairs.

Billy had never felt sadness like this before. He had collected what he wanted from the bedroom.

He knows what I did. He has worked it out because he is a policeman. That's what policemen do, like on the telly. And now he will tell Mum.

'Billy? Are you OK?' said Fergie. His mother was there too, outside the toilet door. And Billy could not bear for her to know what he had done.

'I'll be right down.'

He opened the bathroom window wide; looking down to the lawn, he thought he would ruddy break a leg, jumping from here.

TWELVE

He wasn't hungry.

His head still ached. He tried frying a mackerel but when he looked at it, its opaque stare unsettled him. He put the cooked fish back in the fridge.

After washing up, he checked his email. There was one from the WPC with the red hair and birthmark on her face: '*Here you go. Hope it makes sense xx.*'

It was a spreadsheet of dates, times and locations going back ninety days. He'd never used the ANPR number plate recognition system before; the depth of the data was an eye-opener. Effectively it recorded the movements of every car in Britain, using data from automatic cameras, some at the roadside and some on police vehicles. The list contained details of sightings of the registration he'd written down at Wiccomb caravan site, ordered by date. Only when he printed it out did he realise how long it was; it came to twelve pages. He made himself a pot of tea and sat at his table crossing out all the entries from around Durham. He was left with just eight sightings in the South East, all of them within four days of each other. Two of them were taken by a camera on the Littlestone Road, one of them was taken by a police vehicle on the approach to Ashford, and five were taken by a single camera on the A20, ten miles away.

What did that tell him? It was presumably someone local. And whoever it was had used the fake plates on only four days.

Was it someone buying drugs from Judy Farouk? It wasn't out of the question, though Farouk's clients were not usually the sort who drove in SUVs. A supplier maybe?

Sometime before midnight he put on a jacket and trainers and went out into the night. A run would help stop the thoughts that buzzed around his head. Maybe he could tire himself out enough to get a good night's sleep.

As he left the door, he took care not to look back at the nuclear plant. Staring towards the glare of lights ruined any chance of night vision. Instead, he jogged down to the sea and turned right along the track above the beach.

The sea was black and still. Beyond the nuclear plant he turned inland. At this time of year the nights were quiet. The toads had begun to hibernate. Far off, there were tawny owls, hooting. He ran on up the track parallel with Dengemarsh Sewer.

After half an hour, he lay down on the shingle, panting, and watched the stars moving slowly around the sky.

Bob Rayner had not been who he claimed to be; nor had his sister. It was a shock to find the man he had thought was his friend had as much to hide as he had. Why had Bob come here, to this place at the end of England? He tried to remember anything he had ever said about his past life, but came up empty.

A sigh of a breeze moved through the dead reeds around him. This was a flat land. He had been born with hills around him, but he had liked the flatness. The uninterrupted landscape hid nothing. He had imagined it a more honest place. Like him, Bob had brought his secrets with him here, though. He felt if he could understand what it was that Bob had been hiding, he would understand why he had been killed.

His back was cold; he should start moving again. By the time he turned round at Denge Farm, making his way to crunch along the shingle beach, it was almost two in the morning.

Now the lights of the power station were ahead of him; even a mile away they glared so brightly that they extinguished the stars above him. It was never fully night here. Lit by the industrial glare of the reactors, the scrubby plants cast long shadows across the shingle.

When he rounded the corner of the power station to join the concrete path that led to his house, he noticed a movement to the east. He stopped and squinted into the darkness. There. Someone was down on the beach, close to one of the remaining fisherman's lock-ups about a hundred yards away.

Conscious that the light was now behind him,

silhouetting him, South crouched down and walked off the path, circling round towards the shed.

It was a man. When he was close enough, he saw someone removing something from the open shed, putting it inside a sports bag.

He called out, 'Police. Who's there?'

The man turned. 'Jesus. You give me a shock, Bill.'

'Curly?'

'Only me.'

'What are you doing here, this time of night?'

'I could ask the same. Bloody hell. Good news about the boat, though,' Curly said.

'What news?'

'They found it. Didn't nobody tell you?'

'Nobody tells me anything,' said South. 'Is it OK?'

'Not too bad. A few bumps and scratches, apparently.'

'Did they catch them?'

'No. Just found the boat, that's all.'

'Where did they find it?'

'Way out in the Channel. Hastings lifeboat pulled it in. Coastguard spotted it floating about two miles offshore on Monday evening. I'm going up there tomorrow on the tide to pick it up. If the engine's going OK, I'll motor it back. If not it's going to cost me a few bloody bob in haulage. I was just trying to find the spare key for the engine.'

'Funny,' said South. 'Stealing a boat and then just abandoning it.'

'Kids, I expect. Hope they bloody drowned themselves.

Reckon I'll still get insurance for the damage they done? Bill? You OK? You look like you need a good night's sleep, man.'

'I do.'

South walked away towards his house.

He lay in bed, still awake, listening to the hum of the nuclear power station. It was always loud. He wasn't sure he could get to sleep without its constant roar.

Tonight, though, the hum seemed to be coming from inside his head.

Donald John Fraser.

When he rolled over, his father was sitting on the chair next to him, forehead smashed open. As South lay there, unable to move, his father turned to speak to him.

He tried to scream, but no voice emerged from his throat.

His father raised his finger to his lips.

The second time South tried to scream, his own voice woke him. He sat up with a start, panting, and looked around the dark room.

Nothing but the low roar of the nuclear power station.

But then, from below, the sound of a door closing. Had that been part of his dream?

Now he was fully awake, eyes wide, struggling to make sense of the darkness around him.

If it had been a real sound, had it come from a neighbour's house, or his own? The noise had sounded too precise, too clear, to have come through brick walls.

Swinging his body off the bed, he reached for something he could use as a weapon, but his nightstick was downstairs, along with the baseball bat he kept by the front door.

He stopped at the top of the stairs and strained to hear. Nothing. Then, quietly as he could, he descended.

At the bottom he stopped again and listened.

Still nothing.

He switched on the light; the sudden brightness hurt his eyes.

There was no one. He was the only person in his house.

He didn't believe in ghosts; he lived alone and was used to simple explanations for noises in the dark. He had imagined it, just as he had imagined his father. But then he realised there was something subtly different in the room. A smell; the lingering fragrance of citrus. A woman's perfume? Was he imagining that too? Or was that real?

He went to the kitchen, poured himself a glass of water and then, as an afterthought, checked the kitchen door. It was locked.

He was about to go upstairs to bed when he decided to check the front door for good measure. It was one of those new, UPVC doors. The handle should have been firm; it wasn't. It dropped when he pressed down on it and realised, with a shock, that the front door to the house had been unlocked.

Had he forgotten to secure it, last night, before going to bed? He tried to remember. Locking himself in for the night was such a normal part of his life, and had been for so many years, that he didn't even notice himself doing it any more. But never before had he left the door unlocked.

He opened it now and a wave of cold air rushed at him. Picking up the baseball bat, he stepped outside in bare feet. The lights of the reactor blared.

About seventy yards away, walking calmly towards the beach along the concrete path that ran alongside the power station's security fence, was a figure. He was too far away to see it clearly; just a black shape, silhouetted against the lights.

He stood to see if the shape would turn and look back, but it didn't.

It could be anyone. All sorts walked here, alone, during any time of the day.

Afterwards, he walked around his house trying to see if anything had been taken, or moved, unable to return to bed.

He looked out of the window. He could break a leg, dropping from up here.

'Come on, Billy. God's sake. Come out of there.'

He got into the bath and lay down, staying as quiet as he could.

'Billy?'

Mum rattled the doorknob, yanked it back and forth. It was bolted. There was no way she'd get in without breaking the lock.

'Are you there?'

He heard her saying to Fergie. 'He won't come out.'

'You sure he's in there?'

It would all come out now, he thought. Ferguson had figured it out. He knew what he had done. He was a good policeman. For the first time since his father had died he started to cry.

In the white of the bath he felt a huge sadness overwhelm him. He would be taken away from Mum and put in prison. It's not so much the prison he minded. It would just be a children's prison, not a real one. But that would be the end of it. He tried not to make any noise as he gulped down air.

'He's gone,' said Mum. 'I can't see him. He's jumped out of the window.' She must be looking through the keyhole.

He could hear Fergie running downstairs, yanking open the front door and hurrying outside. 'You think he jumped from up there?' His voice came up from below. 'Where would he have gone? One of his pals?'

'I'll get my coat,' his mother said.

He heard her rummaging, then the front door slamming. And then the house was quiet. They had gone to look for him.

THIRTEEN

The redwings were starting to come through in larger numbers now. He sat in his police car at Greatstone and watched some brent geese passing far out at sea. The swallows were still going south in numbers, later than usual this year. Nothing was reliable. Something was broken.

He was supposed to be briefing neighbourhood PSCOs about data protection but he cancelled it, and instead drove to the locations where the white car had been photographed. Then he tried to guess where the car would have come from. At Sandgate, he drove around, peered into driveways and looked at parked cars. He was surprised at how popular white was as a colour for SUVs.

With the light starting to fade, he drove up Blackhouse Hill to the golf course, to get a better view of the land around him. The club was quiet, a few people were sheltering from the wind in the clubhouse. He counted five white four-wheel-drives just in this car park alone.

The bird was moving through low scrub by the first hole: small, and brown. His first thought was a chiffchaff, but were its legs paler than usual? He reached inside his glove compartment and pulled out his binoculars.

Stepping out of the car, he leaned on the open door and started to focus on the bird.

'I didn't know you played,' a voice behind him said.

He lingered a little while longer on the bird before he turned.

It was Councillor Vinnie Sleight, dressed in just a white shirt, despite the cold.

'I don't,' he said.

By the time he looked back, the bird had disappeared. He lowered the binoculars.

He pulled out his notebook and wrote in it: '*Warbler. Dusky/Rabbes??*'

'Got your eyes on one of those immigrants, Bill?'

'They come over here, with their foreign ways,' said South.

'Don't joke about it, Bill. Enough people take it seriously round here.'

'You're not one of them?' said South.

'I got where I am through hard work,' said Sleight. 'I don't begrudge anyone else who makes their money that way. I read in the papers the murderer killed himself.'

South turned to Sleight again. 'Committing suicide isn't necessarily an admission of guilt.'

Sleight said, 'Well, you looking for anyone else?'

South shook his head. 'Nope.'

'There you go,' said Sleight. 'Good riddance. Is there something worrying you, Bill? You look a bit stressed.'

'Do you know who owns any of these cars?' said South, pointing to three of the closest cars, a Land Cruiser and a pair of almost identical Range Rovers.

Sleight shook his head. 'Want me to ask?'

'What about that one?' A white Qashqai.

'That one?' He smiled.

'Yes.'

'That one's mine. Who wants to know?'

'Just looking for a car that's been driving around with illegal plates,' said South, looking at Sleight.

Sleight frowned and looked at the other cars. 'One of these, you reckon?'

'I don't know,' said South.

'That would be a bit of a shocker round these parts, wouldn't it? This is a golf club, after all.' He laughed. 'Come to dinner sometime, Sergeant,' said Sleight, turning towards the long low black clubhouse. 'My boy's back from Cambridge. Great lad. You ever met him?'

'When?' said South. 'What about this weekend? I'm free.'

'I'll talk to my wife,' called Sleight, across the tarmac. 'I'll be in touch.'

South turned round and scanned the distance again. He waited there for another twenty minutes, watching people swing at balls, but the bird didn't return.

Darkness fell. He drove around the local lanes, exhausted from not sleeping and grateful that it was almost the end of his shift. But then the radio blurted, 'Serious RTC on A259. Junction of Guldeford Lane and Folkestone Road.'

He put on the blue light automatically. Less than a quarter of a mile away, he would probably be the first responder. The worst job of all. If it was a serious traffic accident there would be blood and pain.

As he approached, South added the siren. The traffic was already backed up to the east, drivers leaning heads out of windows. There was always a risk someone would try a U-turn as he approached.

Just as he had guessed, he was the first there. Drivers were standing by their vehicles, dazed, unsure of what to do; this is what accidents always looked like in the first few minutes, he told himself. The far side of the sharp corner, the Subaru was trapped under a scaffolding lorry. The air was still thick with a smell of burnt rubber from tyres that had braked too late.

At odds with the stillness, the crashed car was booming loud music; a thick, pulsing bass.

'He was going way too fast.' The driver of the lorry was a young man dressed in a high-vis vest.

Frowning, South pushed past him towards the matt black car, trying to understand how the accident had happened. He had seen many crashes; this one made no sense to him. It was as if the car had been moving so fast it had somehow forced itself under the safety bar under the side of the lorry, tipping the vehicle sideways slightly. Scaffolding poles had spilled onto the verge. But that was physically impossible. A car would have to be travelling at a ridiculous speed to do that.

The music continued as he jogged towards the car, all synthesisers and stop-start drums. Bystanders stared at him. The whole front of the car was wedged under the oncoming lorry's central section, only leaving the rear of the vehicle accessible. Tinted windows made it impossible to see inside from the back.

'I was changing the tyre,' said the man. 'It was up on the jack. Fluke he didn't kill me.'

He could see it now. A blind corner; an idiotic place to try and fix a broken-down truck. The lorry would have already been lifted high enough to raise the side bars away from the road, allowing an oncoming car to force itself beneath it. The driver could lose his licence and probably his livelihood; he wouldn't be surprised if he served time, but now was not the time for that.

'Give me your tools,' shouted South. 'Quick.' You had to take charge; to be decisive. Civilians could not cope with situations like this. Given a task, the driver rushed to find a large spanner for South.

In those seconds he understood that this is what he did. He wasn't a copper who took on murder cases, delving into other people's lives; he was an ordinary copper who got stuck in to simple situations like this where something needed doing, where one person's action could make some sort of difference. Ugly as the scene was, this was the job he understood, not the one the death of his friend had dragged him into.

Inside the car, his feet still sticking outside of the back window he'd smashed, South heard the other emergency vehicles starting to arrive. The interior stank of hot oil and petrol. The entire back seat of the car was taken up with pulsating speakers which left little space for him to squeeze his body through. As he looked down for a second, he saw the driver's head, lying face down in the footwell. The man had been cleanly decapitated. South looked back up again straight away, stifling the urge to vomit.

The girl in the passenger seat had her head pressed against the lorry's side bar, which had smashed the front window. An inch more and her neck would have been snapped. The first thing she said was, 'Nicky? That you?'

By now, South had wriggled forward another foot, lying along the length of the car, still trying to push himself towards her. Her head was completely trapped, he realised, between the metal and the headrest. Luckily, perhaps, she couldn't twist her head to see the carnage at her right-hand side.

'Don't move,' he shouted above the music. 'We'll get you out of here.'

'I can't fucking move. Nicky? Are you OK?'

'Does it hurt?'

'But I'm fucking cold though,' she said. 'C'n you get me a blanket?'

She couldn't look down either, which was fortunate. As he inched forward he saw that her body had been crushed into the front of the car. The engine had been forced back into the footwell. Fresh blood soaked her legs. Unless paramedics could reach her quickly, she would not have long to live. Even if they moved her now, he guessed she would die soon.

'What's your name?' he asked. He heard men, shouting behind him.

'I'm not saying nothing. Fuck sake. Get me a blanket.'

Finally he found the button on the stereo and pressed it. The silence was good.

'Hey, I liked that,' she said quietly, and then closed her eyes and suddenly started to scream, a loud, high note, as if the pain had only just hit her.

He took a last look and began to scramble back out to brief the firemen and paramedics who were behind him now and to allow them into the vehicle.

By the time he'd finished organising traffic control, she was dead. It took them another hour to tug the vehicle clear. On the girl's ruined lap, a paramedic found her blood-soaked passport in a clutch bag and handed it to South. She had been just eighteen. The young always carried passports these days, he knew, to show they were old enough to buy alcohol.

When, wearing blue gloves, he peeled apart the bloody pages under the glare of an emergency light, he saw the girl lived in his area. He called the name and address through to control, feeling that he was being pursued by something dark and obscure.

South sat in his car watching the men and women measure the skid marks on the road and take photographs while the recovery lorries waited. Distorted metal shapes threw long shadows in the darkness. And all the while, the generator that lit the wreckage purred away to itself in the blackness.

Nobody talked much. It was like that on days like these. It was a bad job that needed doing. They didn't clear the site till after one in the morning.

His mother and Fergie had left the house, thinking he'd jumped from the window.

He dressed, quick as he could. There were no clean socks so he put on a dirty pair from the laundry, taking another old pair as spare. He stuffed everything in a rucksack. Two jumpers, jeans, T-shirts, woollen gloves, a cagoule, his binoculars. Downstairs in the kitchen he found an unopened packet of digestives and, just before he unbolted the back door, remembered the torch from under the sink.

And then he was out the back door. He didn't dare head down through the estate. They'd already be looking for him there. So he threw the rucksack over the fence and pulled himself up, fingers raw on the wire.

He landed badly, pitching face first into the brambles. Thorns stung his palms and face. He got up slowly, disentangling himself. It was no good just pulling against them. They would rip your skin open. From there he didn't stop, taking the steep route straight up the hill to the east, fading light behind him.

He knew all the roads and tracks around here better than they did. This was where he came to go birding.

It would be dark soon. It would be harder to find him then. He could use the night to try and put as much distance as possible between himself and the town.

It took him half an hour to reach a small wood where he'd once seen crossbills. It started to drizzle so he reached in his backpack and pulled out his cagoule. Why did his mother have to buy him a yellow one?

He sat with his back to a tree, sheltering from the drizzle, and realised he was still panting even though he was no longer short of breath.

FOURTEEN

He didn't know it, but Saturday would be the last day William South worked as a policeman.

The vehicle had been uninsured; he was on shift, so the Roads Policing Officer asked him if he'd drive out with him to interview the dead girl's parents.

It was a nice house; detached, with new fashionable wood cladding. The father was quiet and sat at the shiny, polished wood dining table, hands in his lap. The mother wept freely into tissues which she discarded into a wicker waste basket. 'She told us she was babysitting,' she said. 'The policeman who called round last night to tell us she was dead said it would have been instant.'

Two lies within no distance of each other. The officer just nodded, but as he did so South caught the father's eye. He was shocked by the pure fury he saw there; the man was struggling to control himself. The Roads Officer took what details he needed and hurried away, to leave them to their grieving.

His work done, South remembered it was Saturday and he had not done his weekly shop yet, so he pulled into the car park of a Tesco Superstore just off the M20. Inside, he drifted aimlessly, pushing his trolley, trying to remember what he needed but his brain was fogged with fatigue and horror of the previous nights. Did he have bleach?

Normally he was methodical; he went to the same super-market every week with a list, and checked off everything as he went. The layout here was unfamiliar; he couldn't find what he wanted. His hands shook as he reached for a packet of rice. A young woman in a denim jacket was buying ready meals with a boyfriend who kept leaning down to kiss her, and when he looked at them he couldn't help thinking of the couple in the car. He was familiar with this; the delayed shock.

In the household goods aisle, looking for detergent, he was conscious of a woman in a plain blue dress standing next to him stretching to try and reach something on the top shelf, so he reached up and handed the box to her. It was the last box of dishwasher tablets.

'Thanks,' she said.

And then he looked at her for the first time. He could see the shock in her face as she saw his, her smile vanishing instantly.

It took a second to realise who it was, by which time the woman in the blue dress was already tugging her trolley full of goods away behind her and making her way towards the tills.

Gill Rayner. Or whoever she was.

The woman who had pretended to be Bob's sister.

'Wait,' he shouted. A mother with an infant in the trolley looked up, startled at the loudness of his voice.

The woman who had called herself Gill Rayner paused, a panicked look in her eyes.

'You weren't his sister,' he said.

She shook her head slowly, but he wasn't sure whether she was agreeing with him or not.

'What were you doing there? Were you his lover?'

Her eyes widened. She backed away into a throng of children who were chattering and giggling in the aisle. 'Leave me alone,' she said. 'Please.'

'What's your name? I just want to talk.'

One of the teenagers, a boy with low-slung trousers, was laughing at something.

'You were so upset. What did he mean to you? Please. I want to know.'

Her eyes flickered, and he thought she was about to answer, but instead she turned and started to push her trolley away from him, through the crowds packed at the tills. When he tried to follow, she broke into a run, dodging bewildered shoppers, almost tripping over the front of a mobility scooter.

South dropped his basket and followed, trying to keep an eye on her in the Saturday throng. Seeing a uniformed policeman running towards them, the shoppers parted, but by the time he reached the sliding doors at the front of the shop, he had lost sight of her.

He looked left, then right.

'Went this way,' shouted a heavy-looking security guard, pointing towards the right.

Without thinking, South followed him, accelerating into a sprint. He passed the security guard easily but didn't see the woman. At one point he slipped on something shiny on the ground. And again. He realised they were packs of sliced ham lying scattered on the pavement in front of him. What were they doing there? He didn't have time to think about it. Just past the disabled bays, a couple of startled-looking Turkish youths cowered behind a trolley shelter.

'There,' shouted the security guard, catching up. 'Get 'em.'

South stopped.

'We done nothing,' protested the lads.

Confused, South scanned the car park again. On the opposite side, a green Volkswagen Polo was driving away fast.

'I saw you. Empty your pockets for the copper.'

'You saw us what?'

'Go on, arrest them. They're thieves.'

South was looking away at the exit down which the green car had disappeared. His police car was parked more than a hundred yards away. There was no point trying to catch her now.

'It wasn't them I was after. Did you see a woman running? Blue dress? About forty?'

'What you on about?'

South turned back towards the youths. 'Never mind. What did they take?'

'Meat. They take it to sell. I've had my eyes on them.'

'You're joking us,' said the tallest of the pair. 'We weren't even in the shop.'

'Make them turn out their pockets,' said the security guard.

South sighed. 'Go on then. What's in your pockets?'

'Can't search us without a warrant.'

'If I have reasonable grounds to suspect you of theft, yes, I can.'

'Go on then,' said the security guard, urging South on, wondering why he was hanging back.

The boys were looking out of the side of their eyes, calculating whether they could leg it or not. South sighed. Now he looked he could see the remaining packets bulging beneath their baggy khaki trousers. He would now be called to give evidence in a prosecution that wasn't even in his district. And it was a Saturday; he wasn't even supposed to be at work.

After the local police car had arrived to take away the young men, he finally returned to the supermarket to find his basket. For three or four minutes, he walked the aisles, unable to find it before concluding that some staff member must have picked it up and tidied it away. He would have to start again.

So he was surprised to see her trolley, still there by the shampoos. He recognised it. The box of dishwasher tablets he had handed to her was there, sitting on top of a pile of groceries.

He was still standing looking at it when the security guard came up to him, grinning. 'Result, eh?'

'Yes,' he said. He pushed Gill Rayner's trolley to the checkout and started unloading the items, one by one, onto the conveyor belt.

'Need any help, dear?' said the woman at the till.

He didn't answer. He was staring at the items piling up on the counter in front of him, trying to read their significance.

She held up a bottle of Head & Shoulders. 'Two for one on them, if you want it, love,' she said.

He shook his head.

'Suit yourself,' she said huffily. It came to £138.55. He never spent that much in supermarkets usually, but he took out his credit card and handed it to her, then slowly started to put everything into plastic bags. He was holding a box containing a bottle of aftershave and staring at it when he looked back and saw the queue of shoppers behind him, glaring impatiently.

He had stopped panting now. He needed to be calm, to get everything straight in his head. Feeling the bark of the tree pressing itself into his back, he looked up at the blackness of the branches above him and tried to remember everything that had happened; everything that had led him here.

The night he had stolen the Flamenco Red paint had been a week before his father was killed.

Dad had called up to say he was working late at the garage.

'Oh yes?' said Mum, on the telephone, like she didn't believe him. 'Urgent job, is it?'

Dad had been doing that a lot recently. Billy didn't mind; it was better when Dad was not home. But Mum had cooked a beef stew and was annoyed that he couldn't be bothered to even come home for it. She told Billy to take a Thermos of stew down to him, with bread and marge wrapped in tinfoil.

'If he's there,' said Mum. 'If he's not there, then . . . then he won't want the stew, now, will he?'

Why would he not be there if he had said he was? When Billy got there, the forecourt was dark. The electric sign that said *2✱ 76.5 per gal* had been switched off, but the strip light in the office still shone through the glass door. Billy pushed it. It opened.

'Dad?'

The smell was always the same: oil, dirt, petrol and the stink of the paraffin lamp that kept the room warm in winter.

If his mum had thought his dad was lying, she was wrong. Billy could hear his dad grunting at something in the workshop. He would be in his dirty blue overalls, straining at some rusted nut under one of his big Yank cars. Billy put the Thermos on the desk and tiptoed over to the paint rack.

Shiny cans of Krylon spray-paints, all different colours. Dad had them sent over specially from America. Quietly he pulled them out, one by one, then dropped them back in. Antique Gold Metallic, Eggnog, Bright Blue Poly, Tropical Orange. When it came to the Flamenco Red he took it out of the wire rack and held it up. He squeezed the lid and it came off with a small pop, then he held his finger on the nozzle, as if ready to spray.

This was Dad's world, all dirt and grease. On the office wall, out of sight of the till so customers couldn't see it, was a calendar from one of the tyre suppliers. Each month was a different woman with her bosoms out.

'God there!' His dad was shouting, now. When he worked, he often swore, Billy wasn't surprised. Billy could hear him panting, as if straining hard at something.

July was Suzi. Suzi had long dark hair, head slightly to one side, with her hands clasped in front of her so they made her bosoms stick out more than they would have anyway. The skin was smooth and curvaceous, and seemed to shine like it had been polished. Billy stared at the nipples and the big dark circle of skin around them and felt a dull, unfamiliar ache form in his chest. But as he leaned in to get a better view, a clattering came from the workshop, some metal falling to the concrete floor.

'Keep still,' said his dad.

Then a laugh.

And Billy's eyes went wide. It was a woman's laugh.

'Don't move. I'm almost there,' his dad was saying.

And then the panting again. And a woman's panting too.

Billy stood listening to his dad's noise. The breathing gathered pace now.

'Hurry up, Billy, I'm getting cramp here.' He'd have known the voice anywhere. Mrs Creedy wasn't even a looker. She had a squinty eye and was fat from eating too many of her own chips.

Billy leaned forward to hold the spray-can up in front of July's bosoms, and pressed the nozzle down. Instantly a red circle obliterated her chest, paint dripping down onto the grid of black dates below.

The noise of the spray was much louder than he thought it would be. *HSSSSS.* When it stopped, the noises from the workshop had stopped, too.

His dad's voice: 'Who's there?'

And he ran out of the door all the way back home, can of paint still in his hand, not even thinking to pick up the Thermos of stew from the table next to the till.

FIFTEEN

He put the shopping away. Dental floss went in the bathroom cabinet; the frozen onion rings went straight into the bin. The shampoo and the aftershave looked like they were bought for a man. He wondered what kind of man he would be. A husband, a son, or another lover? He put them in the bathroom too. Whoever she was, she didn't live alone.

That evening, he cooked the Tesco Finest Chicken Korma with Pilau Rice for supper and picked at it. After the gore of last night's accident, he had no appetite.

The new set of keys was on the table beside him; yesterday he had had the lock changed. He took one off the ring and went to put it in the kitchen drawer where he had kept the spares. Instead of replacing it he picked out Bob's spare; they had exchanged keys a year ago. Leaving the meal unfinished, he took Bob's key and walked down the track towards Arum Cottage.

From a distance, the empty house was just an absence of light, the gables showing black against the dark grey night sky.

The police had long gone; the house was lightless and dead. Bob had had a security lamp by his front door, but it didn't come on as South approached the small porch. The electricity would have been cut off.

He unlocked the front door and pushed against a pile of post. Inside he shone his torch around the room. He went through the letters. There was nothing special about them: circulars about clothing and pensions. He placed the pile neatly on the kitchen sideboard.

The floor was still a mess. There were books lying, split-spined, on the floor; a pile of china from a broken mug. The forensics team had left the house as they had found it. Where did Bob keep his keys? He didn't know. He started looking in cupboards and opening drawers but didn't find any spares. Had he hallucinated someone coming to his house? Or had whoever killed Bob taken his keys too?

After half an hour he gave up just looking for the keys, frustrated at not being able to find any sign of where Bob had kept them. In the kitchen, he removed cans from the shelves and shook them, looked behind jars of chutney and jam, but there was nothing unusual, nothing hidden. In the living room he peeled back the carpets and looked behind the pictures to see if anything was concealed there, but he found no secretive stashes of letters or photographs that would have explained who Bob had been.

He had trusted Bob, but the man who he had thought was his friend had lied to him, not just about his sister, but about everything.

In the living room, the box Bob had been found in had been removed. The computer, too, had gone from the study. The police had not brought it back.

He moved to Bob's bedroom and peered under the bed, then lifted the mattress. Nothing. He opened one wardrobe door and went through the pockets of Bob's jackets and found only grocery receipts and safety pins. He pulled hats from the shelf and felt his way around the corners.

Then he opened the other wardrobe door and saw a small row of dresses and scarves. Her clothes.

Holding the torch, he stared for a second, then pulled out two dresses and laid them on the bed.

For a second, he wondered if they were even hers at all. They had to be, but these were not the dowdy woollens he had seen her in that first time here, or even the plain but unflattering thing she'd worn at the supermarket. These were expensive, sophisticated, feminine; long pale dresses with spaghetti shoulders, or cool black cocktail numbers.

In the dark, he lifted one up and tried to imagine her in it. These were special clothes; clothes for dressing up in. Like Bob, she had kept this part of herself hidden. She had worn them for Bob; he had kept her hidden, deceiving his friends. He wondered if he had ever really even been his friend at all.

He hung the dress back on the hook and returned to the living room. The place was a mess; searching through it, he had added to the disorder that the Scene of Crime men had left.

Bob would have hated it. He had been a tidy man.

'Tough,' he said, out loud. He felt an urge to yank what remained from his shelves.

He wondered if it was just anger he was feeling at Bob for deceiving him, or jealousy for his relationship.

He shone the torch onto his watch. It would be eleven soon.

The study offered the best view of the route towards the Coastguard Cottages, to South's own house. He lowered the blinds halfway and sat in Bob's chair.

The radio on Bob's desk didn't work without electricity, but he found a small transistor radio in the bathroom, and listened to the midnight news.

He wrapped himself in the duvet he had taken from Bob's bed. It was a double. There had not been a duvet on the bed in the spare room. It had not been made up for a visiting sister.

Birding made you patient. A good birder should be able to sit still for hours, just watching. The trick was not to think too much. It was like a marksman lowering his heart rate to steady his aim. South had learned to empty his mind; leaving his eyes staring, ready to register any movement, any change in the picture. But it wasn't so easy here. He kept seeing Bob's battered corpse. He kept hearing the woman in the car, screaming as she died.

An hour passed; he listened to a business programme on the radio without really hearing any of it.

He kept watch, but nothing happened. If someone had come to his house in the early hours of the morning they had not come back tonight. Beyond the fence, the power station rumbled. For years there had been talk of closing it, but it still remained open. Now, just as the migrating patterns were changing, the sea was too. Since Fukushima, there had been a fleet of lorries coming to bring shingle to build the bank of stones around it higher.

The same day as he stole the paint from the garage where his father worked, he woke in the night.

There was someone on his bed.

He sat up, heart racing.

'Shh.' The smell of sweat and beer and whisky.

His dad, he realised.

'Ye OK, Billy?'

'Was asleep,' said Billy.

The room was black. The street lights must have gone off outside.

'Where's Mum?'

'Asleep,' said his father. He stayed there a while longer, then said, 'Did you say anything to her?'

Billy said, 'What about?'

'Don't fuck about. It was you, wasn't it? Brought me the stew?'

Billy didn't answer.

'Did you say anything to your mother? About visiting me in the garage tonight?'

Billy considered this for a minute. Then he made the only answer he felt he was allowed. 'I don't know what you're on about, Dad,' he said.

Billy's eyes adjusted to the darkness.

'Right,' Dad said eventually, but he didn't shift.

And when Dad finally reached out to him, Billy flinched backwards, assuming his father was going to hurt him, but all he did was ruffle his boy's hair and say, 'Good lad.'

Good lad?

Billy wanted to get up and run to his mother, who was asleep just across the corridor, but he didn't. He was not a good lad. He hadn't told her anything about what he had heard. He had kept it to himself because he didn't know how to begin to say any of it.

So he just lay there, the weight of his father pressing down on the mattress.

SIXTEEN

Cupidi phoned as he was letting himself back into his house the next morning. He looked at his watch. Eight thirty. He had woken, head on Bob's desk, neck stiff.

'What?'

'What are you doing today?'

'It's Sunday. I'm off today.'

'Did you have any plans?'

'Plans for what?' He blinked. 'Are you asking me out?'

'No. I have to work,' she said.

'Oh.'

The night had been a long one. He couldn't shake a growing sense of fear. What of, he wasn't sure. He had watched the track leading to the cottages but seen no one.

She was saying, 'I had been planning to take Zoë shopping in Canterbury as a reward for having a better week at school. But I can't now. I was wondering . . .'

'What? You want me to take her shopping?'

'Birdwatching.'

'Thank God for small mercies. But honestly? I don't think it's appropriate.'

'Appropriate?' She snorted. 'I'm just asking you to look after my daughter for a couple of hours.'

'Weren't you tearing a strip off me for sticking my nose into your business last time I saw you? But now you need a bit of help . . .'

'That was work,' she said. 'It wasn't anything personal.'

'Seems like everything's work. Maybe you should actually be spending some time here with her. She's on her own down here.'

'And you're an expert in parenting now, are you? I'm bloody doing my best here. But something has come up and honest-to-God I have to work. It's not bloody easy, you know? Besides, this is something she wants to do.'

'She does?'

'Believe it or not. I wouldn't ask unless . . .'

Though he'd usually spend a day like this out of doors, today he felt like doing nothing at all. He remembered the look on Zoë's face as she had slammed the door the last time he had seen her.

'William? You there?'

He scratched his chin. 'Has she got any decent wellies this time?' he asked.

Probably because he was bruised and angry, that day he took Zoë inland, up the muddy banks of the Rother, up to Wet Level.

Birders didn't go there much, mostly because there weren't that many birds. He rationalised to himself that this was a kind of test. If she wasn't really keen, she'd soon lose interest there, he reckoned. But maybe he was just taking his foul mood out on her; trying to kill her enthusiasm for birds once and for all.

A damp grey day and there wasn't much around anyway. A couple of anglers grunted at them, sat on the bank, huddled over their rods, but apart from that the place was still and quiet, except for the occasional roar of a motorbike on the Rye Road.

'I can't see anything,' she complained, tramping behind him.

'It's like that, sometimes.'

She would give up soon; ask to be taken home. There was not much cover in this flat land. As he predicted they saw nothing. Sometimes he wondered if what you saw depended on your frame of mind. The birds were a manifestation of how you felt.

He had been looking for birds ever since he was a young boy. Gradually he had ticked off all the regular species. Now it was about looking for rare migrants, birds blown out of their way by storms. What was the point? Right now, on this flat, grey day, he was thinking: maybe Cupidi was right to laugh at him. It was a ridiculous occupation for a grown man. Birding had always been his one safe place. He had been doing it because there was nothing else in his life. And there was nothing else in his life because he had never let anyone in. And he didn't feel very safe any more.

'Did you bring anything to eat? I'm hungry.'

'No. Did you?'

At least she was quiet, after that. He kept his pace, hearing her trudging a few footsteps behind him. When they'd gone about a mile, he said, 'Here then.'

South stood with his binoculars in hand, scanning a small copse. There was little to see apart from a few chaffinches, blue and long-tailed tits and a pair of collared doves.

'So did you grew up in Northern Ireland?'

'That's right.'

'Mum said you were there when all that business was going on. What was it like?'

He focused his binoculars on some sloes, trying to see if any birds were feeding there. All he saw was a blackbird scuffing up leaves beneath the bush.

'Ireland,' she said again. 'What was that like? It must have been mad.'

'Another world,' he said.

'Did you see bombs going off?'

'Heard them. Saw the smoke. Everyone did. It was like that. Didn't happen much. Hard to understand, now.'

'I don't know how people could do that sort of thing to each other. Did you ever see any dead bodies?'

'If you talk, we'll never see any birds,' he said.

'So-rry,' she said, like she wasn't at all. 'Only, there aren't any, far as I can see. Except the same ones we see in our garden.'

'There,' he said, handing her his binoculars. 'Treecreeper.'

All she said was, 'Small, isn't it?' She watched it, and he wished he'd remembered to bring a second pair with him. 'Seriously, though. Did you see any dead people?'

He looked at her. 'A couple.'

'What happened?'

'One of them was my dad,' he said.

'Oh. God. Sorry.' She blushed.

'It's OK,' he said. 'What about your dad? Tell me about him.'

'He's just a lecturer.'

'Do him and your mum get on?'

'What you asking that for? See? You do have a thing for her, don't you?' She smirked.

'That's enough,' he said.

'I bet you do.'

He reached out and took the binoculars from her. 'You can be a precocious pain in the arse if you like, Zoë, but don't be surprised when people don't like you.'

She looked shocked. Her mouth opened, but nothing smart came out.

'Is this what you're like at school?'

The teenage girl looked away suddenly and South wondered if he'd made her cry. Right now, he didn't really care. She stood with her back to him, saying nothing.

'I work with your mother,' he said. 'I think she's a pretty good policewoman, actually. But I don't fancy her, no. And right now, actually, I might have had quite enough of both of you.'

Turning back towards him, the girl whispered, 'It was just, you know . . . a bit of chat.'

He raised the binoculars to his eyes and didn't answer.

'Sorry,' she said.

'Let's forget about it, OK?'

They stood for a long time, seeing nothing. No birds moved.

Eventually Zoë said, 'My dad has a girlfriend. They got kids. If I lived with them, my mum would have nobody. Besides, he lives in Cornwall now. Even worse than round here.'

'Imagine that,' he said. 'Worse than here.'

She giggled. 'And that's saying something.'

'Must be bloody terrible.'

'See that tree?' she said. 'It's like it's got a face in it. Can you see the eyes and the mouth?'

He looked. The smooth bark of an ash had been distorted by lost limbs. A face in a tree; he shuddered, but couldn't remember why the thought was quite so disturbing. There was a dark mark where the forehead should have been.

She was chattering, again, as if trying to pretend nothing had happened. 'That one looks like Mum,' she said, pointing to markings on another tree. 'Why does it grow like that?'

He stared at the tree. 'Trees don't heal their wounds. They can't. They're not like animals who can repair themselves. All they can do is grow a hard skin over them. It's called wound-wood. That's what makes those shapes.'

'Like Mum,' she said. 'She's got a hard skin.'

Like me, he thought, looking at the face in the tree. The longer he looked, the more uncomfortable it made him feel. He should go home. He was not good company.

'Look,' she said, grabbing the binoculars from him.

A firecrest, which she identified correctly without even looking at the book. She must have been looking at bird books. And when a flock of lapwing passed overhead, she knew what they were too.

Eventually they moved on, northwards, where they watched a heron being mobbed by crows. It was perched by the margin of the river, ducking as the crows swooped down on it, cawing.

'Why are they doing that?' she asked, watching the black birds circle round and dive at the heron, over and over.

'They think it's a predator.'

'It's not though, is it?'

'No.'

'They're just bullies,' she said.

'So how is school?'

She glowered at him. 'How do you think it is? I know you think I'm a pain, but I'm not. I just have to get on with it, for Mum's sake. I hate them,' she said, still looking at the crows.

And just by a road bridge she pointed, stopped, grabbed his binoculars again and watched as a large bird drifted low over the land ahead of them, its wings in a shallow V-shape. 'Wow,' she said, her voice full of awe. 'Just, fucking . . . wow.'

He stood looking at her, not the bird, smiling for what felt like the first time in days.

'It was amazing,' she said. 'So . . . amazing. Should have seen it, Mum. It was like, swooping . . . Like, so cool and . . .'

He had dropped her home. Cupidi invited him in and rummaged in the kitchen for a bottle of white wine to give him as a thank you. 'For looking after Zoë,' she said.

'It was beautiful.'

'Amazing,' mocked her mother.

'Shut up. It was. You wouldn't understand,' she said, prising her boots off.

'What would all your grime pals in London have said about you now?'

'They'd say wow too. What makes you think they wouldn't? You never knew anything about my crew.'

It had been a marsh harrier; but watching Zoë's excitement at seeing the bird for the first time reminded him of being a young boy up on the hillside by the town.

'Do you have a minute? I want to show you something,' said South. 'It's in the car.'

'Is it work?'

'Yes.'

She opened the freezer. 'Do I have to? It's been a long day.'

'I've just done you a favour. I just spent my day off with your daughter so you can go to work.'

Holding a packet of fishfingers, Cupidi sighed. 'Fair point.'

'Didn't realise I was ruining your day,' muttered Zoë.

South returned from his car with a printout of the spreadsheet the WPC had sent him.

He laid the sheets out on Cupidi's kitchen table. 'Remember that car was at Judy Farouk's the day we were there? It had a false registration number on it. See? The car was in Durham and Kent at almost exactly the same time. The real car is registered in Durham.'

Cupidi picked up the paper, studied it for a few seconds, then put it back down. 'A pal of a drug dealer has a car that changes plates. I'm shocked. Since APR came in there are tens of thousands of cloned car plates. It's everywhere.'

'Don't be rude, Mum,' said Zoë. 'You think you're the only clever one, don't you?'

South said, 'Bear with me. From where it's been spotted I'd say the cloned one is from somewhere around Folkestone.'

'How do you figure that?'

'Look here,' he said. 'See the first and last sightings on both the days the car is spotted down here? Before it arrived here, the number plate was registered on this camera. That's got to be close to where the driver lives. We can request the images and maybe if one's any good, we'll know what make of car it was that the guy was really driving.'

He lifted up the paper and took out a printout of a Google map. He had drawn a ring in a five-mile radius around the cameras that had spotted the car.

'If we're able to find the make, all we need to do is find out who owns that type of car in that colour around here.'

'All we need to do? It's a town. If you're right, and it's just a hunch that the car is from round there . . . you have any idea how many white four-wheel-drives of any make are going to be in that circle?'

'Well . . . No.'

'Even if we get the make, I bet there will be a hundred. At least. Maybe two hundred. How many hours do you think it's going to take to go through all those? You planning to send a copper round to each house for a crime that we don't even know has been committed? And there's no actual connection to her anyway.'

'Mum. You tell me to be nice.'

Cupidi sounded tired. 'Nobody's even reported Judy Farouk missing. She's not even a case.'

'No, but there's something else. Look at the dates,' he said. 'See?' He ran his finger down the left-hand column. 'I don't think this is just about Judy. I think it may have something to do with Bob; I think there's a connection. That —' he pointed to the top of one sheet — 'is the day we think the assault on Bob started. And the last date, here, is when Judy Farouk disappeared. I don't think Donald Fraser is who you're looking for.'

He looked up. The expression on Cupidi's face was one of sympathy. Pity even. 'Look, William. There's nothing suspicious about Judy Farouk's disappearance. And the case on your friend is officially closed.'

'What?' said South.

'Oh God. Did no one tell you?'

'Tell me what?'

'The DNA on the weapon is Donald Fraser's. His DNA is all over Bob's house too. It was him. Without any doubt. He's the killer. And the autopsy found bruising on Donald Fraser's body, but nothing to suggest that it wasn't self-inflicted, or that he didn't just commit suicide. It's over, William. You shouldn't be doing this anyway. You're not part of any investigation. Leave it alone.'

South sat on her kitchen chair, mouth open. He had been sure it had not been Fraser. 'Is that it?' he asked. 'You're not looking for anyone else?'

'A hundred per cent. Well, nothing's ever a hundred per cent. But close enough.'

'Listen. OK then. Maybe the registration number means nothing. Yesterday I saw Gill Rayner. She was in Tesco's. When I saw her she scarpered.'

'Did she recognise you?'

'Yes. I think she's married . . . from what she was buying.'

'Somebody married having an affair. It's not a surprise, is it?'

'Says you,' said Zoë.

Cupidi glared at her daughter, then said, 'I feel sorry for her, whoever she was. It must be awful when your lover is murdered but you can't grieve. But we're not interested in Gill Rayner, William. My advice is to leave it alone. If you're not careful this will turn into a disciplinary issue.

Whatever her relationship with your friend was, it's not our business.'

'We could see if there's CCTV of her car at Bob's house. Track it via the plates. It's a green Polo.'

'We have the killer.' She looked at her wristwatch. 'I need to cook now, William.'

South stayed sitting at the kitchen table, trying to make sense of the evidence that Donny Fraser killed Bob Rayner. He said, 'Another thing. I think someone was in my house last week.'

'Someone broke in?'

'No. They let themselves in.'

'You leave the door unlocked?'

'No, it was locked. At least I think it was. They must have had a key. I've been thinking . . . I kept a spare key for Bob in case he locked himself out. I think I must have given him a spare for my front door in return. I never thought to check whether it was missing.'

'So you actually think the person who killed Bob stole your front door key?'

'Yes. Maybe. From Bob's house.'

She squinted at him for a while. 'So this person . . . Did they steal anything from you?'

'No. Nothing.'

'And did you see them?'

'No. Well. Maybe. But . . . not in the house, no.'

There was a little too much sympathy in her glance, he thought. And he wondered whether anyone had been in his house at all. Perhaps he had just left his front door open.

She reached out her hand and laid it on top of his, like someone visiting a patient in a ward. 'I heard you had to take on a bad RTA, William. Was it grim?'

'Very.'

'I think you're stressed. This thing with Bob and Judy Farouk. You want there to be a connection. But there isn't.' Her face had softened. She spoke quietly. 'I'm sorry, William. You should try and get some help. Maybe see a counsellor.' She reached out. 'Call the DCI. Tell him you need a break. He'll understand. Tell you what. I'll call him first thing in the morning. I'll tell him I spoke to you. Take a couple of days off. There's no shame in it.'

South looked at the paper. 'There's a word for that in birding. We call it a "string". When someone so badly wants to be the one to spot a rare bird they start to see it, even if it's not there.'

'What did you call it?' said Zoë. 'A string?'

'You get a reputation for stringing and your name is mud. It's the worst thing that can happen to you in the birding world. Once you've been labelled as someone who makes up reports, everyone turns their back on you. Mostly those people just disappear from the scene. It's happened to a few people I've known.'

'Let it go,' said Cupidi. 'OK?'

He picked up the paper, crumpled it into a ball, and put it into Cupidi's kitchen bin.

As he was about to reverse out of the cul-de-sac, Cupidi emerged from the front door, holding the bottle of wine he'd left behind. He wound down his window. 'I meant to say, I'm getting the files on your father's murder sent over from the PSNI. Just so we can tie things up with the Fraser case. Routine, you know. But thought you'd want to know.'

South's hands tightened on the steering wheel. 'Look after yourself, OK?' she said, but he was already winding the window back up and putting the car into gear again. Half an hour later, drawing up at the back of Coastguard Cottages, he found his fingers aching from clutching the wheel so hard all the way.

And as he walked in the darkness, stumbling sometimes as the land began to rise in front of him, he put it all together, everything that had happened in the last few days. In the blackness it became vivid.

Two days before the 12th of July, the day before his father was killed, Billy knocked on Rusty's door.

A Monday evening after school. 'Can Rusty come out?'

His brother Stampy was there in the kitchen, smoking cigarettes without anyone bothering him for it because Mr and Mrs Chandler were both at work. The brother walked to the door and shouted up the stairs. 'Rusty? Little Billy from across the road's here for you.'

'Can I have one of your fags?' asked Billy.

'Bog off and buy your own.' Stampy wore denim baggies and had a Rod Stewart haircut. On anyone else they'd have looked stupid.

'Only asking.'

'Only telling you to get lost,' said Stampy, affably enough.

'Can I see your new jacket? I heard it's ace.'

'It's at the cleaner's.'

Rusty arrived at the kitchen door. 'Coming out?' said Billy. 'I got something we can do.'

'What?'

'Better not say.'

'Very *Twilight Zone*,' said Stampy.

'Don't mind,' said Rusty. 'Nothing else doing.'

'Don't you go getting into trouble,' said Stampy, and he pulled out a pair of cigarettes for them. One each.

'Thanks.' Billy grinned, sticking his inside his jacket for later. Sometimes Billy wished he had an older brother too, even with the Rod Stewart hair.

'Well?' said Rusty, when they were outside.

Billy opened his jacket wider and pulled the can of spray-paint out a little way.

Rusty's eyes widened and he said, 'Superb. What we going to do with it?'

And Billy led the way down to River Street where that dank path took him to the back of the old lock-ups that stood between the river bank and the street.

There, like an invitation, was a long, even, bare brick

wall. What was great was that in winter you would be able to see it from the car park on the other side of the river, but right now it was hidden by all the trees. Nobody would see until the leaves dropped.

'Me first,' said Billy. 'Then you, OK?'

Rusty nodded. 'What you going to paint?'

Billy popped the cap off the paint and stood in front of the wall, shook the can and thought of Mrs Creedy and the naked bosoms of Suzi July. And then he started. First thing he realised was that if you held the can too close the paint dribbled. And as he stretched higher, as the can angled, the paint sprayed wider and thinner, which actually looked OK. The plastic chemical tang of the paint and the heady smell of solvent filled the air. By the fourth letter he was getting the hang of it, angling the can to give the letters a kind of style. The bottoms of the letters widened like flared trousers.

Billy stood back. Fuck Fuck Fuck, he thought. Fuck his dad. Fuck everything.

In bright Flamenco Red the letters spelled FUCK. The K looked great, but the other letters weren't as good, so he wrote it again. Twice. And, thinking of last night in the garage he sprayed another word: CUNT. Rusty laughed.

'Cunt.' Rusty said the word out loud.

It felt great.

'Won't sneak, will you?'

'Bog off. Come on,' said Rusty. 'You said I could have a go.'

'My paint,' said Billy. SHIT was his first S. Some letters had a great shape for spray-paint, he decided.

'It'll run out,' complained Rusty.

Billy shook the can, listening for the small ball bearing they put in to keep the paint mixed pinging around inside the metal. 'There's loads.'

PRICK. He stood back and added an S for good measure.

'I'm bored. I'm going.'

'Here then.' Billy finally handed over the can, and when he did, Rusty noticed how his right hand was red from where the paint had bounced back off the wall. 'The Red Hand of Ulster,' Rusty said, giggling.

'No surrender,' shouted Billy, all deep-voiced.

They moved up a few yards to where there was fresh wall, and Billy stood, smoking Stampy's cigarette with his red hand while Rusty held the paint can, squinting at the bare brick wall. 'What shall I write?' Rusty asked.

'I don't care. Write whatever you want.'

When they got back to Rusty's, Billy tried washing the red off with hot water but it wouldn't shift. He tried Fairy Liquid, then Vim, which made his skin itch.

Stampy came in. 'Billy, what's that on your hand?'

'We been painting.' Rusty held up the can.

'Shut up,' said Billy.

'Where did you get that?'

'Filched it,' said Billy.

'You're too young to go nicking stuff.'

'Well I did, matter of fact.'

'Any left?'

'Quite a bit,' said Billy.

Stampy grabbed the can out of his brother's hand and shook it. 'C'n I have it?'

'It's mine,' said Billy.

'Go on.'

'Why?'

'Shh!' said Stampy, holding his finger to his lips.

'What are you going to do?'

'You'll see.' Stampy grinned.

Billy looked at him, half nervous, half excited.

'I'll give you another fag if you like,' said Stampy.

From somewhere, far off, the sound of flutes. A pipe band was rehearsing, all high notes and snare drums, and straight-backed old men in bowler hats. It was marching season. Billy felt a tingle of excitement in his spine. Fuck all that. Fuck it all.

SEVENTEEN

The doctor prescribed Ativan.

He didn't trust the pills, so didn't even bother picking them up from the pharmacy. Back at home, he was boiling a kettle for a Thermos of tea when Eddie knocked on his door.

'Heard you were off sick. I've got something that'll cheer you up. Come on down the beach, Bill, quick. There's a pomarine skua,' he said, fingering his binoculars.

Standing next to him was his girlfriend, pierced nose and coloured mittens, one of the women who regularly took part in the sea watches. She said, 'We were worried about you. We've not seen you around.'

South stood in his porch, not inviting them in. 'No. I'm just taking a break . . .'

'Pomarine skua offshore,' said the man again. 'Want to come and take a look?'

He shook his head. 'You're OK.'

Eddie blanched. 'I just left the beach to come and tell you about it,' he said, offended. 'Don't you want to come and look at it just for a bit?'

'I don't think so, really,' South said. 'I'm sort of busy.'

'What about sometime this week? I wanted to check your numbers against mine.'

'Maybe,' said South.

Through the window, he watched the couple trudging back to the beach, bemused. When they had disappeared over the shingle bank, he finished making the tea, put it into his small backpack and put it into his car.

He was driving past the lighthouse when he noticed Curly running up the beach towards the road, waving. South stopped, winding down the window. 'Got something to show you.' Curly grinned.

South got out and followed him back down the beach, past rusting cables and old abandoned nets. Curly had winched the Plymouth Pilot up the beach and had piled beer crates against the side of the hull.

'Go on,' he said. 'Look.'

South climbed up onto the crates and peered over the edge of the fibreglass boat.

'See?'

It was wet in the bilges; that meant that some of the blood hadn't dried properly. It was still lividly red against the white fibreglass of the hull.

'Fish blood?' said South.

'You'd have to catch half a ton to leave that much in a boat.'

'Someone fall in there, and cracked their skull?'

'Hopefully,' said Curly. 'The boat was nicked. Reckon

you can get a sample and do a DNA thing? Find out the cunt that nicked it.'

'That's assuming it's the criminal's blood,' said South quietly.

He turned and called down to Curly, 'What date did your boat disappear?'

'Thursday, last week.'

'So it was stolen on either Tuesday or Wednesday night, yes?'

'Suppose.'

That was the week Bob Rayner had been killed. Below, Curly was rubbing his hands together. 'Reckon you'll catch him?' Wednesday would have also been the night Judy Farouk disappeared.

'Was there any diesel in the tank when the coastguard found it?'

'The tank was empty and the tiller was lashed straight. Cunts had just let it go until it ran dry.'

He stood, looking down at the pale red against the whiteness of the fibreglass. He remembered Cupidi saying, 'You want there to be a connection. But there isn't.'

The flat marsh offered little shelter but today there was a thin mist hanging over the land. He left the car parked in a lay-by and walked back up the lane towards Puddledock Sewer. There was no easy route to get to it, but he had found he could push his way backwards through dead blackthorn and bramble to reach the field edge that ran parallel to the water. The marshes around here had been drained five hundred years ago, leaving these silty water-ways between the fields.

The farmer had ploughed close to the edge, so there wasn't much left to walk on. South followed the winding waterway northwards. At a curve, the dead winter grass had been flattened from when he had been here on previous days. He unfolded a small tarpaulin from his backpack and laid it onto the same place on the steep riverbank, then lowered himself onto it, leaving his head just above the top, looking over the parapet of land towards Nayland's Farm.

Three hundred yards away there were three high-sided vehicles parked up in a row on the concrete of the farm-yard; as far as he could remember they had been there, in the identical position, last week. He focused his binoculars. There seemed to be power lines held up on poles, running into the back of lorries. Why?

Flocks of lapwings rolled in the sky. Somewhere behind him, some mammal was splashing. Vole probably. He ignored it. Cold seeped into him; he didn't mind. He stayed, just watching the farm. Nothing happened.

The days were short already. He wore full thermals under his waterproofs. If you lay still for long enough, you'd see things no one else did. The light was going when the white car appeared, driving down the long track towards the farm.

That night he walked back over to Bob's house; there was dry wood stacked outside in a lean-to on the north side of his house. He grabbed an armful and took it with him inside.

The stove was an expensive one; some Swedish model. The Scene of Crime team hadn't found anything significant, but at least they had cleared out the ashes, in their search for anything that Bob's killer might have tried to destroy.

He found some kindling in the basket next to the stove and lit it, watching the flames take hold. While the fire was still warming, he started going through the books, still trying to discover some sign of who the real Bob had been. He yanked out hardback books looking for any names inscribed on the endpapers, or slips of paper tucked inside, but found nothing. He piled the books untidily on the floor. They were mostly novels he had heard of, but had never read. He searched through the shelves too for books that might have come from Bob's childhood, but saw nothing. There was nothing.

He went back to close the fire down. The flames slowed. Heat began to fill the room.

He returned to the shelves. At one side, there were half a dozen books of poetry. At first he thought they were all the usual collections – Wordsworth, Shakespeare's Sonnets, *The Oxford Anthology of English Poetry* – but one volume was further back than the rest, spine facing in. He pulled it out. It was the work of a South American poet.

This book had a dedication. It was the first – the only – aberration he had found. It was a simple heart drawn in pencil and in the centre, the number 142.

He turned to the page. There, on page 142, a verse had two lines underscored in the same pencil:

I love you as certain dark things are to be loved,
in secret, between the shadow and the soul.

It was a short, passionate love poem, just four verses long. He read it twice, thinking of the woman he had seen in the supermarket, the woman whose clothes were in Bob's closet.

The wood in the fire would last for a few hours, until it had burned itself out, warming the small house, keeping it dry.

The night passed. He woke in Bob's chair, body stiff from the cold, the radio chattering out the morning's news. That morning, avoiding Eddie, he made himself sandwiches and tea and headed off again with his binoculars.

Birdwatching had taught him to believe in patience; the longer you looked the more you could see. But in the evening he returned again to Bob's house, tired from sleeping poorly the night before, from straining his eyes in the low winter light.

It was Thursday morning when the radio he had left on for company jolted him awake. He blinked. It took him a second to realise he was in Bob's chair again. Something about the Dover lifeboat and a body. By the time his eyes were fully open, to see the first light bleeding red at the edge of the horizon, the presenter had moved on to the weather forecast.

He was at Dover by 8.30, unshaven. There were four police cars parked behind the lifeboat station on a harbour arm, just past a pontoon of yachts.

South parked a little way off, got out of his Micra. To the sound of rigging tinking on the swaying aluminium masts, he jogged towards the lifeboat station. At the best of times, there was nothing pretty about Dover; the port was huge, grey and functional. The lifeboat station sat in the middle, a small pitched-roof building dwarfed by the white liners that lay along the two cruise terminal quays on the far side of the south docks.

The orange lifeboat was moored alongside the station. The craft was an ungainly one, designed with a high prow at the front and a low sheer-line to the rear, to make it easier for the crew to pull bodies out of the water, thought South. And right now they were heaving the body-bag off the back. Six crew members, all brightly dressed in yellow drysuits and fluorescent lifejackets, and a single black bag, three handles on each side.

They laid the black shape on the jetty; the forensics team were there again with the white van.

Cupidi was talking on her phone. South waved at her. She frowned, shook her head, turned her back.

South approached the huddle of forensics officers and lifeboat crew as they were lifting the bag onto a gurney, ready to slide it into the van.

271

'Why didn't you call me?' said South.

Cupidi was standing with her arms crossed. 'Why are you here? This is nothing to do with you,' she said. There was a frostiness in her voice he had never heard before.

'I heard about it on the radio.'

'You're completely out of order, Sergeant,' she said. 'Even if you weren't off sick, you're a neighbourhood policeman. This is not your responsibility. You need to leave.' This coldness was new; only last weekend, he had been looking after her daughter.

'What's the problem, Alex?'

'This is a crime scene. You are not a serving officer right now.'

'And just when did you become such a stickler for the rules?' he said. 'I'm here . . . so I might as well look.'

'You shouldn't be.'

'What's wrong? Something's happened.'

She didn't meet his eye. 'I'm sorry, William. This is a serious development. The DI will be here any second. Please go.'

Herring gulls swooped over the lifeboat; the regular beat of dull metal travelled across the water from docks where coasters were being unloaded. He stood his ground, looking at the bag they were lifting out of the gurney. 'Man or woman?' asked South.

'Woman,' said one of the crew, a tall bearded man with long curly hair. Cupidi glanced at him.

'Young? Old?' she said.

'Hard to tell.'

'Decomposed?'

'No. Just all wrapped up in wire.'

'Chicken wire,' said another.

'A trawler pulled her up in the nets just a mile out,' one of the men said. 'Called us out.'

'Beam trawler,' said the bearded man. 'So she must have been close to the bottom.'

'What do you mean?' said South.

'When we pick bodies up they're always on top of the water. Swimmers, suicides. Beam trawlers scratch their way along the bottom. Complete fluke.'

Cupidi approached the long dark bag.

'Can we open it?' she asked.

The pathologist was a young woman whose pink lipstick made her look too feminine for the kind of work she did. 'Do you think you know who she might be?' she asked.

'Maybe,' said South.

'Though I doubt you'd be able to recognise her. Shall I?' The pathologist directed the question at Cupidi.

Cupidi rolled her eyes. 'I suppose it's possible one of us might know who she is.'

'I want to see,' said South. The young woman shrugged, leaned forward and unzipped the top of the bag, then rolled down the black plastic.

The body had been wrapped in wire. There were stones too, as if they had been added when the body was encased to help weigh it down.

'Shingle,' said Cupidi.

South nodded. The corpse was naked; the skin the yellow of marzipan. She's fat enough to be Judy Farouk, South thought; but it was hard to tell. The body was bloating, pushing at the criss-crosses of wire that held it in.

'What happened to her face?' he asked.

'Most of it's been eaten away already,' the pathologist said. 'If it was on the bottom, sea lice and crabs will do that. Is it someone you're looking for?'

He stared at the pale shape of nibbled flesh beneath the wire. There were dark holes where her eyes had been. He had seen too many dead people already these last few days. 'It could be,' he said.

'Now get lost,' said Cupidi. 'Don't call me. Stay away.'

'Look. If it's Judy Farouk, I'm right. We should be doing something.'

'Fuck off, William. OK? Go home. Don't do anything.'

'What's got into you?'

'Nothing. Look at some birds. Don't call me. Don't. OK? Please.'

Even the lifeboatmen looked shocked at the sudden anger in her voice. South walked back to the car, hurt and confused. When he passed the turning north, towards the Army Cadet Force hall where he'd stopped, he U-turned and drove back towards it. He parked at the gates facing the hall and turned off the engine hoping for thoughts to form, but they didn't.

He reached in his jacket and pulled out the book of poetry.

I love you as certain dark things are to be loved,
in secret, between the shadow and the soul.

He looked for meaning but couldn't find any. But when he closed the book and threw it onto the seat next to him, he found it. He saw a sticker with the name of the book-shop and the price: £10.99.

'Have you seen it?'
   'What?'
   'Superb.'
   'Disgustin'.'
The morning of the 11th of July on the way to school, it was there for all to see. In big red letters next to 'NO POPE HERE'.
   'Oh sweet fuck,' said Billy.
The 12th and the days before it were always mad around these parts. Remember the Boyne. There would be fight-ing and marching and protests. But nothing like this. All the boys around him, swinging satchels, were thinking it was the most outrageous, most shocking thing they'd ever seen.
   Even the timing could not have been more calculated

to insult. To do something like this at the very height of marching season.

Just three words, but everything about it was brilliant: 'LUCKY BLOODY POPE'. Unlike the stodgy letters his father inscribed all those years ago, which had been tidied and bodged over the years, this was beautiful. It was proper graffiti, all angles, swoops and swirls, like it was by some cool Bronx boy, not a lad from some shitty estate in Armagh. They had never seen anything like it.

'Surprise me if someone's not going to get bloody 'capped for that,' said someone. Billy looked round and saw Wally, the eldest of the Creedy children. 'Fair enough,' said the Creedy boy. 'I mean. You can't go round sayin' things like that, can you? It's a disgrace.' He peered at Billy. 'You OK? You look like you just sicked something up.'

'Nothin'. Leave us alone.'

'Who d'ye think it was? They'll be fucken creamed.'

'Fuck off, Creedy.'

And he walked down the hill past the graffiti, feeling sick to his stomach. It wasn't Stampy's fault. He wasn't to know that Billy had filched the paint off his own father.

EIGHTEEN

Harbour Books was on a one-way street next to a shoe shop, its windows full of birthday cards and local history. It was Friday; his week off work was drifting away from him, and nothing was any clearer. South held out the book of poetry.

'We don't take second-hand books,' the woman on the till said. She was middle-aged, dressed in arty pinks and oranges.

'Do you remember selling this?' he asked.

The woman wore glasses on a silver chain that swayed as she shook her head. 'I've only been here a couple of weeks,' she said.

'Would anyone else know?'

'Is it important?' She lowered her spectacles and peered at South.

'Very,' he said. He produced his warrant card from his wallet and showed it to her, though he had no right to.

She peered at the card, as if taking in all the details on it, then said, 'I could ask the owner, I suppose, but it's unlikely he'd remember.'

'Never mind.' South looked around him. Most of the small bookshops in the area had closed in recent years. This was one of the few that had survived, but it seemed to have been a wasted journey. Out of habit, he walked towards the Natural History section for anything that he didn't already have, pulling out a book about British butterflies.

The woman was still talking to him. 'We don't really do much in the way of poetry. It's so hard to sell; no one's that interested. Certainly not Neruda. I'm wondering if it was a special order. Unlikely I suppose, these days. People just buy everything online, don't they?'

He turned to her. 'Do you keep a record?'

She stood up and bent over to open a drawer at the bottom of her desk and pulled out a blue hardback ledger of some kind. 'If it was an order, it would have been in here, I think.'

He put the book back onto the shelf. She turned past lists of handwritten entries. 'There.' She smiled. 'I was right, after all. Would that be it? February this year.'

February. Valentine's day. 'What name?'

'Gail.'

Gill. Gail. Similar at least. He was sure. It was her. 'What about the last name?'

'No. She paid for the item in advance apparently. All she left is a contact number. I don't suppose I should give that out, should I?'

'This is important. It's a murder investigation,' he said, though he had no right to say it.

'Ooh,' she said, and without asking any more, she turned the ledger around and showed him the telephone number. It was a mobile. He wrote it in his notebook.

'Do let me know if you catch him,' said the woman. 'Or her, of course,' as if this was some game she had been invited to play. She waved at him as he left.

Outside, he pulled out his phone and dialled the number. It rang out, unanswered.

With nothing else to do, he wandered the high street, then went and sat in an empty tea shop for a while, wondering what he should do with the number. He tried calling it again but still no one picked up. He texted Cupidi: '*I think I have found Bob's girlfriend's number.*'

He ordered walnut cake because it was half-price and waited for her answer. On the opposite side of the road, on a boarded-up shop, someone had tagged the word 'KILLJO'. He wondered who Jo was. And then he realised the vandal had just run out of paint or been disturbed before they'd finished.

A woman PSCO came into the shop for a can of Coke and glanced round. 'Sergeant South?' she said. 'What are you doing skiving here?'

'I'm on sick leave.'

'Oh yeah?' She winked at him. 'Proper poorly.'

The phone vibrated in his pocket. He pulled it out and read the message: '*Don't contact me again.*'

He blinked, stung.

'I won't tell if you won't,' said the PSCO.

He ignored her. When she'd gone, he walked out of the shop and stared at the graffiti on the opposite side of the road. The paint was red.

He must have been standing there a while before a small woman with a huge double buggy said angrily, 'Excuse me. I'm trying to get past.'

He watched the white van through his binoculars. Lit by the low afternoon sun, it slowed, then sped up, then slowed again. Side on, he couldn't read the registration, but he opened a notebook and noted the time: '*Fri. 4.28 p.m.*'

Over the course of the week, returning here each day, South had learned the way vehicles slowed and sped up again, weaving as they drove down the lane to Nayland's Farm. There were potholes too deep to drive over at any speed. Instead of parking alongside the lorries, or by the office, the van drove into one of the decrepit barns and parked under its rusting roof.

The barn door closed behind it.

As soon as that was done, a man climbed into one of the lorry cabs and started the engine, reversing it out of the yard and swinging it round into the lane. It stopped about two hundred yards away from the farm and the driver got out and walked back to the farm.

Why? Had the driver forgotten something? But if so, why didn't he just reverse the tractor unit back down the lane? There was no trailer attached, so it wouldn't have been hard. Or perhaps there was some kind of mechanical problem with the truck?

But the man didn't return. The lorry cab remained where it was, not moving. And South realised that it was like locking the gate. No other vehicle could pass it. The farm was effectively cut off. The distant silhouettes of lorry cabs looked like gravestones, lined up against the pale horizon.

Lights came on in Dacre's yard. He could see new figures moving around between the lorries, but could not see what they were doing; they were just silhouettes now. Some of them were gathering around a brazier; he could see the glows of their cigarettes as they smoked.

Some sort of delivery had taken place; he was sure of it. And it was enough for him to use to stir things up a bit, at least. Garage doors opened and the white SUV emerged; it drove towards a diesel tanker and a man got out and started to fill the car. South focused. It was Dacre.

Lying on the tarpaulin, South picked up his phone and called the station, asking to speak to DI McAdam. It took a few minutes to get put through. The first thing McAdam said when he answered was, 'I thought you were on leave, South. Post-traumatic stress, I was told.'

'I am, sir. Only something's come up.' South could hear the familiar babble of the police station in the background. 'I think I've just seen something.'

He described what he had witnessed.

'And you were simply there by chance?' said McAdam.

'Birdwatching, sir.'

'Really?'

'Just by chance.'

'And you think there might have been a delivery of narcotics to Mr Dacre's farm?'

'Yes, sir. I think so.'

'Birdwatching?'

'I'm very keen, sir.'

There was a long pause. 'Leave it with me,' McAdam said, without enthusiasm. 'I'll pass the information to the team.'

On Monday Eddie had arranged to come round to discuss bird records. Now he was back with his notebooks and spreadsheets. 'The swallow migrations are definitely later and later,' said Eddie. 'Look at the figures.'

Eddie had an extinguished roll-up cigarette in one hand and a wad of migration statistics going back for the last ten years in the other. 'What about your numbers?'

'I haven't had so much time this year,' said South.

Eddie loved figures in the way a lot of birders do. Eddie liked to compile them and interrogate them. He was like this every spring and autumn, recording the emerging patterns, trying to discern the difference between natural fluctuation and radical change. He put the half-smoked cigarette in his tin and set to rolling another. 'I mean. Look at these figures for ring ouzels.'

With nicotine fingers, Eddie started picking through his piles of paper.

South wasn't paying attention. He was thinking about the phone number. It was a mobile, so the phone number he was calling from would show up on the screen. Whoever he had rung had not recognised the number that was calling.

South stood. 'Excuse me,' he said, suddenly. 'I just need to do something. I'll be back in ten minutes.'

'Take a look,' said Eddie. 'It'll only take a sec.'

'Sorry. It's important.'

'Thought you were on a sickie?'

'Make yourself some tea. Or there's beer in the fridge.'

Eddie sat there, looking offended. 'I've other things to do too, you know.'

'Ten minutes,' said South, and he took Bob's keys off the hook and went out into the chilly evening.

Despite the fire he'd lit, Bob's house felt colder and damper than it ever had. Bob was an old-fashioned man. He had an old-fashioned phone, still hard-wired to the wall. He lifted it and put it to his ear; the electricity had been cut off, but the phone was still connected. He took out his notebook and dialled the number he had got from the bookshop.

He let it ring again, ten, twelve times. Still, nobody picked up. He waited a little longer, then put the phone back down again, disappointed.

It had just been an idea; to call from Bob's line would have been a signal: I know who you are. Bob's number would show up on her screen. But again, it had rung and rung, and nobody had picked up.

He sighed. Looked round at the mess. Maybe he should clear it up, but not today.

He was just locking Bob's front door to return back to his house to hear Eddie talking about his statistics when the phone inside the house began to ring.

The lock was stiff. It hadn't been used much. With so much salt in the air, everything here seized up fast. He swore, struggling with the key, but got the door open and ran towards the phone, knocking the receiver off the telephone stand.

Grabbing it from the floor he lifted it to his ear.

A breathing.

'Hello?'

'Hello?' a woman whispered.

'I'm William South. Bob's friend.'

'Yes.' Just one word.

'Who are you?'

There were no words, just the breathing. He was exhilarated.

'I need to know,' said South. 'If we are ever going to find out who killed Bob, I need to know.'

Still nothing.

'I think the person who murdered him wasn't the man the police think it was. And I think you can help me. Gill. Gail. Whatever your name is.'

The breaths were unsteady, broken, as if the woman was crying.

'Christy Dacre. You know him?'

'Who?'

'Christy Dacre.'

'Never heard of him. Why are you asking this?'

'You sure?'

Silence. But she was still listening, at least; her presence on the other handset felt almost tangible. He closed his eyes and tried to picture her: the woman in the supermarket. 'I think you want whoever killed Bob to be caught.'

'No. I don't.' Her voice was anxious, panicky.

'You don't?'

'You wouldn't understand. It's . . .'

'It's what?'

'Nothing. I can't talk to you. You don't know what you're doing. Please leave us alone.'

'Who is us?'

She didn't answer. He could hear her so clearly, shifting the phone in her hand as if she were about to disconnect the call.

'You loved Bob, though, didn't you?'

A pause. 'Yes. I loved him.'

'What was Bob hiding from?'

'No. I have to go.'

'Who are you? Please.' But she had cut off the call.

He dialled back but when the phone connected, it just rang. She had switched off the phone, he guessed. He did not understand. Cupidi had told him not to do anything. He had the feeling he had set something terrible in motion, but he was not sure what.

Billy walked on in darkness, legs aching now.

It had happened that same evening. Eleventh Night. Mum had been out at the Tuesday bingo. Dad had come in raging, slamming the door. He had been drinking with the boys.

Billy had been expecting it. All day he had been sick with the worry of it. He had tried to run upstairs to lock himself in the toilet, but hadn't made it in time. Dad's fat hand had grabbed his shirt and pulled him back down, knocking his head against the step. Billy could hear the shirt fabric strain, then start to tear. His father smelt of bonfires; the stench of rubber from the tyres they built the Eleventh Night pyres out of was in his skin.

'Oh no ye don't. So it was you, then, was it, Billy?'

Of all the people he didn't want to cry in front of.

'What? Was what me?'

'Don't fucken act smart with me, you wee get.'

'I don't know what you're talking about.'

Though he knew; and his dad knew that. The first punch came hard in the stomach and all the air left him. When his father let go of his collar with his left hand, Billy slumped to the floor in the hallway. When he touched his forehead, he felt blood. There was a small cut just below his hairline; usually Dad was more careful than this, bruising where it didn't show. Tonight he was livid; anything could happen.

'Get up,' said his father.

'Honest. I don't know what you're on about.'

'Liar.' And he picked up the walking stick he kept by the door, like men in these parts did. 'It was you that filched the paint, wasn't it?'

'What paint?'

He lifted the stick and whacked him hard once with it across his chest where it wouldn't show. The skin beneath his shirt stung, and the tears he didn't want to let go of started to fall. 'Don't hit me, please,' he cried, bubbling snot.

And it went on like this for a little while. 'Lie still, ye little bugger.' At one point, Billy remembered wishing his mum had been there, then that he was glad she wasn't, because he'd have probably given it to her too. He remembered noticing how Dad's boots were all polished up for the marching season too. 'You're a weed. You can't even stand up for yourself. Come on, get up.'

But Billy remained on the floor at boot level. 'It wasn't me. I promise. Swear to God.'

'You nicked the paint. I know ye did, thieving shit. Don't lie to me.'

And the boot lifted and hovered above his head. He was going to die.

'I'm not lying, Dad. It wasn't me.'

His dad leaned down, face close. 'Well, which of your degenerate little bastard friends was it then?'

'Can't tell you. That would be sneaking.'

'I'll fucken kill you, Billy. I swear.'

And the boot quivered in the air. And Billy couldn't help himself and he whispered the name.

Stampy had done the best thing ever. Better than all those words Billy'd written in the alley by River Street. And it had looked magnificent, he had thought, though he'd known the moment he'd seen it, that it was going to end badly.

'I will lamp the fucken bastard. Fucken kill him.'

He would kill Stampy. And it would all be Billy's fault.

In the bathroom upstairs, he dabbed witch hazel on the cut. His mother had taught him how to cover the signs of what went on when his father was angry. Below, he heard his father roaring still. He was getting drunker, fetching another bottle from the kitchen.

And even if he didn't actually kill Stampy, everyone would know that Billy had told on him.

Pausing in his work at the bathroom mirror, he noticed it had gone quiet downstairs. Listening, he caught the sound of steady snoring from below. Billy breathed out. Dad would have passed out in the chair, at least.

That's when he made the decision to go back downstairs and lift the manhole cover, just as he had seen his father do. There was nothing else for it. His mother was not back for another hour.

He was still trudging along the black tarmac when, up ahead in the dark, he heard the voices. A loud laugh.

As he got closer he realised the accents were English. Squaddies. There must be a roadblock up ahead. He would have to go round it, through the fields now. It was time to leave the road anyway, to head up the hillside. It would be getting light soon.

Tired now, he wished he could lie down and sleep, and stop everything from going around in his head.

NINETEEN

He was still at Bob's, waiting for the phone to ring again, when his mobile rang instead.

It was Cupidi.

'What happened to "Never contact me"?' he said.

'Wait,' she pleaded. It was loud in the background. The chatter of angry voices. 'Has Zoë been in touch with you?'

'Me? No. Why?'

'I just wondered.' She sounded odd, distracted. 'I know you think I'm a terrible parent, but . . .'

'What's going on there?'

He could hear the sound of someone wailing in the background. 'The place is full of bloody Chinese. Some idiot decided to send a car down to some farm because of a tip-off about drugs. Turned out the farm was full of migrant workers and they brought them all here. No bloody drugs. Now we're waiting for Immigration to turn up and process them. It's bloody chaos here.'

'Nayland's Farm? Christy Dacre?'

'Did you know something about this, William?'

So that's why Dacre had looked so nervous when he had

visited him: the white van hadn't been carrying drugs. It had been full of workers; illegals. Someone was running immigrant farm workers out of his buildings. That's why they had closed the road.

'What were you saying about Zoë?'

'She's not at home. She's not picking up her phone. I just thought she might have called you. She likes you.' On the dockside at Dover she had sounded cold and hard; now she sounded anxious.

'No. I'm really sorry. She hasn't.'

'Right. Well, thank you, anyway,' she said stiffly. 'I better go then.'

'Do you want me to go and look for her?'

'Where would you look?'

'I don't know.'

'No,' she said, voice thin with nerves. 'No. I'm sure she'll be back.'

'I don't mind. It's no bother. I'd like to help.'

'I shouldn't have called.'

'Please, let me.'

'I need to go.' And she put down the phone.

He walked slowly home. He had assumed there was a connection between Dacre and Judy Farouk, that if there was it might explain why she had disappeared; but it seemed that Dacre was just a desperate man trying to keep a business afloat.

South was ten feet from his front door when he saw

something dark in the shadow of his porch. His first thought was that someone had dumped a black bin-bag there, but as he dug the key out of his pocket, getting closer, the black shape moved. A white oval appeared at the top of it.

'Zoë?' he said.

He could make out her face now.

'I'm sorry,' she said. And she was crying.

'Your mum just called me. She was worried sick. Where have you been?'

'Can't say. I'm sorry. I'm a bit stoned.'

'Stoned?' He hadn't thought her that kind of girl. 'What did you take?' he asked, opening the front door, and regretting having said that; it was such a policeman thing to do.

'Don't tell Mum,' she said. 'Please don't. I'll be OK.'

He led her, blinking in the light, to the kitchen. He helped her take off her cold coat and sat her on a chair. He'd only ever seen her in a school uniform or jeans before: she was wearing a short black skirt and dark blouse and her face was made up, trying to look older than she was, but the make-up had run from the rain, or because she'd been crying. She looked suddenly very like her mother.

'I'd better call her and tell her you're OK. She's worried.'

'I've been really stupid,' she said.

Cupidi answered her mobile straight away.

'She's here. At my house. She's fine.'

'Oh, thank fuck. What the hell was she doing?' said Cupidi over the hubbub of voices at the station. He could hear the tension leaving her.

'I don't know. I didn't ask. Shall I take her home?'

'Why did she come to you, not me?'

'It's not important. She's here.'

'You're right. I'm such a bad mother. Christ. I'll be home in fifteen minutes,' she said. 'Will I meet you there?'

Zoë sat at the kitchen table shivering. 'How did you get here?' he asked her.

'Taxi. I thought you'd be in. Once I was here I didn't have enough left to go home.'

'I'm sorry.'

She looked exhausted and cold. He went upstairs, fetched a blanket from his spare room and wrapped it around her.

Zoë said she felt sick so South drove slowly. 'I've cocked it all up.'

'I'm sure it's OK.'

'No, it's not.' She seemed younger now; more childlike. He turned the heater up, but she was still cold. 'These girls at school,' she said. 'See, I wasn't really worried about them. They're just idiots. But they hated me. Ever since that first day. When Mum put the siren on.'

'I know,' he said. 'It's OK.'

'No it's not. They hate me because I'm a copper's daughter. I just wanted them to leave me alone. So me and Mum could get on with our lives.'

'What did you do?' he asked again.

'I'm really tired now. I don't want to explain.'

She picked up the paperback that had been lying on

293

her seat and switched on the interior light as he drove. Opening it she saw the big hand-drawn heart. 'Is someone in love with you?'

'No. That's my friend's. Bob's.'

She pouted. 'Shame. It's lovely. You should be in love with someone.'

'This is the bit where you usually mention your mother.'

She giggled. 'Yeah. I've stopped that.'

'What about you?' he asked.

She said, 'Yeah. Well. There's this bloke. Only he turned out to be a knob.'

'Oh.'

'Do you like poetry?'

'I don't really understand it,' he said.

She turned to the page with the poem on it, and read the two lines. 'Oh. So your friend had a secret lover?'

'Yes, I think so,' he said. 'But I don't know who she is. I'm trying to find out.'

'How exciting. She bought this book for him?'

'Why did you come to see me? Is it because of that boy? Did he sell you the drugs you had tonight?' he asked.

She glared at him.

'Sorry.'

She reached up and switched the light off. They drove in darkness, the only car on the road. 'These girls hate me. I tried to get along with them like Mum asked me to. That's all I did. I did it for her. She needs to make it work down here.'

'What are their names?'

'Don't be a bloody policeman, please. They're just girls, at school. Their names aren't important. And they made my life hell. But I didn't want to worry Mum about it. So I tried to get along with them, like Mum said, because otherwise they were going to fight me.'

'They take drugs?'

She nodded.

'You know those crows we saw that day? They're all black make-up and they're fat like crows.' She giggled. 'That's what I call them. The crows.'

'They gave you drugs?'

'No. God. Everyone takes drugs.'

'I don't understand.'

'I started buying them cigarettes. One break I said, "I don't want to be your enemy. Can we make friends?" And I gave them a packet of cigarettes.'

'I thought you hated smoking.'

'I do. Anyway, they took my fags and shared them out. And then they told me to fuck off. God I hate them. So it's become a routine. Sometimes I buy them a packet of cigarettes and they . . . you know, call me names. But they don't pick fights any more. It was one way to keep them off my back.'

'You can't buy a packet of cigarettes every day. That's a fortune.'

'I know. But if I stop, it's going to start up again. And Mum's all pleased because it's all been going OK at school this last week. And then, Friday, I'm giving them the cigarettes and they're smoking one and this boy comes up. He's from the sixth-form college. He's actually kind of nice-looking. Groomed, you know? Not like all the boys at school. And these girls all go nuts and wave at him and everything, and he stops. And he comes up to me and asks my name. So that really pisses them off to start with. So I make the most of it.'

'You flirted with him?'

'God, no. I just said hello. Told him my name. Asked him his.'

'Which is?'

'I'm not telling you.'

'OK.'

'So then after school he's hanging around again.'

'How old is this boy?'

'Seventeen. And he comes up to me and says, "I got a motorbike. You want a ride?" I said, "Not likely." Then he said, "Want to come to a party?" And one of the crows is right there. Like, furious. You should see the look on her face. She's spitting sparks from her eyes at me. So I turn to her and say, "Can my mate come too?"'

South laughed.

'I know,' Zoë said. 'So all of a sudden she takes my arm and says, "I'll come too then?" Job done, I thought. If only I knew . . .'

'Knew what?'

'He has this friend whose parents have a big house and he's going to have a great big party there . . .'

'This is yesterday, right?'

'Mum would never let me go to a party. She lets me swan around with a birder twice my age in the middle of nowhere, but she wouldn't let me go to a party.'

'And you wanted to, yes?'

She shrugged. 'This boy was inviting me to a party. Course I was happy about it. What are you, an idiot? But Mum calls up and says something has come up, some big thing that's going to take hours, so I decided to go off and meet him in town and we caught a bus out towards Folkestone. And I think he's funny, and kind of sweet, and he's telling me about what music he likes, you know, the kind of things boys talk about, and then we walk up this big hill to this other boy's house . . . And the party's already on. And it's cool. The boy whose party it is – his parents are away, and we're all sitting around and there is loads to drink. And other stuff.'

'Other stuff?'

'You know. Drugs. That's what parties are like. Normally I would be nervous at a place like that. But actually, you know what? It feels good. Until me and the boy go into this room and the crows are all there. The crows from school. And they're all stoned, and talking to the guy who's throwing the party and they're all smoking this big bong. You know what a bong is?'

'Well, yes. I do, actually.'

'Course you do. You're a copper. Anyway, they're only there because I got the boy to invite them, but they all stare at me like they hate me for even being there too. And one of them, the one I had a fight with on my second day, says, "She's the copper's daughter." '

Zoë shrugged.

'And just then the music finished and there was like this silence in the room, everyone just looking at me. I was bloody dead, you know? It's all they had to say. "She's the copper's daughter." Thanks a bunch. So the guy who's smoking the bong with the crows, it's his party. He's an older guy, maybe eighteen. And he starts screaming at the boy for bringing me along and calling him an idiot. It's not his fault. I didn't tell him. I was afraid if I did he wouldn't like me. So I said, "It's OK. Pass me the bong." And I took a great big suck on it and everyone just laughed.'

'You took drugs to try and be cool?'

'Don't be so stupid. I hate drugs. I took drugs so they'd know I couldn't tell my mum about the party. It was horrible. And stupid. Really stupid. But I was just so desperate to get along, I wanted them to know I was OK. So after a bit I started feeling strange and they were all staring at me. And it felt really bad. I couldn't move. I hadn't had that much. And I was passing out and everything.'

'They spiked your drink?'

She nodded. 'Think so. And I got the feeling everyone was laughing at me. I don't know. It may have been the drugs. I remember I was crying and asking the boy to take me home. He was just embarrassed to have brought me there. I think I fell asleep for a while. And when I came to, some boy gave me ten pounds and put me in a taxi. You found me.'

'I'm sorry. You don't have to tell your mother anything. You just need to steer clear of those people.'

'You don't get it. I can't steer clear of them. They're my life. And it's just so fucked up. Because they're all such vile people.'

They were outside her house now. He switched off the engine.

'They got photographs,' she said, quietly.

'Of you taking drugs?'

She nodded. 'They said they'll put them on Facebook. The boys said it as a joke but then the crows said they were serious. They're going to. I know. Because they're crows. And Mum will lose her job.'

They sat in the car and he realised how scared she must feel.

'I'm going to do like you. Go to the other end of the world to get away from all this. I just wanted to tell you. To explain to someone. To stop myself from going mad, you know?'

'Running away doesn't help,' he said. 'I tried that.'

She let herself into the house and walked straight up to her bedroom. He followed to make sure she got there all right. At the door to her room, he asked, 'Would you like some water?'

She kicked off her shoes, flopped down on her bed fully

clothed and pulled the duvet over her, closing her eyes. 'I just want to go to sleep,' she said. 'Can you switch off the light?'

As a policeman he had been inside a few teenage girls' rooms. He was used to the outsize stuffed toys piled on a bed, or the mess of knickers and moulding food on the floor, apologised for by the parents. Zoë's room was surprisingly neat; bare, even.

What he wasn't prepared for was the walls. They were covered in drawings of birds. He recognised some of the images. They had been copied, painstakingly, from the *Pocket Book of British Birds* he had given her.

They were just plain pencil drawings, but in some ways they were better than the ones in the notebook. She was a natural. His own drawings, the ones he had surrounded himself with as a child, had been awkward and shaky. He had always been frustrated at never being able to capture the character of each bird. Zoë's were confident. Her lines were strong. She understood the shape of the bird, how the feathers lay, the whole feeling of motion that each bird had. What birders called the 'jizz'.

Among them, there was a shelduck, a green sandpiper, dated from weeks earlier, copied from the book she had kept on her lap in the hide. But there was another, of lapwings in flight. That cannot have been from a book. She had caught the peculiar swept back curve of the raised wing; the chaotic nature of their flock. It was all in there, captured in simple lines.

His drawings had been more than just a way of seeing birds. They had been about making his own world. Hers must be the same, he supposed. And then he remembered Sergeant Ferguson looking at his own drawings in much the same way, and gulped in air.

His phone vibrated. A text message from Cupidi: '*Five minutes away.*'

The girl on the bed was fast asleep already, fully clothed. He switched off the light.

Cupidi came downstairs red-eyed. 'Was she on something?'

South stood in the hallway, whispering back. 'She just wanted to talk to someone, that's all.'

'And why didn't she want to talk to me?'

'I can't say. She made me promise not to tell you.'

Cupidi looked first stung, then shocked. 'Oh Christ. She's not pregnant, is she?'

'It's nothing that bad,' said South. 'Trust me.'

'I hate it,' she said. 'I don't even know you, really.'

'She has her reasons. I promise. And she loves you a lot, you know. She's pretty extraordinary, you know that?'

She stood there stiffly. 'Thank you for bringing her home.'

'Right,' he said. Then, 'Did I do something wrong at some point? You seem really pissed off with me.'

She didn't answer.

'I can take her birding, if you like. She enjoys it.'

'I don't think so.' She went to open the door. 'I think it's best if she hangs out with people her age more.'

'You're joking, aren't you? That's what she was doing tonight.'

'I'm tired,' she said, holding the door open for him. 'I'm very grateful for you bringing her home, but you have to leave now.'

Like he was a stalker or something. And he drove back home in the black night, muttering to himself, angry, as the first ice of the year glittered on the road ahead.

Billy walked into morning.

The early farmers were up, picking up churns and dumping them at the gates.

Nobody paid him any attention. He was invisible. The land rose and he started to climb, first stony track and eventually slender footpaths dotted with sheep shit, black dots on the grey soil.

Halfway up Tornamrock, he was scanning the sky as the early light began to pick out the shapes of the mountains around him. The binoculars were heavier than they had ever been before. It seemed a struggle to lift them to his eyes.

There was no shelter here. He would have liked to have made it round to the south side of the mountain, so that he wouldn't have been so visible from the roads below, but first the night walk and then the climb had exhausted him and he was only taking a few steps at a time now before having to stop. His stomach hurt; he tried to remember when he had last eaten.

If he stood for too long the cold began to seep into him, and he wasn't sure that if he sat he'd ever get up again, so he kept on, but slower and slower.

As the sun nudged up he could see how little progress he was making now. He would have liked to have found a better place, but this would have to do. He collapsed onto the coarse grass to get his breath back.

When he finally sat up, there was a buzzard over the col towards Rocky Mountain, circling slowly in the rising air. It felt good to rest for a while.

The huge ache that had followed him ever since he killed his father was always there. It was something he could talk to nobody about because there were no words for it.

His mother would be crying but it was best for him to go completely.

Further out he saw another buzzard; then, towards the west, a peregrine. He was too tired to even care about them.

It was still summer. With the light, the mountains were coming alive. Bees were already searching for heather. Wood ants scurried around him.

He scanned to the south and thought he saw movement; something pale flying low. His heart jumped, but the bird was half a mile away and the shivering meant he found it hard to twist the focus. Frustrated, he lay on his stomach and, with what seemed like a huge effort, managed to steady the lenses on a rock. But as the damp from the earth seeped into his jumper he only saw a third buzzard; it was not even a barn owl.

The moment he sat up, the shivering started again, worse this time because his chest was cold from lying on the wet ground.

Crouching, he panned across the sky again from left to right and back once more, struggling to stay awake.

He didn't deserve to see the snowy owl, anyway.

The drizzle started to fall again and the cold began to drain his last energy. It was calming. The colder he became, the smaller the ache seemed to be, as if it were moving into the distance.

He thought he saw an ouzel, but couldn't be sure and realised he didn't really care.

He had come here to see the owl, but maybe that didn't matter at all either. LUCKY BLOODY POPE.

Below, the pale buzzard was still there in the dark of the unlit valley. It had perched on a dead tree.

The pink sunlight was slowly making its way down the hillside towards it. But when it hit the bird for the first time, he noticed something strange and beautiful.

It was a buzzard, not an owl. And completely white. A pure white, tinged salmon pink by the first light.

For a second, he couldn't believe it. Thinking it was just

his tiredness, he closed his eyes, scrunched them tight, then opened them again.

But when he looked, the bird had gone. He traced the hillside looking for it. Where was it? He had lost it.

He moved the binoculars cautiously left and right, looking for a hint of motion, but the bird had vanished.

TWENTY

It was the first night he had not camped out at Bob's house in days. He woke early, feeling angry, ineffectual and dirty. The last one, at least, he could do something about. Bob's house had no hot water; he had not showered or shaved in days; he had gone straight out to see the body the lifeboat had brought in, then gone to lie by the edge of a muddy river.

He ran a bath and lay in it, trying to make sense of everything that had happened in the last two days. It was as if Cupidi had changed into a different woman. Before, she had been friendly, now she was hostile; on the dockside she had been frosty, and at her house curt and dismissive, even though he had brought her missing daughter home.

Nothing made sense: Bob's murder; Judy Farouk's disappearance; Donny Fraser's death. If it was Farouk's body, and if Fraser had been killed, then three acts of violence had taken place within days of each other. He was sure the killer had deliberately made only a half-hearted attempt to conceal Bob's body, but the other two murders — assuming they *were* murders — had been meticulously covered up, so meticulously that the police didn't see the connections he did. But then they didn't know that Donny Fraser had not killed South's father.

South got out of the bath and stood in front of the steamed-up bathroom mirror. Is it just that he wanted to believe that Fraser hadn't killed himself? Because, in some way, if he did, it was South's fault? By letting Fraser go to prison for a crime he had not committed, he asked himself, had he created the monster that had killed his friend?

Wiping the condensation, he looked at his face and tried to see the faint line of a scar where his father had hit him, but couldn't.

He picked up his razor and shaved. On a whim, he took the bottle of aftershave he had bought in Tesco's out of the box and unscrewed the lid.

When he splashed it on his cheeks, relishing the sting of it, his nostrils were assailed by a sharp, chemical smell. But there was something familiar about it. For a second he couldn't place it.

Citrus. Then he stood there looking in the mirror, open-mouthed.

It had not been a woman's perfume in his house that night. It had been a man's aftershave that he had smelt. Alongside the tang of chemicals, there was a faint smell of orange. Of some kind of spice, too. He looked at the bottle: 'Instinct'. And the man had been Gill Rayner's other lover, or husband, or son. He was the man she had bought the aftershave for. Suddenly he felt tantalisingly close to the woman Bob had loved.

Had Bob known about this other man? Had she been cheating on Bob, too? Or had she been cheating on the man whose aftershave South was wearing now?

He was standing naked, trying to fathom what this meant, when the doorbell rang. When he opened his front door, wrapped in just a towel, Eddie was standing there, grinning, holding his spreadsheets.

'I know you've been busy . . .'

'Not now,' South snapped.

'Sure. Shall I come back when you're dressed?'

Looking at Eddie, all hopeful, South almost said yes, but then he changed his mind. A thought had occurred to him. 'No.'

'When, then?'

'Another time.' He went to close the door, then opened it again. Eddie was still there, a worried look on his face. He said, 'Look, Eddie. I am sick of just looking at things. All we do is look. Do you understand?'

From the hurt expression on his face, it was clear that he didn't, but South closed the door on him anyway.

There was at least one thing he could do, he realised, if not for himself, or for Bob, or Donny Fraser.

He hadn't switched on his computer for a week. He opened a browser, found all the local taxi firms and started working his way through them, phoning each one up.

'No, it's nothing serious. I need to find the address a driver picked a young woman up from last night . . . No, she hasn't made a complaint. It's nothing like that. I just need to speak to the driver.'

He gave each dispatcher his mobile contact and his warrant number and then set about reading through the unanswered emails. The HR department had mailed to say they required a second letter from his GP if he was going to have any more time away. He wouldn't bother. It was driving him crazy not working; tomorrow he would declare himself fit again and turn up for work.

He dressed and switched on the radio for the news, which he listened to as he made himself a fried egg sandwich. Lorries were queuing on the M20 again because of another strike at Calais, another young immigrant had been found dead after trying to hide on a Eurotunnel train.

He was thumping tomato ketchup onto his sandwich out of a bottle when the third item was read out. It was about the body they had recovered from the sea that week. 'Kent Police confirm that the body belonged to 43-year-old Judith Farouk.' Nothing else; nothing about who she was.

But he had been right about that after all.

He considered calling Cupidi, but what would be the point? They would be working on it now, at last.

Instead he walked over to Bob's house to light another fire there. Somebody had to look after the place.

There were new letters behind the door. He stacked them up and put them with the others. He should probably shut the water off. If it got any colder it would freeze and the pipes might burst.

On an impulse he picked up the phone and dialled 1471. Bob's house had been called an hour earlier, but the number had been withheld. Could it have been the woman he had spoken to last night calling him back again? There was no way of telling.

He sat in front of the fire, watching the flames build. Around three in the afternoon, his mobile rang. It was a man with an Asian accent who called him 'sir'. 'Of course I remember the house I picked the young lady up from, sir,' he said, as if the suggestion that he had forgotten it offended him. South noted down the name of a road to the west of Sandgate. 'She was very sad,' the taxi driver said.

'What kind of house was it?'

'A big house.'

'New. Old?'

'New. Like James Bond would have.'

'What do you mean?'

'You know. Like James Bond.'

He left the fire to burn itself out and walked to the beach. Curly's boat was out there, bobbing in the ocean. That was the boat that dumped Judy Farouk's body, he thought. The forensics team would want to impound it now, to search it for traces of the victim and her killer.

It was one of those bright days of early winter. The sun was low and caught the shape of the hill that rose above him.

It was a private road, neatly hedged. The houses were set back, with large leaf-bare trees silhouetted against a bright sky. He walked down the road trying to guess which house the party would have been in. If he did find out which house it was, what was he planning to do? He was not sure. People here had money. This was an enclave of the rich. *Excuse me, but are your friends bullying a policeman's daughter?*

Reaching a gateway, he peered in. A large, yellow-bricked house with a green tiled roof looked deserted. The next, a mock-Tudor mansion had four cars parked outside it on gravel. Was this the driver's idea of a James Bond house?

He doubted it. But there were not many homes in this road; it had to be one of them. The next house had a solid gate, steel and pale wood, with an entryphone to the right. He approached the centre of the gate, hoping to find a gap to see through.

It was a low, white, modernist house, glass doors extending out towards a swimming pool. The lights were on. Cool Danish chairs were arranged around a free-standing stove, in which a wood fire burned. He could see no people though.

A James Bond house, thought South.

He rang the doorbell and waited. A woman's voice came through the intercom. 'Hello?'

'Sergeant William South,' he said. 'Kent Police.'

Something buzzed gently, and the gates swung slowly open. He walked up a short drive towards the neat house.

Even the pale ochre gravel seemed to have been tastefully chosen.

In a stone wall, a big plain door opened: hinged towards one side so that while one part of the door swung out, the bigger part swung back inside the house. Holding it was a cool-looking woman in her late fifties. She was dressed in black; reading glasses tucked into her hair.

She looked puzzled. 'Yes?'

'Are you the owner of this house?'

She looked him up and down. 'What's this about?'

He held out his warrant card. 'We've had reports of some suspicious youngsters hanging around this area. May I ask your name?'

She had perfect, uniform teeth that showed as she smiled. 'Suspicious youngsters?'

It was a poor invention, but it would have to do. He looked from left to right, along the long low building. 'Have you seen anyone suspicious in the neighbourhood?'

'Are you expecting to find them in my house, officer?'

'Do you have any children?'

'Yes. Why?'

'What were they doing last night at round midnight?'

'My name is Olivia Gemmell JP. Justice of the Peace. I would expect you to know that if you want to ask questions like that about a minor, you would need to tell me the reason. I would also expect you to be in a uniform unless you're with CID and I doubt this is a CID matter. If you don't explain what this is about, right now, I shall ask you to leave. And I shall call the police.'

A magistrate; she knew the way these things were supposed to work. He would be in trouble now, but he had come this far. 'We have reports of some young people in the area after dark. Of a nuisance.'

'Young people? Whatever next?' She sneered at him. The middle classes were always the worst. 'Oh,' she said then. 'Don't say you've had complaints about my son's party?'

'Your son's party? Was that last night?'

'Who complained? Did someone complain?' He looked past her. On the wall was a family portrait. He recognised her in it; there was also a man with hair down below his ears and a young son.

South smiled. 'I really can't say, madam. Is your son in?'

She reddened. 'No. He is not. He's back in . . .' She looked at her watch, then changed her mind. 'Have you finished?'

'I can wait till he's back, if you like.'

'I don't think so,' she said. 'Can I ask you to leave now?'

He kept his smile. 'Thank you for your time.' He turned and walked back down the immaculate driveway.

'Which bloody arsehole complained?' she called after him.

He returned to his car, the gate closing behind him. Releasing the handbrake, he let gravity take him a little further down the hill. Sure enough, around the corner as they approached the golf course, there was Vincent Sleight's house. They were neighbours.

He sat watching it for a while.

'Bungalow' was not sufficient to describe it. It was only one storey high, but the house sprawled across at least an acre, with a swimming pool to the left that was sheltered from the far side by a separate guest house. With its terracotta tile roof and its arched portico at the front, the house looked like it should be in Spain, not here in Kent. To the far side was a huge garage.

The house sat in an immaculate garden of rolling grass that curved around the house, dotted with neatly clipped shrubs.

South was wondering how much a house like this would cost when he saw a figure at the window looking back at him. He squinted but could not see if it was a man or a woman.

He looked at his watch. When he had asked about her son, the woman in the James Bond house had done the same, as if she was expecting him home at any minute. He would give it another hour, he thought.

He waited. Every now and again, as the evening darkened, the figure returned to the window as if checking he was still there.

It was dark by the time he heard the motorbike approaching up the lane. It was one of those 125cc bikes made to look like it was something bigger, and on it sat a young man with black helmet and a full-face visor. He paused, headlight playing on the gates of the James Bond house as he leaned over to the keypad.

'You. Wait.' South got out of the car and ran back towards him, holding out his ID.

When he lifted up his visor, South saw he was only a boy of seventeen or eighteen.

'A word,' said South.

'What?'

'You had a party here yesterday.'

'So?' the boy said warily.

'There was a young woman here called Zoë.'

The man took off his helmet and put it on the petrol tank. He was good-looking, dark-eyed and deliberately unshaven.

'I don't know all the names of the girls that were here. News got around, you know?' He talked slowly as if he couldn't be bothered to hurry the words out.

'Were you providing the Class A drugs, or did someone else bring them?'

The boy didn't miss a beat. 'I don't remember there being any drugs at all,' he said. He smiled at South; the young and the rich thought nothing could touch them.

South stared into his eyes. 'Which is odd. Because you took photos of your guests taking drugs.'

The young man's gaze flickered for a second.

'I didn't. I suppose someone might have.'

South nodded slowly.

'Let's hope they don't make it onto the internet then.

You being a young man who probably knows about these things would know that any photos your friends take on a smartphone would probably have location data on them, wouldn't you?'

'Yes,' said the youngster. 'I mean . . .'

'And your mother's a magistrate, I understand.'

The boy nodded.

'Location data can be pretty accurate these days.'

'Right.'

'Word to the wise.' South leaned forward. 'It would be in your interest to contact everyone who came to your party and insist they delete their photos. OK? Imagine what the local press would make of it.'

'Right,' said the boy again, sounding less cool by the second.

'I'd get straight on to that, if I were you. Call up everyone you know and beg them not to put anything they took at your party that shows anyone doing anything illegal onto the internet, OK? Tell them that it's for their own protection.'

'Right. Um, thanks.'

South winked. 'And I wouldn't tell them that a copper told you to do this. That would be embarrassing, wouldn't it?'

The boy giggled nervously. He suddenly looked quite young.

'And between you and me, a colleague of mine is monitoring the social media of some of the girls who turned up here last night. And if they post anything that's relating to the party, it's going to come straight back to you.'

The boy nodded.

'Good lad,' said South, and continued to stare at the young man as he waited for the gate to open.

And he felt pleased with himself. Smug even. He had enjoyed the power he wielded, for that second. And in his pocket, his phone vibrated but he didn't want to look at it in case it spoiled the moment.

The moment did not last long. He was just returning to his car when he heard footsteps behind him. He turned; lit by street lamps, Vinnie Sleight was striding towards him.

'Sergeant South? What are you doing in our neighbourhood?'

'Your neighbourhood, Vinnie?'

'This isn't your usual sort of area. I know it isn't.'

'Complaints of noise. At a party,' South lied.

Sleight squinted at him. He seemed to be considering what South had said. 'But like I said, this isn't your patch, is it? Is there something else going on that I should know about?'

South ignored the question. 'Did you hear any noise of a party? Last night?'

Sleight wrinkled his nose and shook his head. 'It's the trouble with people round here. They think they've bought the whole area.' He smiled.

'It was teenagers, from the sound of it. Your son's back from college, isn't he? Maybe I could ask him?'

'I don't approve of snooping,' said Sleight, eyes narrowing.

'It's my job.'

Sleight stared at him. He stepped closer. 'I'm not sure it is your job, Sergeant. Why aren't you in uniform?'

And as he leaned forward, South saw something vicious in his expression, and caught the hint of orange in his aftershave. Just for a second. And then Sleight's face was calm again.

The roaring came from far away, pulsating and low. His first reaction was annoyance; the sound would scare the birds away. But as he looked, the pure white buzzard launched itself from a fence post on the hillside opposite, heading high into the air, hovering for just a second, then dropping away out of sight behind a rocky outcrop.

He saw it long enough to be sure. An albino. A freak.

He raised his face into the drizzle and felt the rain dropping on the balls of his eyes.

The racket was suddenly closer now, no longer a single continuous brash note, but a noise broken into little tiny pieces, an angry stuttering. Billy's heart beat faster.

He could not make any sense of it. He looked around but couldn't see the source, only knew that it was coming towards him.

And then from behind the crest of the ridge, the rotors appeared, then the bulbous nose of the army helicopter. It was close; only a couple of hundred yards away.

He ducked straight down again, flattening his body into the grass as the machine rose up, not daring to look for showing the white of his face, but surely it must have been above him now. All round him the wildest wind he had ever been in was knocking the grass round him flat in ripples, spreading away from him.

The rush of air froze him, pinning him to the ground. The noise was unbearable. The chopper seemed to hang above him, stationary, for minutes. He thought of raptors hovering above prey, waiting to kill. They are silent at least; an owl could swoop without making even the noise of a single wingbeat. This made his whole body shake.

And then the machine peeled suddenly away to his left, lifting itself a little higher, and hung there for another few seconds before its tail raised slightly and the whole beast started to move forwards again, back the way it had come.

The noise diminished. Only when his muscles un-tensed did he realise how frightened he was in those seconds. A scared mouse.

Have they seen him? He is not sure.

TWENTY-ONE

Did Sleight register the look of shock as everything fell into place?

He looked up. Sleight's own face was blank. Behind him, the figure was at the window of his house again, watching. South breathed in. 'Excuse me a minute, Mr Sleight,' he said, as calmly as he could. 'I just need to check this message.'

'Why don't you come round now?' said Sleight, unsmiling. 'Nice cup of tea.'

South took the phone from his pocket and swiped the screen.

'Something stronger if you like.'

It was a message from the woman who had loved Bob: 'HE SEEN U WATCHING US'.

But he hadn't been watching them. He had simply been in the area by chance. Until that moment, he hadn't known that was where the woman who had called herself Gill Rayner had lived. Sleight must have seen him walking up and down the lane, waiting outside his house. Sleight was the one.

He glanced back at the window, but the figure had gone. He knew who it was now.

'I would love to come round,' said South, as evenly as he could. 'But in five minutes, OK?'

His phone vibrated again.

'Don't go, Bill,' said Sleight, looking around, as if checking whether South was alone. 'Stroke of luck you being here. I've got a few things I need to talk about.'

Cautiously, South dropped his eyes down to the screen: 'HE HAS GUN'. He blinked. 'Maybe later tonight. I just have a couple of things to do.'

'I don't think this can wait,' said Sleight. 'I'll show you what I mean if you come round to my house.'

South looked back at his car. There was no point just following him into the house; he would be walking into a situation he didn't fully understand. He needed to call the police; to get an armed unit here as soon as he could.

'Give me ten minutes,' said South, trying to smile. This was the man who had killed his friend. He was sure of it now.

The phone went again. This time he didn't even conceal his glance at the illuminated screen: 'PLEASE!!! HELP US'.

He could feel the tension between them; each unsure how much the other knew.

Sleight frowned. 'Who are you texting?'

South shook his head and said, 'It's just work. Nothing important.' But before the words were out, his eyes had betrayed him. It was just for a tiny part of a second, a fraction of a glance up at the window of the bungalow where the woman stood again. 'Why don't you come with me, instead?' said South, trying to make it sound like everything was fine and they were just at one of their quarterly Neighbourhood Panel meetings. 'I really think you should.'

'I don't think so,' said Sleight. And slowly he turned to look at his house. The figure at the window darted behind the curtain. Had Sleight seen South's eyes move? Had he given her away?

And then Sleight smiled too. 'Come round another time then, OK?'

And he turned and headed calmly back towards the house.

'Stop,' shouted South. 'Vincent Sleight. I order you to stop.' But Sleight carried on walking.

The moment Sleight was back inside the gate, South dialled her number.

The woman answered straight away.

He said, 'He's coming back. Get out of there.'

'I can't,' she whispered. 'He's already in the house. I just heard him come in.'

'And you're sure he has a gun?'

'Yes. He got it out when he saw you first. You've got to help us,' she said.

'Why didn't you tell me? You knew it was him all along, that first day at Bob's house.'

'I'm scared,' she said. 'He's my husband.'

'Who else is in the house?'

'Our son. Cameron. He's in his bedroom. He's playing a game. I tried to call him just now, but I think he's got his headphones on.'

'Get him and then leave the house.' He was at the gate, crouching behind the post.

'It's too late,' she said, so quietly that he could barely hear. 'He's here.'

And then the house went black; all its lights went off at once.

'What happened?' she said, her voice suddenly loud and high. 'He's switched the lights off.'

'Keep calm. You need to move,' said South. 'I'm coming in, but you know the house better than I do. Get out of a window. Anything. Any way you can.'

'I can't leave my son with him.' She was crying now.

'You have to.' He was keeping his voice even. 'I will look after your son. I promise.'

'It's too late,' she whispered.

'No. It's not. If you're inside, you're in danger.'

Her voice dropped lower. 'Outside our bedroom door. I can hear him.' He could hear the breath in her voice; it was as if she was right next to him.

'Talk to him. Be calm. Tell him everything will be OK.'

'He's not like that,' she said. 'He's angry with me. He says all this is my fault. I've ruined everything. I have to go. He's here now.'

He heard another voice; it was controlled and even. 'Who are you talking to, Gail, love?'

'Hello, Vinnie,' she said. 'I was just . . .'

'Don't end the call. Keep talking,' said South; but she had already done it. All he heard now was a long beep.

He ran towards the house, phoning the station as he did so. They picked up straight away.

'Don't interrupt. Just listen. Get this to OPS-one. Armed response required,' he was saying, repeating his name, rank and warrant number into the phone as he entered the gateway. Using all the right words. Trying to sound as normal as possible in order to get things done. What was the address? the woman asked. He had visited the house, but couldn't remember the name. 'Ridge Lane. Registered home of Vincent Sleight.' He spelled out the last name.

'Say again.'

But there was no time.

Unless you're close to them, the noise of a shotgun is not loud. Muffled by the walls of a house, this was only a dull thump. But it was unmistakeably a gunshot.

All the curtains and blinds were closed. Inside, blackness and silence.

To the left, a swimming pool and a guest house. To the right a huge, four-car garage.

He tried the front door. It was locked, of course.

'Sleight. Let me in.'

He heard a voice say, 'Dad. Why have all the lights gone off? I was on the computer and then it . . .'

'Get back in your room,' South shouted through the

door. He could see nothing. He pushed the door with his shoulder, but it wouldn't shift. There had to be another entrance.

He ran to the garage but the swing door was locked. Desperate now, he hurried round to the back door on the opposite side of the house. That too was locked. So was the side entrance towards the back of the garage.

There was a water butt on the side of the garage. He grabbed the downpipe and hauled himself onto the metal barrel, switched on the torch on his phone and shone it through the high window that ran along the wall.

Inside were three cars. A white SUV, a grey Audi estate and a green Polo. Gill Rayner's car. The one he had seen outside Bob Rayner's house; the one he had seen at the supermarket. There was a door from the garage into the house, but apart from the locked swing door, there was no other way into the garage.

Holding his phone in his mouth he tried to prise the window open, but it was locked.

Shit. He was losing precious time.

Jumping down he ran back to the front door again, pressed his face against it and shone the light through the glass. An empty hallway; a huge vase of dried grass by a doorway. No sign of anyone.

Then he thumped on the door with the side of his fist. 'Sleight,' he shouted. 'Open the door.'

Nothing. The house felt deserted; but it couldn't be. Somebody moved. 'Dad?'

'Get out of the house,' South shouted through the door.

There, leaning against the porch wall was a bag of golf clubs. He pulled out a driver and, in the limited space he had, swung it at the bevelled glass. The first impact bounced straight off, but the second cracked it. A third smashed through.

Reaching through he found a Yale lock and twisted it. Luckily there was no mortice; the door swung open. He was in. He stood for a few seconds, listening, eyes adjusting to the dark.

'Police,' he shouted.

No answer.

'Cameron. Can you hear me?'

The house seemed oddly silent. What had happened to the boy? He tried the light switch. Nothing.

There were four doors off the hallway. All were shut except for one, slightly open. He didn't know the house. Trying to navigate it in the dark would put him at a disadvantage to anyone who lived here.

He tried to remember what he knew about the layout. He had been to Sleight's house once; to check on Sleight's gun safe. It was in the basement, he remembered. He guessed that's where the fuse box would be.

If he was right, that was the door that had been left slightly open. Pulling it back he shone his phone down into the black.

'Hello?' he called.

Taking a breath, he walked down the steep stairs. The basement was large. There was a dartboard and a table-tennis table down there, and an old sofa against the wall. A draught blew through it; there must be some ventilation to keep the place dry, he figured.

At the back of the room, the gun safe was built into the wall. Its door was wide open. He tried to remember how many guns Sleight had had. Was it one, or two? He was shining his torch around the walls to try and find the fuse box when the door at the top of the stairs closed.

Shit.

'Who's that?'

No answer. The room was instantly still. The draught he had felt had stopped. He raced to the top of the stairs, club in his hand, expecting to find the door locked, but it wasn't. Cautiously he emerged into the hallway. Wind gusted through the front door. It must have just been that breeze, he supposed, that had slammed the door on him.

He stopped again to listen. The house was bizarrely quiet. What had happened to the son?

He looked at his watch. How long would it take for the police to arrive? In theory an armed unit was always ready to move, but there were protocols. The Ops One officer would have had to sign off on it.

Golf club still in his right hand, he turned left into the living room. He remembered; he had not been invited into it when he visited last time.

The living room seemed empty. He looked around.

She was there above the mantelpiece. The woman he had met as Gill Rayner. In a family portrait, painted more than competently in oils, she was there in the centre. He shone his light on her. This was not the dowdy middle-aged woman he had met at Rayner's house; here she wore a low-cut bright green dress and wide smile. This was the trophy wife of a successful businessman. Sleight was behind her, grinning in an open-necked brightly striped shirt, his hand laid on her shoulder. Moving the torch beam to the right, it fell on a dark-haired boy who looked about fourteen, standing in front of them. It must have been painted a few years ago; the boy was at least twenty-one now.

The room which this happy family looked out onto was comfortable, wealthy. There was a cut-glass decanter full of some spirit on a table, a flower print on the wall.

And then, unmistakeably, the sound of a door closing. South tensed.

He inched back to the hallway. Head back against the wall, he called, 'Who's there?'

Nothing.

At the top of his voice, he shouted, 'Armed police are on their way. Show yourself.'

There was a long corridor that ran down through the centre of the house. Keeping flat against the wall, he edged down it, trying to guess which door would be the master bedroom's.

He dialled again. It rang. At the end of the dark corridor a song started to play. '*Some day, when I'm awfully low . . .*'

Fred Astaire's voice was coming from the room at the end of the corridor. It was her ringtone, he realised.

'*When the world is cold . . .*'

He moved towards the door, golf club raised, pressing himself up against the wall. With his left hand, he twisted the handle and then kicked the door open.

'*And the way you look tonight . . .*'

Was he still in there with her? He had to risk it.

'*Yes you're lovely . . . Never ever change . . .*'

He stood in the room, holding his phone in front of him to create a dim light. Her phone was shining too as it sang. In their pale light, the redness shone. She was in a yellow dress, lying on her back, eyes open wide, on the double bed.

The white linen around her was dark with blood. Her hands lay on the deep cavity of where her stomach would have been; all soft tissue had simply been blasted away. Sleight must have held the gun close when he pulled the trigger. She would have bled to death in a matter of a minute or two.

The phone she had called him with was still on the bed, close to her hand, playing its tune. He switched off his phone. She must have known she was about to die.

He reached out and took her hand. It was still as soft and as warm as if she had still been alive.

Poor Gill. She had loved Bob; Bob had loved her. She was dead, and he had not been in time to save her. If he had been cleverer, he could have. He felt the weight of it, heavy on him. Both lovers were dead now.

But if not from in here, where had the noise he had heard come from? He dropped her hand back onto the bed and moved out again into the hallway.

Stupid.

Sleight would know exactly where he was. He should have looked before he'd gone back out there.

The doorway opposite was Cameron's room, he guessed. When he'd last seen it, the door had been closed. It was open now.

'Vincent,' he said.

No answer.

'I know you're in there.'

A slight creaking sound. He moved forward.

'You need help, Vincent. Please let me help.'

Nothing.

'You're upset. Your wife was having an affair. It must have been a shock to you.'

He caught a glimpse of something moving; shining the torch he saw a small glinting figure-of-eight and in that second realised he was staring at the twin barrels of a shotgun.

He jolted right and started to sprint for the front door, expecting the explosion at any second. The door was swinging open in front of him. He dived through space, straight onto the porch floor just as the gun fired. Wood and glass sprayed onto his back.

He scrabbled back onto his hands and knees, then

330

upright, and ran towards the pool, ducking into the shadows on the far side of the house.

His brain felt sluggish. Think, he told himself. Think. It was a twin-barrel hunting gun. There would be another round in the other barrel. Or was there another weapon too?

Pressing himself back against the wall of the house, he heard steps on the gravel to his left. What had happened to the boy? He remembered what Cupidi had said at the start of all this. *Someone who literally cannot control themselves, or doesn't want to. Someone who is so consumed by anger they cannot stop.* Cautiously he peered round the corner.

Lit in the orange of the street light, Sleight was calmly opening the gun. He pulled out a cartridge and slotted another round into the empty barrel, then turned towards where South was hiding.

'Stay in the fucking house,' Sleight shouted over his shoulder.

Who was he talking to? His son of course. Cameron. The university child. The Cambridge boy Sleight had always been so proud of. Where was he now? He must be terrified.

South shrunk himself into the darkness; but a light came on in the James Bond house, shining on the pool and illuminating his darkened corner.

'Come out, Bill,' said Sleight. 'Not going to hurt you.'

South stayed as still as he could. The empty swimming pool was in front of him. If he fell into that, he would be trapped. To his right was the guest house which was joined to the main house.

If Sleight rounded the corner, he would be able to see him. If he ran to the left, he would be heading straight towards Sleight. If he moved to the right side of the pool he would have to run alongside the far edge, by the guest house. He would come into view after just a couple of paces. For fifteen yards, until he made it into the blackness of the garden beyond, he would be an easy target.

'Come on, Bill. Things have just got a bit confused. You and me got to talk, like you said. You know me. You can trust me.'

He stayed as still as he could, calculating. The police would be here soon. Could he risk waiting?

The wind made it hard to make out footsteps.

And then, lit by the street lamp behind him, Sleight rounded the corner, gun at waist height. He looked South in the eye, then raised the gun.

A shout. 'Dad. No.'

In Sleight's flicker of hesitation, South took his chance. He sprang away to his right, up alongside the pool. He heard the gun boom and simultaneously felt the crackle of shot pellets around him, but didn't stop to look back. As he reached the end of the pool, the gun fired a second time but this time the miss must have been wider. How? It was hard to miss with a shotgun. That was the point. Rather than a single bullet, they emitted a cone of pellets that sprayed out, catching everything. Sleight must have shot wide. His luck was in.

At least he would have a couple of seconds while Sleight reloaded.

Then, as his ears got used to the ringing that that shot had caused, he realised someone was screaming in pain, but it was not him. He squatted behind one of the small conifers that dotted the lawn and took a second to look around and figure out what had happened.

Looking back at the house, he saw, sprawled on the gravel in front of it, a dark shape, lit by the neighbour's security lights.

It hadn't been him that Sleight had fired at the second time. The son was lying on the ground a few feet away from Sleight, his arms moving slowly, as if swimming, but going nowhere. It was him who had taken the second shot.

Sleight seemed to have pockets full of shells. He had cracked the gun open already and was methodically reloading. Before South understood what he was doing, he had lifted the gun, and was pointing it at the body on the ground.

South had speed at least. As he ran, Sleight must have heard him because he looked up. By now South had gathered pace and was sprinting in his direction. Sleight was just beginning to swing the barrels up towards South, away from the man on the ground, when South hit him, knocking him flat.

'Dad,' said the sprawling man. 'Dad.'

South had no time to process the horror of it, of the fact that Sleight had just tried to kill his own son, because Sleight was on the ground now too, next to him, kicking hard as South clutched his waist. South was trying to look upwards at him, attempting to see where the gun was, if there was any chance of grabbing it, when Sleight's shoe caught him on the bridge of his nose. Once. Then twice.

Though Sleight held the gun, South was too close – and the shotgun too long – for him to aim the barrels at South's head. For anyone watching, South realised, there would have been something almost comical about their struggle, had it not been so deadly. Sleight writhed to try and put enough distance between him and South so he could get a shot in. South, the stronger of the two, grasped Sleight's waist, clinging on as hard as he could.

'Fuck off,' screamed Sleight.

As long as there was a small space between them, he was safe. But he had to try and get the gun. Sleight's shoe kicked his face again. He couldn't hold on much longer.

With no time to think, he let go of Sleight to try and grab the barrel of the gun, but knew it was a mistake the instant he'd done it. It gave Sleight the freedom to yank his body back. The barrel swung wildly. South's hand grabbed air instead of metal. With a loud crack, the gun went off again, but the first shot went wide, spraying gravel onto the lawn ten yards away.

South lunged again for the gun, knocking it upwards just

in time as the second barrel exploded, this time smashing a window above him.

Again, two shots. Sleight would have to reload. That gave him a few seconds.

South tried to get to his feet to throw himself onto Sleight again, but as he did so, the young man grabbed his arm, holding him back. 'Help me,' he pleaded.

With Cameron clutching him, instead of catching Sleight, he clawed at empty air.

Sleight was getting to his feet.

South turned and shouted, 'Let go,' but when he looked back again, Sleight had vanished. South twisted his head round to the left and right.

Shit. Shit. Shit. Where had he gone? He would be reloading his gun.

His first thought was to get the wounded man indoors. But what if Sleight had gone inside himself? To be safe, he needed to know where Sleight had gone.

'What's going on?'

A woman's voice from the road beyond the gate.

South looked up. A woman was standing in the road, her back to the street light. 'Police. Get back in your house,' shouted South.

South scooped Sleight's son up and, stumbling with the weight of him, headed to the gate where the woman was standing. He recognised her; it was Olivia Gemmell, the JP.

'Come on,' he shouted. 'Get inside.'

South looked back just in time to see Sleight emerging

from the light of the house behind him with the gun raised.

The woman seemed to stand there, reluctant to give any ground.

'Run,' he screamed at her. The boy cried out, wide-eyed, in shock from the pain. There was no time to get into his car. The James Bond house was their closest shelter. He heard a roar of anger from behind him.

'What's going on, Mr Sleight?' called Mrs Gemmell towards him. 'Is there a burglar?'

'He's got a gun,' shouted South, struggling to run towards her with the young man in his arms.

She hesitated, trying to make sense of the situation, and was still standing rooted to the spot as South passed her. With the young man's weight, every pace seemed like an effort.

'Vincent?' the woman said. 'Is this man bothering you?'

South made it down the short driveway towards her house and the open front door and he turned to scream at her to follow, one last time, just as the gun fired.

The shot hit Mrs Gemmell's head, snapping it backwards. Her dead body dropped straight backwards out of sight.

South tore himself from the horror of what he was seeing. He had to get the boy to safety. He manoeuvred himself through the massive door, the bleeding boy in his arms.

He turned. They were inside and he went to lock the door.

336

When he stepped back, Sleight was at the gate. He stood with the gun, panting, looking at them through the big glass walls.

'Fuck you,' he mouthed, then refilled the empty chamber.

The only thing separating him from Sleight was a sheet of glass. It would be no protection.

From behind him, a door opened. A pale boy in low-slung underpants came out, yawning. It was the boy on the motorbike. He looked at South and the young man in his arms and said, 'Jesus. Cameron. What's wrong?' The half-naked boy looked around. 'Where's Mum? What are you doing here?'

Somewhere down the hill South noticed the bare winter trees were being lit by distant blue flashes. The police were coming at last. But it would be too late.

'Get back,' he shouted.

With a tremendous bang, the entire glass wall seemed to turn pale. The shattered glass hung for a microsecond, then dropped, scattering onto the bare floor.

He could hear Sleight clearly now. 'Fuck you all,' he shouted, and pointed the gun directly at South.

It was as if they were suddenly in the open; the roar of the wind was on them. The room where they were standing was effectively now just part of the garden. And for the first time South could hear the sirens too, getting closer, but still too far away.

South watched Sleight, hair matted against his scalp by the rain, tightening his finger on the trigger, the gun pointed at South's head. Sleight was going to kill them all, starting with him.

But he didn't. Sleight heard the distant wail of sirens and stopped. He stepped forward, still pointing the gun at South.

'Inside,' he shouted. 'Everyone.'

For a second, South was puzzled. They were already inside, even with the window smashed down.

Then he realised that Sleight wanted them to move further into the house, out of sight of the approaching police. Holding the wounded young man, South looked around. The room was open plan. A dining room and living room all in one. But there were two doors leading off it.

'Get in there,' Sleight shouted, nodding towards the door nearest them.

The boy from the house looked paralysed with fear. 'Where's Mum?' he asked again.

'What's in there?' South shouted.

'Kitchen,' he said. 'Is she OK?'

'Move!' screamed Sleight.

South led the way, moving sideways through the door. 'Do as he says.'

'He's going to kill us,' whispered Cameron Sleight.

The kitchen was large, set around a huge marble island. As gently as he could, he laid Cameron down on the stone floor. Sleight closed the door behind them.

'Everybody get down,' Sleight shouted, waving the gun.

The young man winced, clutching his leg. This was the first time South had had a chance to look at him. The leg was bleeding, but from the amount of blood South guessed the shot had flayed muscle, but didn't appear to have damaged any major blood vessels. He would live, he guessed.

'My mum's dead,' Cameron whispered. 'Isn't she?'

South nodded. He was trying to remember everything he knew about hostage situations. He had had a briefing once about them but had assumed he would never have to use any of that knowledge. He was just a neighbourhood cop, after all. What were you supposed to do? These first minutes were the vital moments when you were supposed to take any chance you could to escape, he remembered, before they were trapped here as hostages. But Cameron could almost certainly not walk much, if at all. He could not just leave him and the other boy here. They would be killed.

Sleight opened the door a crack, looking into the living room.

'You stupid cunt,' he was saying. 'This is all your fucking fault. Everything is your fault.'

'What's happening? Tell me what's happening,' cried the half-naked boy.

South said nothing; he was looking around to work out where they were, work out where the exits were.

Outside, he heard cars skid to a halt and cut their sirens; over the rising wind he could hear the instant chatter of radios, the crunch of boots. The police were finally here; they would be trying to work out what had happened. Sleight's house was dark, but this one was blazing with light.

Had they brought a firearms unit? He couldn't be sure. If not, it would be here soon, when they saw Mrs Gemmell's body sprawled out on the road.

Sleight had opened the kitchen door a crack, looking out. South spoke. 'Give yourself up, Vinnie. It's the only thing.'

'Shut your mouth,' said Sleight, not taking his eyes off the scene outside.

'Dad,' said the boy. 'You shot me.'

'You knew, all along,' said Sleight.

'Shh,' whispered South. 'Don't talk.'

'You killed Mum.'

South raised his finger to his lips.

Hadn't he grown up knowing that this was what men could be? He knew this rage and fear. His father had had it; and he had, too.

Without even realising, South had backed Sleight into a corner. When backed into a corner, these men became monsters. They did terrible things. He knew that. Sleight had killed his own wife, he had killed Bob and would have killed his own son if his aim had been better. It would not stop here. The presence of the police outside would only make things worse.

Sleight turned. 'Is there a back door?' he demanded.

The boy sitting on the floor looked confused.

South repeated the question in a quieter voice.

'End of this corridor,' the boy said.

'You,' Sleight said, pointing at South. 'Go take a look. See where it goes. No more than ten seconds. Or I kill the boy.'

'Don't kill me,' cried the boy. Sitting on the cold floor, shaking, the boy was panting so hard he could barely breathe. He was panicking. He would have to be calm or Sleight would find his own way to shut him up.

'What's your name?' asked South.

'Axel,' he said.

'Axel. It's OK. The police are outside. Everything will be OK,' he said, though he doubted it would. 'Trust me.'

'Fucking go,' shouted Sleight.

South stood and walked slowly, as calmly as he could, down the corridor and out of sight.

A single door with a key in it. He turned it and pushed the door open and looked at the quiet darkness beyond. Behind the house was the golf course. Maybe Sleight was planning on trying to escape, to lose the police there. The police hadn't made it to the back of the house yet; they had seen the body. That had altered the rules of engagement. They would now need a clear plan; clear orders on the use of weapons. All this would happen fast, but it would still take precious minutes. They wouldn't approach the back of the house until they were sure it was safe to do so.

He himself could run now, he thought, leaving the others behind. That way, at least, the police outside would know what they were facing. But Sleight would then kill those who were left behind, he was sure of it.

In the darkness of the corridor, he took his phone from his pocket and texted DI McAdam's number: '*1 man with shotgun. Pass intel to Ops 1.*'

He took a last breath, put the phone on silent, locked the door again, turned and went back, still walking slowly, trying to look calmer than he felt. 'Door into the back garden,' he said. 'The key's in it.'

Sleight nodded.

'Can they see through it?'

'No. It's wood. At the moment there's no one there.'

'Bollocks. You're trying to trick me.'

'No. I promise. There's no one. You could escape if you wanted to.'

'Close the blinds,' Sleight said.

A long window ran down one side of the kitchen. If the police could not see in, they would not be able to assess the situation. South hesitated.

'The back is clear. The police aren't there yet. You'd have a clear run out onto the golf course if you leave now.'

Sleight turned away from his crack in the door and pointed the gun at South again. 'Don't you start telling me what to do.'

South raised his arms. 'I'm not.'

'Shut the fucking curtains, then get on the floor.' He was staying. Which meant this could only end with more blood.

South walked over to the blinds and started to draw them, taking his time.

When he'd finished, he sank down on the floor between Cameron and Axel.

'Your dad's gone fucking nuts,' said Axel.

Cameron nodded.

'How's the leg?' South asked.

'Fucking hurts.'

'What are they doing?' said Sleight.

'They'll take their time,' said South, from his position on the floor. 'They'll be wanting to assess the situation. Establish a chain of command. In a minute, the phone here will go.'

'You answer it. Talk to them. Tell them I've a gun. Tell them I'll kill you if they try to kill me. And the boy.'

Axel started to sob.

But the phone didn't ring yet. Nothing happened. Each slow second seemed like an age.

The thin sun emerged on the skyline of the mountain above him, warming him a little. He thought of his mother and of the way she hugged him. And then he must have slept. Because a voice was saying, 'Billy. Wake up.'

And someone was shaking him.

He looked up and there was Sergeant Ferguson in his peaky cap, but he had no jacket on and his shirt was half untucked, flapping in the wind.

'I guessed you'd be here. I told them that's where they should look. The helicopter spotted you. I ran up here ahead but there are soldiers coming after me. So we have to be quick.' He was panting as if he had run hard.

Billy wished he had tried harder not to be caught.

'Glad I got here before they did.'

He looked down and realised Sergeant Ferguson's jacket was wrapped around him tightly to keep him warm.

'I saw it, Fergie,' Billy said. 'Only it wasn't what people thought.'

Ferguson didn't seem interested. 'Where is the gun? Tell me, lad. The gun that shot your dad?'

Fergie knew. He was so ashamed of himself.

'Quick. Before anyone gets here. I had to run like fuck to get here first. My heart is going to bloody explode. Tell me, God's sake, it's important.'

'The gun?' Billy's brain was sand.

'Please, Billy. I can save you both if you do this.'

'Save me?' Billy was surprised to hear how little strength there was left in his voice.

Ferguson leaned in closer. 'Save you and your mother. I don't want to see her go to jail.'

'Why should she go to jail?' asked Billy, bemused.

'That's what I say. I understand what she did. None of it was her fault. She's been through enough. It was him or her. I know that. That's why I want you to tell me where the gun is.'

What was he on about? Billy didn't understand. 'Down the drain,' said Billy.

344

'Where? Was it you got rid of it?'

Billy nodded. He could hear more voices now, shouting.

'It wasn't her fault Billy. You don't have to run from her.'

'From her?'

'Sometimes we have to do bad things, Billy. Especially times like this. You'll understand when you're older. She thinks the fucken world of you, Billy.'

The thin policeman reached down and placed his hands under Billy's armpits to lift him.

'I have to tell you this, Billy. You know that your father was not a good man, Billy. You have to understand that. He was a killer. I figured it out, you see. It took me a while. It wasn't anyone else. It was him killed those Catholics. Must have been.'

'But—'

'It's the truth.'

And with what seemed like an enormous effort, Ferguson lifted him up, his jacket wrapped around him.

The shouting was getting closer. 'Over here. The copper's got him.'

'So if it was the same gun that killed him, it must have been his own gun. I didn't want to believe it at first. And if it was his gun that killed him it had to be someone who could find the gun. God knows, she had reason enough to do it. I've always known . . . And you have to understand too, OK?'

'But . . .'

'Which drain? Quick. Before they come. Which drain?'

The soldiers were running, bounding over the uneven ground.

'I can make everything better if you let me know where the gun is.'

'I saw the bird, Fergie.'

'Never mind the fucken bird, Billy. I don't care about the bird.'

Billy looked at him. A grown man in tears. Why is that? What is wrong with the man? 'At the back of the house.'

The soldiers were here now, all around.

'A drain at the back of your house?'

Billy nodded.

'Good lad,' said Fergie, and gave him a wink.

And then they were all around him, rubbing him on the back, shouting orders. The squaddies took him from Sergeant Ferguson and two of them made a fireman's chair, crossing arms, while a third placed Billy on it. 'He's got exposure, I think,' said Ferguson.

'We'll get him down. Stand back.' To Billy they said, 'Grab on, laddie.' And placed his arms around the two soldiers' necks.

'Got the poor little bastard, Sarge.'

Billy said, 'They got it all wrong. It wasn't what they said it was.'

'What's the lad saying?'

'Nothing,' said Fergie. 'He's delirious. Get him warm, quick.'

The Englishmen's accents seemed so strange and alien.

Next thing he was off at a lick, the soldiers striding fast back down the mountain, bumping up and down.

When Billy stretched his neck to look round at Fergie, he was standing there with a strange smile on his face and a finger up to his lips.

It was the last time he ever saw him.

TWENTY-TWO

Sleight was still at the door trying to see the police outside.

'What are they doing?' Sleight called.

'I don't know.'

South leaned down to Cameron. 'Are you OK?' he whispered.

'My dad killed Bob, didn't he?'

'Yes,' said South.

'I liked Bob,' said Cameron. 'He was a nice man. He got me into uni.'

'Yes,' said South. 'He was my friend. I liked him a lot.'

Cameron nodded. 'My leg really hurts.'

'I know it does,' said South. 'You're doing great. Bob was your teacher, then?'

Cameron nodded. 'My tutor. He used to live in the guest house. He was like part of the family.'

'He loved your mother. Did you know that?'

'They tried to hide it. I knew. I don't think Dad ever did. He's God's gift. Why would she love anyone else? They were childhood sweethearts, my mum and dad. Before he ever got money. There are photos in their bedroom. A couple of teenagers. He always said he did all this for her.'

'What are you talking about?' shouted Sleight, still at the door, trying to look out.

'I need to put a bandage on him. He's still bleeding.'

'No talking,' Sleight shouted. 'I can't see them. What are they doing?'

'They'll be getting in position around the house,' said South. 'I expect they'll be at the back by now.'

And then the phone finally rang.

'Pick it up,' said Sleight. 'Bring it here.'

It was a modern phone, all black, on a silver stand, a red light pulsing as it rang.

Standing, South picked up the phone, still ringing, and walked towards Sleight, holding it out. If he took it, South might have a chance to grab the shotgun, but Sleight seemed to have made that calculation already. 'Answer it,' he said, raising the shotgun and pointing it at South's head. 'Tell them who you are. Then give me the phone.'

He did exactly as Sleight said. 'This is Sergeant William South. Kent Police.'

'Now give it to me. Slowly.'

He passed the phone to Sleight, who took it with his left hand, gun still aimed at South.

'Stand here, Bill. Don't budge.'

'If I stand between you and the police, you don't have to keep looking round at me.'

Sleight squinted. 'What are you trying to pull, Bill?'

'Nothing, Vinnie. I just want things to go OK.'

Sleight shouted into the phone, 'I've got a gun pointed at your copper's head. Come near and I'll fucking kill him, OK? And then the rest.'

And he ended the call.

'That it?' said South.

'For now,' said Sleight.

And the phone started ringing again, but Sleight ignored it.

The phone kept ringing and ringing. South stood with his back to the half-open kitchen door. He had made himself a human shield. This way Sleight didn't have to turn his back to keep an eye on him, and the police would be able to see him; that way, at least, the gun was not pointing at the two boys. The barrels of the gun were pressed against South's forehead. He felt oddly calm for someone about to die.

Overhead he heard a helicopter. Light blared suddenly through the blinded windows.

'Why are you fucking smiling?'

'Know what? I just remembered something from when I was a boy,' said South. A scared little boy up on a mountain. He was not scared any more, though.

'Well, don't.'

'You killed Judy Farouk too, didn't you?'

A whisper. 'Fuck off.'

'Why? Because she'd seen your wife with Bob? That's

what happened, wasn't it? She was walking her dogs at Dungeness and she saw your wife going into Bob's house.'

Sleight said nothing.

'How did she know you? I don't understand. Was she trying to blackmail you?'

'Judy wasn't a blackmailer.'

'So you did know her, then?'

'You don't understand anything.'

'But when she told you, you killed her and you dumped her body at sea. You seemed to know how to do it. Have you done it before?'

'Fuck off.'

'You know what? I bet you have.'

Inside South's pocket, his phone started vibrating. They would be trying to call him on that, too. 'And poor Donny Fraser too.'

'Who?' Sleight was staring straight at him down the grey metal barrels of the gun.

'The homeless man. You framed him for Bob's killing.'

'Oh. Him. They know that, do they?'

'I do. They'll figure it out soon. It's over.'

'Fuck off.'

Afterwards the reports in the papers would have Vincent Sleight's picture. They would have quotes from colleagues and friends that would say, 'He was always so friendly to us. He invited us round for dinner. A lovely wife and son. We never had any idea.'

'You don't have to do any of this,' said South.

'Oh shut your dull stupid mouth,' said Sleight and with a vicious dig stabbed the barrels upwards into the skin they were resting on, knocking South backwards so his head hit the door jamb and he slid, dazed, onto the floor. He had a memory of his father's shiny boots.

'Get back up,' said Sleight.

The sound of a megaphone's feedback outside. South felt blood on his cheek from where the barrels had cut his skin.

'Hello. This is the police. My name is Michael. Tell us what you want in there. I'm going to call you now. Pick up the phone and we'll talk.'

Sleight started laughing.

Struggling back upright, South started laughing too. Michael would try and empathise. Those were the techniques. They would try and build a rapport. Fat chance.

The phone rang and Sleight didn't move to answer it. It kept ringing for a couple of minutes, then stopped.

'This is Michael. Please answer the phone. Then I can find out what you want.'

'I' and 'you'. Personal words and first names. These were the techniques they used to try and build empathy, but they would have no effect on Sleight. He had gone too far. He had done too much. There was no going back. This is what these men did. It would not be long before he did the calculation. There was no way out; he could never get away. He might as well kill them all.

While Sleight looked out of the door, South had a view of the kitchen behind him. Sitting with his back against the

352

kitchen island, Axel was crying quietly. The fear had made him wet his pants, the poor boy.

'Bob was my friend,' said South.

'You chose shit friends then.'

'He got your son into Cambridge. That's what you wanted, wasn't it?'

'I didn't ask him to fuck my wife. She had everything she bloody wanted. I gave her that.'

'That must have hurt a lot when Judy told you what she'd seen. They must have been very frightened of you to keep it quiet for so long.'

'So long?' Sleight's eyes narrowed slightly. 'Did he talk to you about it? Did he boast?'

'No. He never told me.'

Sleight chewed on his lip. 'Your mother,' he said to Cameron, 'was a lying bitch. Every fortnight she said she was going to see her poor bedridden sister. All that charade about looking after her since the stroke.'

'That's what she told you she was doing? Looking after her sister?'

'Like she actually cared. She made a big fuss about buying medicines for her. Bandages. Everything. And all the time she was fucking that useless old . . . old . . .'

South remembered the package of unused bandages in Bob's bin. It had been part of her decoy.

'So why did you kill Judy?' said South, as much to himself as to Sleight. He was trying to figure it out when the megaphone started again.

'Is anyone wounded in there. Do you need medical attention?'

That's when South noticed that Cameron was moving. He had a look on his face, half determination, half fury. Using the distraction of the megaphone's blare, he was forcing himself upright. The first time he slid back down again.

'Please let us help, Vincent.' First names. They had figured out who the man with the gun was.

The second time Cameron tried to lift himself, he caught hold of a drawer handle and started to pull himself upwards.

Converse. Keep him distracted. If he sees Cameron moving, he will kill him.

'You were watching me all along, weren't you?' he said to Sleight. 'You came to my house.'

'Wasn't sure how much you knew.'

'It was you, wasn't it? In my house?'

'I could have killed you then,' he said. 'Should have.'

With Sleight facing him, South kept his face as expressionless as he could. He had made that mistake once already tonight. His first thought was how he could tell Cameron to get back down. Stop him doing anything that would make his father even angrier. But he could say nothing, do nothing, as the boy pulled open the drawer he had lifted himself up on, then closed it again.

'Do you need medical attention?' repeated the megaphone.

The helicopter approached overhead again, adding to the noise.

Sleight was looking anxious for the first time; he shook his head quickly as if trying to clear his thoughts. They did not have long. He would be figuring out that he had no options. There was nothing left. He would kill them soon. With a growing sense of anxiety, South watched as Cameron found what he needed in the next drawer. If Sleight became any more restless he would look around. Any second now he would turn and see his own son, propping himself upright against the kitchen units. Keep your face straight. Show no emotion. Don't look at Cameron. Don't give him away. How could he keep Sleight focused on him?

'I killed a man once,' said South quietly.

For the first time in a few minutes, Sleight looked him in the eyes.

'With a pistol. He was as close to me as you are now. I just shot him in the head. Once.'

'You? You're shitting me,' said Sleight. 'You couldn't hurt a fly.'

'It was pretty terrible. But at the time, I thought there was no other way out.'

'You killed a man?'

'And you know what? They never found out.'

'You're making this up.'

'No.'

'Who was it?'

Empathy of a kind at last; one killer to another. Cameron was already halfway across the room now, leaving a smear of red behind him on the brown stone, the knife held at head height. Don't look. Don't even let your eyes flicker to the side.

'My own father,' said South. The first time he ever said it out loud.

'You killed your father?'

'I did.' Behind Sleight, he could sense Cameron's hesitation. He was holding the knife up, but would he have the guts to bring it down?

'Why?' asked Sleight.

'He was a bad man. He killed other people. At the time, I felt I had no choice. The only way I could be safe from him in the end was to kill him. And you know what? It was easy to do it.' The knife was still there, harmless in the air. The boy was hesitating. 'Do it,' he urged this time, louder.

By the time Sleight heard the movement behind him and went to turn, it was already too late. It was that slight stirring to the left that saved South's life. As Sleight swivelled to see what was happening behind him, the gun moved off South's head, just as the long kitchen knife stabbed into Sleight's collar, travelling down into the soft skin, slicing muscle and tissue and blood vessel. And though pellets tore at South's ear, the full blast of the gun smashed harmlessly into the plaster wall, and South just watched as Cameron yanked the knife back upwards, out of his father's wound, and the blood began to fountain outwards over them both.

Sleight lay quivering on the ground, dying, as the red spread out across the perfect kitchen floor.

South looked up and saw the boy's tears rolling down his cheeks, and he wanted to reach out and tell him that it would all be all right, but before he could say a word, the room was full of noise and smoke.

The stun grenades blinded them. Someone pushed South to the floor. He fell hard again, this time onto Sleight's trembling body and his spreading blood; and when he looked up, the room was full of men dressed all in black, holding automatic weapons, pointing them at Cameron and screaming, 'Drop it. Drop it. Drop it.'

And South was trying to scream back at them to leave the boy alone, but the air had been knocked out of him and he seemed to be making no sound at all. Beside him, Sleight's body stilled and his wide-open eyes, just inches from South's own, slowly dulled.

They took him to the hospital and fussed over him a while. Mum came and squeezed him and cried. She was dressed in the same clothes as she had been wearing yesterday; a yellow blouse with red flowers on it.

'I was so worried,' she said. 'Fergie dropped me here.'

'Is he here?' asked Billy, anxious.

'No. He left. He said he had something important to do.'

In borrowed pyjamas that were much too big for him,

he lay in a small iron bed painted white, a locker next to it with a jug of Robinsons Barley Water and a glass on it. They had curtains all around him. The nurses had taken his temperature and a doctor, who had called him a brave little soldier, had listened to his heart. They said he would be fine.

'Mum? Can I come home?' he asked.

'Of course you can!' And she looked shocked. 'Why wouldn't you?'

And he realised that Ferguson had said nothing at all to her, not yet at least.

She cried a little more and asked him, 'Why did you run away?'

He couldn't begin to tell her, so he said, 'I wanted to see the snowy owl. Only it was a buzzard.'

She laughed. 'You and your birds,' she said. 'I would have taken you, if you wanted. All you need to do is ask. I'll do anything for you, Billy.'

If she wanted to ask more, she didn't. If she knew that there was more to it, she was pretending that there wasn't. He could pretend too, if she liked.

They caught a taxi home, which was good because he didn't feel he had the strength to catch the bus. His legs felt like they were made of wood. When she paid, Billy saw that her purse was bulging with notes, and he frowned, but he said nothing.

'I'll give you soup, then straight to bed with you,' she said.

All this love and fuss and he deserved none of it. While she was opening a can of cream of tomato and putting it to heat on the stove he unlatched the back door.

'What are you doing?' she said, feeling the draught.

'Just looking,' he said.

'What would you be looking at out there, you daft boy?'

'Nothing.'

It was mild outside. There, beyond the concrete of the back yard, was the drain cover.

'What's wrong, poppet?' his mother asked.

'Nothing,' he said again. He looked closer. Next to the cast iron manhole cover, blades of grass were bent and trapped under the lid.

'Stay inside,' she said. 'I'm not having you running off up the mountains again.'

The sound of a wooden spoon slopping soup into a bowl.

It burned his tongue, but tasted fantastic. He had two bowls and three slices of bread and butter and held the bowl to his face and licked the bottom.

The climb upstairs felt like a mountain, his legs were so stiff. The stairs were just bare boards now. She had ripped the entire carpet away. His mother tucked him up in bed like she used to do when he was a little boy. She had a smile on her face.

'Tell you a secret,' she said.

His eyes widened.

'Only, you have to promise not to tell anyone.'

'OK.'

'I'm serious, Billy. Can you keep a secret?'

'Yes, Mum. I can keep secrets,' he said, which was so true it hurt to say it.

She leaned closer and whispered, as if the whole world would hear if she talked any louder.

'We're going away. Leaving this dump. You and me. We're going some place amazing.'

'I thought . . .'

She grinned. 'I borrowed it. We should go as soon as we can. There's too much trouble for us here.'

'Where?'

'Somewhere where it don't rain as much,' she said. 'Somewhere with no bloody mountains.'

And she was still talking when he fell asleep; the kind of thick oily sleep where there was no space for any dreams.

He slept through the afternoon and the night and when he woke it was just after five in the morning, when the first light was rich and red.

He dressed in jeans and his red jumper, went downstairs and quietly pulled the bolts on the back door. This time the cover lifted easily and he peered down into the darkness.

The string was gone, and along with it, the plastic bundle that had lain at the bottom of the drain. He did not understand.

A light came on in the upstairs bathroom and he dropped the manhole cover back down just in time for the window to rattle open and his mother's head to emerge.

'You're not going again, are you, Billy?'

'No.' He shook his head.

'Come back inside then. You hungry?'

'Starving.'

'Me too.'

After he bolted the door behind him, he noticed that the Reader's Digest atlas was open on the kitchen table. She must have been looking at it last night. It was open at Africa, for God's sake.

With the radio on loud, even though all the neighbours were asleep still, she pulled out the pan and set it on the cooker. 'Boogie oogie boogie,' sang Mum as she fried the bacon, even though she was way too old for disco and didn't know the words. Billy usually hated disco but he didn't mind now. She would have never played music like this when Dad was alive.

'Dance, Billy.'

'No.'

'Do you think I'm a good dancer, Billy?' She wiggled her hips like she was doing some old sixties' moves from ages and ages ago when she was young.

'Stop it, Mum,' he said.

'I used to go dancing all the time.'

Then Plastic Bertrand came on and she pulled him up and began yanking him around the kitchen. He broke away and started to pogo around the kitchen by himself, twisting his body as it sprung into the air.

'What kind of dancing is that?' She laughed. 'That's not

dancing. That's stupid. This is dancing.' And she twisted and shimmied away in front of him, laughing, until the bacon started to burn in the pan and the record stopped and the seven o'clock news came on the radio.

'Fergie used to be a good dancer. Can you imagine that? And Zeb Chandler, Rusty's dad. He never missed a dance. I don't know what happened to all the fellers around here. They all got so old.'

The radio was saying, 'Mr Heath pledged his support to Conservative Party leader Margaret Thatcher. He said that during the general election campaign he would fight just as hard as he had ever done for a Conservative government.'

'He used to love all them black singers, Zeb did. He had all the moves. James Brown, you heard of him? Your dad hated that. He had no taste.'

Out of nowhere, Billy heard his name on the radio: 'Billy McGowan', loud and clear. He wondered for a second if he was going nuts, thinking the radio was talking to him and then it said the name again. 'Hush a sec, Mum.'

'James Brown did this one called the Mashed Potato. Let me show you.'

'Mum. Shut up!'

And she looked at him, suddenly shocked. Surely him being up a mountain the night before last wasn't on the news? But the radio was saying, 'The twenty-one-year-old man was taken into custody in Armagh last night.'

'What?' said Mum.

'Shh.'

It wasn't his name; it was his father's name he had heard. 'I think they said they arrested someone.'

'What?'

'I don't know. For killing Dad, I think.'

And, after she had switched the radio off, she took the eggs out of the pan and put them on a plate, next to the bacon, and sat with the food in front of her. 'I don't care. I don't even want to think about it any more,' she said. 'All I care about is leaving this place.'

And she banged the ketchup bottle so too much sauce spurted all over the bacon, and then picked up her knife and fork to eat it anyway.

A group of young men and women he didn't recognise were outside the house, deep in conversation, as if Billy and his mum were an exhibit of some kind. It had been like this before. Not much went on around here and when it did, everyone wanted to know your business. Billy peered from behind the living-room nets at them.

When Billy put his head out of the front door to fetch the milk, Mrs Creedy, out on her front step with the paper, didn't smile and say hello. She just concentrated on the paper even harder, pretending not to notice him.

On his way down to buy bread for lunch, he picked up the *Reporter* at the Spar. The same photograph of his father that they had used when they had reported his death, and under it the single word: 'Murdered'. He read down. The article said the Constabulary had found the gun concealed in Donald Fraser's house after an anonymous tip-off.

'*An RUC spokesman says initial forensic tests confirm that it is the same weapon that fired the bullet that killed Protestant paramilitary Billy McGowan.*' They never called him 'Mr McGowan'; people like his father were low men, unworthy of the respect. '*A source close to the security forces speculated that the killing was part of an internal feud within the Ulster Volunteer Force.*'

When he looked up, the girl behind the till was staring at him reading the paper. He shoved it back into the pile and put his bread on the counter.

At home, Mum was already packing a suitcase upstairs in her bedroom. When he told her what he'd read in the local paper, she said, 'Donald Fraser. I never even heard of him. Don't want to even know. There's a suitcase on your bed. Get a move on.'

He was trying to figure it out.

In his room, he started taking the bird pictures off the walls. After a while, she came with a big old envelope for him to put the pictures in. 'About us moving; where did you get the money, Mum?'

'It's not important,' she said. 'We'll pay it back. What's important is we have it now.'

'Where are we even going?'

She smiled. 'I can't decide. Just the two of us. What if we went to France?'

'Don't you need a passport for that? I can't even speak French.'

Taking down a dipper he had drawn, he tore it in half. It was all wrong anyway. He crumpled it up and threw it on the floor. 'Was it from Mr McGrachy? The money?'

'God, no. Why do you think that, Billy?'

'Because he said he'd give you it.'

'I wouldn't take it from that bastard, even if he gave me a million.'

Leaving here wasn't just a game any more. It was real. He sat down on his bed and tried to imagine living somewhere else and couldn't. 'Was it Fergie?' he asked.

She didn't answer, just looked at his walls and said, 'Want me to help you doing this?'

Why would Fergie have given her the money? To get her away from here. Why, though? Because he fancied her, obviously. Loved her. But why the hurry? It was because Ferguson believed Mum had killed Dad. And now he was helping her get away with it, Billy thought. He must have taken the gun and planted it on Donny. And now Donny would be sent to jail because of him. An act of love. But he was a policeman and policemen always found out the truth. He had sent them away, but when it all died down he would come and find her because he loved her. What would happen then?

'Do you like Fergie?' he asked.

'Course I do. He's a good man.'

Billy pulled open one of his drawers. 'I mean, really like him?'

'I suppose I do.'

'He fancies you, you know.'

She smiled. 'I know that.'

The upstairs room was hot now. A wasp flew in through the open window. Billy shooed it away. 'Does he want to marry you?'

She said, 'I wouldn't be surprised.'

Billy thought about it for a while. If they married, one day he would tell her how he saved her, and it would all come out, wouldn't it? But she looked happy when she talked about him.

'Aw. Poppet. Don't look so glum. Don't worry. I won't go around getting hitched again in a hurry, mind,' she said. 'Once bitten. He says he'll come and see us in a while though. A few months maybe.'

Accidentally, he ripped another of his pictures, a dunlin, and was so overwhelmed with sudden anger at himself he started tearing the last few pictures down carelessly so they ended up in shreds on the floor.

'Billy,' she said. 'What's wrong?'

'I made a bloody mess,' he said.

'Don't cry, poppet. Doesn't matter. We're leaving it all behind anyway. Is it about Fergie? Don't you like him?'

'No. Fergie's great.'

'It's OK. You'll make new friends. You'll be fine. You're a great wee boy. Everyone says so. There,' she said, tightening a belt around his suitcase.

'What about everything else? The furniture and the pictures and the plants.'

She said, 'Fresh start, Billy.'

The wasp pinged against the unopened half of the window. Back and again, against the glass it went, trapped inside the room, only inches away from the open pane.

TWENTY-THREE

South didn't sleep. The rattle of hospital trolleys and bleeping of equipment kept him awake; his mind's eye re-ran the slaughter of the previous night – Gill, the magistrate, and finally Sleight – and each time the result was the same.

The hospital came to life while it was still black outside. The bandaged side of his face was swollen and his throat was painfully dry, but the nurses said he was nil-by-mouth.

After the consultant had been to inspect the wounds on the side of his head, South asked to see Cameron. A nurse found him some slippers and showed him to a pale-painted side room in a ward on the next floor up of the hospital.

Cameron was on a drip; his wounded leg was bandaged. He looked red-eyed either from lack of sleep or from crying. The first thing he said was, 'I had to do it.'

South knew the copper who was sitting next to him, reading a Kindle. He said, 'Give me five minutes, will you?'

When the officer had gone to stand outside in the corridor, South took his chair by the boy's bed and said, 'You did absolutely the right thing.'

'He killed Mum.'

'I know. I'm sorry,' said South. 'She was a good woman.' Moving his jaw to talk was painful. The consultant had said they were going to operate in a couple of hours.

'Putting up with all his shit for all those years. I suppose, you know, I'm an orphan now,' he said.

South nodded. 'Is your leg going to be OK?'

'They said they think so. They arrested me. I've been charged with murder.'

'They have to do it. You'll be OK. You did what you had to. You were incredible,' he said.

'I killed him.'

'I gave them a statement last night. I'll back you up. As a matter of fact I came to thank you. You know you saved my life?'

'I thought he'd killed you too.'

'The doctors say I'll be fine. Just not as good-looking.'

Cameron looked away. 'I keep going over it in my head,' he said.

'Me too. That's what happens. You'll try and think of ways in which it might have happened differently. You could spend your whole life doing it. But you have to come to terms with it in your own way. Find someone you can talk to about it. I never did.'

The boy was frail, thought South, but that was no surprise, given what he had been through. But he was a handsome boy; he had his mother's face.

'That thing you said. Was it true? You said you'd killed your own father,' asked Cameron.

'Yes. I did.'

'Did you go to prison for it?'

'No. I didn't. They never found out,' he said.

'Oh. Was it supposed to be a secret?' He coloured. The police would have questioned him already, thought South.

'Not any more.' South smiled at him. 'No harm done.'

'Will I go to prison?'

'No. You won't. I promise,' said South.

When he walked back out into the shiny, polished hospital corridor, Alex Cupidi was there waiting for him, hair a mess and make-up rushed. He was pleased to see her. She was wearing the same bad linen suit as she had done the first time he had met her. There was another uniformed constable standing awkwardly next to her. He looked embarrassed to be there.

'I went to look for you, but they said you were here,' she said. 'Then I saw you two were talking and thought I should leave you alone till you'd finished.'

'Thank you. You come for me, then?'

'I'm afraid so,' she said quietly.

They stood in the busy hospital corridor, a couple of feet from the bustle of the nurses' station.

She sighed. 'I don't like doing this, William.'

'Just do it, OK? It's your job.'

She closed her eyes and then opened them again. 'William South. I am arresting you for the murder of your father, William "Billy" McGowan on 11 July 1978. You don't have to say anything but it may harm your defence if you do not mention, when questioned, something which you rely on in court.' She took a deep breath. 'Sorry. I'm crying now. I didn't mean to.'

'Anything you do say can be given in evidence,' he prompted.

'Yep,' she said. 'That.'

'Did the boy say?'

She nodded. 'But I had my suspicions before. I just kept them to myself.'

It all made sense. 'Right. That's why you were being such an arse to me?'

'Yes. I had to keep my distance. If I found out for sure . . .'

Because if she was right, she should have arrested him then. Or if the force had found out she'd known all along, she could have been chucked out too.

'You're a good copper. A good man. And I'm sure you had reasons.'

'How?'

'Because when you said you thought that Donald Fraser didn't do it, I took a good long look at the files from PSNI. Given what was happening back then I thought they'd be a right mess, but they weren't. There was a sergeant there who had put together the evidence about the gun that killed your father. His notebooks were in there. Nobody had ever even bothered looking at them, as far as I could see, I suppose because the case against Fraser was open and shut. But it was all there. Within a couple of days of the murder he had worked out that the gun was your father's.

It was never Donald Fraser's. But then all of a sudden the gun's at Fraser's flat. I couldn't work it out.'

'The sergeant planted the gun on Donny,' said South. 'I suppose he was going to fix his notes later, but he never had the chance. He was killed.'

'Why?'

'Long story. How did you guess it was me?'

'So if it wasn't Fraser, it had to be somebody in your house. You or your mum. So I assumed your mother. And you were protecting her.'

'That's what Sergeant Ferguson thought too.'

'But you wanted so badly for me to know why you thought Fraser was innocent, why he wasn't the kind of man who would have killed Rayner. It was going round in my head. Why didn't you find some way of telling me that you knew for sure Fraser hadn't killed your father? Because your mother is dead. No harm would come to her. So I began to wonder if it was the other person who could have got hold of that gun.'

'That's right. You worked it out.'

'I'm so sorry,' she said.

'I'm glad, really,' he said. They walked down the corridor and waited for the lift.

The lift took a long time to arrive. An elderly woman lying on a trolley was there with them, the hospital porter gently stroking her hand as they waited for the doors to open.

'You know, I think I always knew you'd figure it out,' South said. 'Moment I saw you, that first day.'

'Really?' she said.

The lift doors opened and they waited for the trolley to be pushed into the lift before they too stepped inside.

They caught the ferry to Stranraer. Billy had never been on a ship before. The air was full of new smells: diesel fumes, fresh paint and salt. As they left the loch and entered open water the boat started to judder and roll, and to Billy, it felt like it was shaking the whole old world away.

'Excited?' she said.

'Can I go outside?'

He found a door and when he opened it, wind flattened his cheeks. It was brutal. Out on the deck, he tried to spot gulls but it was too rough. He watched the low green hills disappear into the gloom and felt exhilaration and fear; he had never been anywhere different. Would they talk in hard accents and eat strange food? Where would he go to school? He would miss his friends; some of them, at least. He had known them all his life. How did you go about making new ones? He had no idea. What kinds of birds would there be? Everything was being ripped away.

'Hungry?' His mum was at the door to the deck. Others were looking pale and miserable; she looked great.

'Starving now,' she said. 'Fancy egg and chips?'

The cafeteria was on the next deck down; they sat at a

table of lorry drivers who crowded round her, offering to buy drinks.

'Guinness? Hate the stuff,' she said.

'Bloody hell, girl. Don't think they sell Babycham on this boat.' And they were all laughing and she was laughing with them.

'Don't get him another Coke, lads,' she was saying. 'He's had two already. All his teeth will turn black.'

They were loud, friendly men who pulled out battered black-and-whites of their own sons and daughters and waited as his mum complimented each one for having such handsome and good-looking children, even though some of them weren't.

By the time they arrived at Stranraer she had accepted a lift in a lorry from an old man with naked women tattooed on his arms who was going to Birmingham. 'In one go? That's miles.'

'Don't worry about him. He's got them pills that make him stay up all night.'

'Pills for his VD most like,' joked a younger man with long hair and sideboards.

'Cheeky fuck.'

By the time Billy went out on deck again, they were already sailing down another loch, the water calm again.

They sat side by side in the cab of the big blue Bedford lorry, high above the other vehicles, Billy passing the driver lit cigarettes whenever he asked for them. He had wanted to sit by the window but his mum said he had to sit in the middle.

'Why?'

'Just do it,' she'd said. 'OK?'

They drove into the night, on winding roads. To be up here, above all the cars, felt special, like they were arriving in this new country in style. Lights of towns and cities appeared in front of them; they passed closed shops with strange names, their windows still bright, and pubs, doors wide open so you could see the men all packed inside. Everything looked fresh and different; the street signs seemed bigger, the roads wider.

Around midnight they stopped in an all-night cafe by a dark roadside. Where he was from, nothing stayed open all night.

The driver drank two cups of coffee and wrapped a meat pie in tissue, then they were off again. Billy fell asleep in Scotland and woke in England.

In Birmingham, they spent two nights in a bed-and-breakfast run by a black woman. Billy had never seen anyone black close to before and was fascinated. He helped her with the washing-up while his mother dried.

'Such a polite, handsome young man,' the woman said.

'Are we going to live here?' he asked, when the landlady went to finish clearing the tables in the front room.

'I don't know. What do you think?'

'What do I think?'

'Why not?' she asked.

'I don't know neither,' he said, thinking the fact that she was even asking him showed how lost they were. She had no idea what would become of them. All he wanted was for her to know what would happen next, and she didn't.

'What about London?'

'London?'

'We're the lucky ones, you and me, Billy. We are free of it all. We can go anywhere. I'll have to earn some money of course. Find a job.'

'Get a job? You?'

'What did you think I was going to do?'

He thought about how Donny would be telling the police how he didn't do it.

In a Wimpy in London they met a woman who wore a feather boa and who had a dachshund called Nathaniel. She laughed at everything Mum said and looked shocked when Mum admitted they didn't have anywhere to stay yet.

'Oh crikey. I have a whole empty flat in my house. Why don't you come and stay for a couple of days?'

'Oh no. I wouldn't like to impose,' Mum said. Billy was relieved, because he didn't like the woman's loud voice, and from under the table, the dachshund was growling at him.

'Quiet, Nathaniel,' the woman said. As she yanked on the dog's lead, he noticed how dirty the woman's fingernails were. 'It wouldn't be any trouble at all. It would be fun, wouldn't it, Nathaniel, some company?

You finish your dinner and I'll just put the bags in the boot of my car. I'm parked just outside.'

'You're so kind. I really hadn't expected the English to be so kind.'

'Oh no. We're a terrible lot, mostly.' The woman laughed.

'You help her with the bags, now Billy,' said Mum.

'No. You finish your meal, son. It's not a problem. I'll be back in one minute.'

Billy wiped the remains of the egg up with his last chip and the waitress took the plate away.

Ten minutes passed.

'Did she mean for us to meet her outside?' Mum wondered.

When she went to the counter to pay, she found that the woman had not paid for her meal; it had been added on to their bill.

'No problem at all,' said Mum.

Outside, they looked to the left and right but they couldn't see her, or her dog. Mum walked a little way up the street, standing on her toes to look past the crowd, then returned and did the same in the opposite direction. They peered into all the parked cars but after an hour Mum said, 'You know, I think she robbed us.'

Billy had been thinking this for a while.

'All your drawings, Billy,' Mum said sadly.

'They weren't very good,' answered Billy.

'London's not our place,' she said.

They spent the night asleep on a bench in Victoria

Station waiting for the first coach to Dover. It was in the morning that Billy saw the copy of the *Daily Mail* lying on the bench next to them. In smaller letters, next to the headline 'TORIES ATTACK LABOUR'S JOB RECORD':

TWO RUC KILLED BY IRA SNIPER

And the photograph of two men. One of them looking like any other copper, the other with his hat slightly cocked, and a half-smile on his lips. Beneath it, the caption: '*Sergeant John Ferguson.*'

All the way to Dover, the other passengers watched Mum crying, embarrassed by her noise. She didn't stop for an hour. She tried to keep her voice quiet, but occasionally another howl escaped her and people pretended to concentrate on their newspapers or knit. An Indian man with a beard gave her a purple handkerchief and told her she could keep it.

The details in the newspaper were slim. They had been on patrol in a car on the edge of a town when a sniper shot the driver, Sergeant John Ferguson, dead. The other man was killed as he tried to leave the vehicle. That's all they said. The IRA claimed responsibility for the attack.

'We going to go back for the funeral?'

'Never going back to that place,' she said, and held the purple cloth to her eyes.

And soon Billy started too, like he had never cried before. And now he had started, he found he couldn't stop.

'Don't cry, Billy,' said Mum.

'I liked him,' he said, which was true. It was not just that that made him cry, though. Without him, this secret was his to keep forever. It was going to be with him always, now. But she didn't know that. This cold stone was going to be inside him for ever.

But she thought he was just crying for Fergie and she put her arm round him and hugged him so tight he felt his bones were going to break.

The first operation was later that morning.

When he woke, face singing with the pain, he too had a copper sitting next to him.

'Sorry, mate,' said the young policeman sheepishly. 'Orders, you know?'

'You're OK,' said South. 'I'm not going anywhere.'

Cupidi came to visit every day. On the third day she brought Zoë. She leaned across him and kissed his good side.

'Don't flinch.' She laughed. 'I'm really pleased to see you.'

'I made a cake,' said Cupidi.

'It's horrible,' said Zoë. 'She's a terrible cook.'

'Did she put a file in it?'

'Don't joke. You won't have to serve time. I'm sure of it.'

The doctors had done their work. He would be discharged tomorrow. The Northern Ireland police were flying over

379

this afternoon to take him back over there. They did things differently there.

'I mean, they won't really put you in prison, will they?' said Zoë. 'Not after what you did. Not after what your dad did.'

'Yes. They probably will.'

'So unfair,' said Zoë.

'That's great news about Bob's house,' said Cupidi, trying to change the subject; if he did go to prison, it would not be easy. Nobody liked a copper in prison.

'Yes, isn't it?' They had finally read Bob's will; he had left everything to South. Rayner had no relations. So Arum Cottage was now his. It felt like an apology of sorts; proof that, for all the deceit, they had been friends.

'Will you sell it?'

'I don't think so. I'd like to live in it, when I get out.'

Cupidi looked away. 'Zoë's right. They wouldn't dare give you a custodial sentence. Your dad was a monster.'

'They still might.'

'What about your own house?' Zoë asked.

'I don't know yet. Sell it or rent it. I'll need the money now.' He had been served notice. He would be off the force by the time he came out. 'I don't want to live there any more. I think I prefer the cottage.'

'Want me to keep an eye on it?' Cupidi said. 'Just in case?'

'That would be good. Curly and Eddie said they'd keep an eye on it too. I'll tell Eddie to let you have a key.'

'Just thinking. Can *we* rent his house, Mum?' said Zoë. 'The one he's in now. Much better than that poxy house we're living in here.'

'Jesus, I'd hate it there,' said Cupidi. 'All that bloody nature everywhere.'

'Oh, Mum. It would be great. Please?'

'What are you going to do now, anyway?' said Cupidi, adding, 'When you get back . . .'

Nobody knew when that would be. It could be months, or years. 'I don't know,' said South. His career in the police was over. There would be a dismissal hearing, but it was a foregone conclusion. 'I'm not really worried. I can manage from the rent on the house, I guess. Something will come up.'

Cupidi went to fetch tea from the machine.

He said to Zoë, 'You going birding again?'

'Course,' she said. 'I'm up to sixty-one already. Will catch you up, easy.'

'There's a guy lives at Dungeness,' said South. 'His name's Eddie. I've told him all about you. His girlfriend is a birder too. He says the three of you should go out.'

'Cool,' she said. She looked down at the floor. 'It's like, I'll watch them for you while you're away. The birds. I'll write about them, maybe.'

'I'd like that very much,' he said. 'You seen a redpoll?'

'No.'

'There's some there now, Eddie says.'

'Maybe Mum and me can go there after . . .' She tailed

off, reddening. *After the police have come to take you away*, she must have been going to say.

Cupidi saved her embarrassment by returning with two cups of tea in paper beakers. 'Turns out, Sleight was big in drugs in the nineties, or so we think,' she said, sitting back down in the plastic chair. 'He ran clubs in North Kent when all the ecstasy boom happened. He was around at the same time people were making hundreds of grand. Never arrested, though. We guess that he got away with it. Married his childhood sweetheart . . .'

'Gill?'

'Gail. But Sleight wanted to go respectable, so bought a posh new life for them, moved into scaffolding, big house in Sandgate for her. There's no indication of where the money came from.'

'And hired a personal tutor to teach his son.'

'That's right. He didn't want Cameron growing up like he'd done.'

'Bob,' said South.

'Yes, Bob was the tutor. Cameron says Bob lived with them for almost eight years. Cameron was home-educated. The deal was, if Bob got Cameron into Oxford or Cambridge Sleight would give him a hundred grand on top of what he'd already earned.'

'Jesus.'

'Bob kept his part of the bargain.'

'What a snob,' said Zoë.

'A control freak,' said Cupidi. 'He wanted a perfect

family and that's what he got. They had to be it, whether they wanted it or not.'

A nurse came in to take his temperature and blood pressure. She stood by the bed saying nothing.

'So he'd have known Judy Farouk from the old days when he was a dealer?' asked South as the nurse strapped the cuff around his arm.

'We think so,' said Cupidi. 'It would make sense. Bob and Gail or Gill had fallen in love. When Cameron went to university, Bob used the money Sleight had given him to buy a place so they could still be together. What she didn't know was that Judy Farouk lived so close. We know for a fact she had been on the drug scene back then. We reckon she knew Sleight from those days. She must have spotted them together, recognised Gail, and gone and told Sleight about it.'

'Sleight would have hated that.'

'Imagine it. Having that drug dealer tell you your wife is having an affair. Confronting him with the fact that everything he'd built up was a lie.'

'Is that why he killed her?'

'We don't know. I don't think she was stupid enough to try to blackmail him.'

'No. During the siege, he said it wasn't blackmail. Maybe she thought she'd get him on her side. Maybe it was just because they were old mates.'

Cupidi nodded. 'Either way, Cameron said he noticed his dad had changed when he came back from university. Went from being his usual Jack the Lad self into being violent and angry. He saw him assault Gail one day. Slapped her. When Cameron tried to intervene he beat him as well, and blamed him for being too close to Bob, too. Didn't like to let her out of his sight any more. He was screaming at her, threatening her. She was scared of him. They both always had been, by the sound of it. He killed Bob, then made it look like Fraser did it. And he fooled most of us, too. What was Fraser even doing there?'

'I think he might have been looking for me, but I don't know. He might just have been unlucky. He always was, I suppose. Can you prove Sleight killed Judy Farouk?'

'That was easy. Her DNA is all over the back of his Audi. And it was her blood in your friend's boat. We think he must have killed her not long after we saw her. When Bob turned up dead, she would have known it was Sleight. Like I said, he was a control freak. He controlled his wife, his son, everything. If Judy knew about Gail and Bob's affair . . . He didn't want anything out of his hands, so I think that he killed her, stole the boat and dumped the body at sea.'

The nurse left the room.

'I think he'd seen us in the car outside her caravan. Maybe he thought I was on to him from the start.'

'That would make sense.'

'How?' asked Zoë. 'How did he kill Judy?'

'It's hard to say. The autopsy suggests he strangled her.'

'Poor woman,' said Zoë.

'She was a thug,' said her mother. 'She got what she deserved.'

'Nobody deserves that.'

'Maybe not.'

He sat up in bed, shifted a pillow.

'How's school?'

'Shit still,' said the girl.

'Don't use that word,' said her mother.

'I'm getting through it, though. I'm picking biology A-level. I like it. The teacher's OK, too. Maybe do zoology at college.'

'What about you?' said Cupidi. 'You and your father. You never said why.'

'Maybe he doesn't want to talk about it,' said Zoë.

'It's OK,' said South.

So, lying in the hospital bed, with the sutures on the side of his face starting to itch beneath the dressing, he tells them about Mr McGrachy and Donny Fraser and the white bird and the red paint, all about the Sergeant in the peaky hat and the flappy trousers. And he tells them how he shot his father on the night of the 11th of July and how he got away with it because Sergeant Ferguson loved his mother.

They listen without interrupting until he's finished. And it's great to get it all out, because he has not been able to tell anyone the whole story before. 'What happened to the policeman – Ferguson?' asks Zoë.

'He died. He was murdered, as a matter of fact.'

'God,' says Cupidi. 'By the UVF?'

'No,' says South. 'It was an IRA sniper. Nothing to do with anything except he was a policeman. He was just unlucky. Dead unlucky. In those days people there died all the time.'

'So he died thinking your mother had killed your father?'

'I assume so,' says South.

'And that he'd saved her,' says Cupidi.

'Yes. And he did save her, really.'

'Amazing,' says Zoë.

'Unprofessional,' says Cupidi.

'Who cares? He was fantastic,' says Zoë.

'Yes,' says South. 'I think he was.'

'He sent someone to prison for something they didn't do,' says Cupidi.

They sit together in silence by the bed. The Northern Ireland police will be arriving soon from the airport to take him away. Cupidi thinks they will go easy on him because he has been a good copper all his life and because he was so young when he killed his father and it is all such a long time ago.

He is not so sure. He deserves to go to prison, not so much for what he did to his father as what he did to poor Donny, though he is frightened of it. Either way, he thinks it's wiser to assume he will not be back by the time the birds come again.

But Zoë will be here, he thinks. Eddie's girlfriend and her will get on fine. She will watch the birds for him, she says. That is good.

The house on the beach will stay locked up. They will keep it ready for him. It will be here for when he comes back.

ACKNOWLEDGEMENTS

Firstly, I must thank many people from the UK's extraordinary birding community who freely offered their advice. The exceptional Anne Cleeves kindly put me in touch with the excellent birder Tim Cleeves; Grace Packman put me in touch with Mary Faherty of the RSPB at Dungeness. Jonathan Cook, also of the RSBP, was my saviour on warblers, dusky or otherwise, and had some great insights. Sylvia Patterson put me in touch with Chris Hocking, whose suggestions were consistently thoughtful and clever, and reminded me why I admire naturalists so much. Thanks too to Neil Ansell, Mark Adams and my old Palimpsest pal Al Kitching and for their extremely useful observations.

Thanks to the great Roz Brody, Mike Holmes, Janet King and Chris Sansom for strong-arming me into returning to a half-finished manuscript and for their input into it over several incarnations. Graham Bartlett kindly offered wonderful advice on policing detail; I'm looking forward to reading his book. Una Conway, Deborah Sharpley and my colleague Steve Cavanagh all offered wise, though conflicting advice on the ending, which is to be expected as they all work in the law. The title was given to me by fellow writer Cal Moriarty.

The errors that remain are all mine. And finally huge thanks again to my editor Jon Riley and Rose Tomaszewska of Quercus, to Nick de Somogyi, to Jane McMorrow and to my agent Karolina Sutton.

On the lookout for more by William Shaw?

Catch a Breen & Tozer investigation

And watch out for more with Alexandra Cupidi,

coming soon

Follow William Shaw for news, videos, competitions and more

f /WilliamShawWriter

t /@william1shaw

williamshaw.com/subscribe

Follow riverrun for more outstanding fiction and non-fiction

t /@riverrunbooks

riverrunbooks.co.uk